The Shepherd of the Blue World

Jay Sauls

Dedication:

To my wonderful wife for believing in my vision, and to my daughter Dakota for helping me make some last-minute editing decisions. You ROCK, Cuddly Cactus!

Chapter One

Captain P'tonich walked the bridge of the Firestar Confederation heavy-cruiser Star Crucible, his home for the past twenty-seven solar cycles. He knew every weld, every weapon-scorched meter of its hull. She has been his home through five battle campaigns and eight complete refits. By the vibrations pulsing through the hull, he knows if her cannons are firing at full power or pulling their punch. And he knew the hum of the slipstream drive when it was operating flawlessly.

He paused and cocked an ear to the ceiling. Sensing a subtle compression of the ship's atmosphere. "Pilot, status of the drive?"

The pilot, senior class, with half as many war campaigns as the Captain, responded at once. "Slipstream currently operating at ninety-nine point oh-nine-eight percent of efficiency. Currently on course for Shovain. Current estimated arrival is one-hundred thirteen hours."

P'tonich walked to the NavCom board, stood beside it, and stared at the main viewer. The screen covered the warship's bow, providing a panoramic view of the universe outside his command. Icons marked the location of planets, stars, and vessels in their sector. The Captain's armor crinkled

slightly as he turned to view his crew, all handpicked for this mission. Their body language did not show the tension they were under, but their body chemistry pulsed with the tang of war pheromones. He returned his gaze to the main viewer. In null space, the screen displayed jetting streaks of colors, the computer's interpretation of the slipstream spacial strings they traverse from one corner of the galaxy to another.

He crossed his arms and sniffed the air again, his flat, gray nostrils flaring. "Pilot, status of the slipstream drive?" He grimaced slightly, his thin lips pulling back to expose a row of narrow, sharp teeth.

"Sir?"

"Status of the drive!" P'tonich turned to face the pilot. "Are we still functioning at ninety-nine point-oh-nine-eight percent of efficiency?"

The pilot glanced at the Captain as he refreshed the engine's output display. "Yes, sir, the drive is still operating at…." He paused, turning his attention to his display, his ridged brow pinched.

"Pilot, is there something wrong?"

"One moment, Captain, we seem to have an anomaly in the drive. Efficiency has dropped…."

"That's not an anomaly, pilot." P'tonich sprinted back to his command chair and palmed the battle alert. Across the bridge and at every station, alarms blared as warning lights flashed. "The Galv have found us and are trying to pull us from slipstream. Full power to the drives!" He closed the containment braces across his thighs as the bridge crew prepared for battle.

"Lieutenant Kooraht, drop transmission buoys and broadcast our situation. Open ship-wide communications." The lights change on his display, showing that all comms are now open. "Battle stations! Fire control arm the Quantum charges." He ordered. "Engineering, prepare for sustained maximum burn."

The Captain closed the channel as the ship slewed to port.

"Here we go. Let's all be sharp, and we might just escape. If not, we want to look our fiercest when we pass over to Valcianna. Hopefully, our sacrifice will please her."

"Captain, the slipstream is collapsing, searching for alternate strings." The navigator's fingers danced across the display as the transit lines on the main viewer faded. "Sir, detecting zero slipstream vectors for parsecs. The Galv has flooded this sector with capnium radiation. We'll have to clear this sector before a new transit point will develop."

P'tonich slammed his fist against the arm of his chair. "I'm releasing power restraints from the drive. Push through the stops. If we go nova, then so be it. Releasing control in 3… 2… you have it all, pilot."

"Pushing through the stops now, Captain." the pilot shouted over the whining and creaking of the bulkheads as gravitation forces tried to crumple the ship. "Slipstream is holding—barely."

"Navigation, do you have the location of the Galv vessel?"

"Yes, sir. They are seventeen degrees to port on our y-axis and closing. Recommend turning to starboard and running evasive maneuvers."

Explosions ripped through the forward consoles, knocking out the bridge lamps and sparking fires. "We are reverting to normal space, Captain"

"Bring us around, pilot. I want to run The *Crucible* up their collective snouts. Weapons officer, prepare a new firing solution." The officer nodded, his hands splayed across his control panel, moving in a blur.

The bridge display changed from slipstream to a close-up of the Galv vessel. It dwarfed the *Star Crucible,* resembling a trio of 'X's layered on top of each other. Weapon ports jutted from all corners.

"Engineering, whatever we have left, I want directed to the subspace drives."

"Aye, sir,"

"Weapons, officer, are the pods ready?"

"Aye, sir, they are armed and manned."

"Very good," replied the Captain as he leaned back in his chair. He purged the smoke from the bridge and silenced the klaxons. The automated fire suppression system extinguished the rest of the smoldering consoles. "Pilot, over-charge the sublight engines and prepare to launch at my command. Aim for their bridge on a direct-intercept vector. Weapons on standby."

The bridge lights changed again as power was routed from the support systems to the weapons.

P'tonich released the leg restraints and stood with his armored fist on his hips, staring at the viewscreen and the Galv battle platform. "Griv'dr, what are your scans telling you?"

The weapons officer glanced up from his console. "Sir, their weapons are powered and targeting our engines."

"Capabilities?"

"Sir, they could turn us to slag, then slag our molecules."

"Absolutely. So why don't they attack?"

"They desire our capture, not destruction."

"You are correct. Until they have what they want, we will continue to live. So, let's *not* give them what they want without a fight." P'tonich sat back in his command chair, the restraints closing automatically, then tapped his heavy fist on the armrest. "At my command, target their bridge with everything we have. Let's see if we can get their attention."

"Aye, sir."

"Pilot, let's see what you can do. Makes us very hard to hit."

The pilot nodded. "Executing evasive routine now."

On the forward viewer, the Galv vehicle rushed toward them, then suddenly slid off to the right.

"Griv'dr, show us what you've learned."

Green bolts of proton energy fired from the weapon emitters, striking the Galv ship and making it briefly list.

"Damage report, Griv'dr!"

"Direct hit to their bridge and forward cannons. Shields flickering but holding."

"Very well, keep firing!"

More green lances of supercharged protons streamed out, stitching a blistering patch across the bow of the Galv ship. Their shields rippled, dispersing the waves of green energy. "Launching missiles… banks one, two away. Targeting engines." Eight fiery stars shot out from under the bow, toward the enemy ship. On the forward viewscreen, small flashing red icons raced toward the battle platform before vanishing one by one. "Sir, all missiles destroyed before contact. The Galv are locking weapons."

"Pilot, keep us clear!"

The *Star Crucible* rocked and seemed to drop a thousand meters.

"Direct hit to drives. Aft shields have fallen, attempting to rebuild." Several streaks of crimson energy skated off the shields, not penetrating but pounding the much smaller vessel.

"Captain, I'm picking up gravitational distortions," Commander Anorak advised. "The Galv are preparing grappling beams."

"Pilot, don't let them…" The crew was slammed against their restraints as the warship stopped abruptly .

"Sir, we are being hailed," Kooraht announced with a cough, smoke again pouring from the ventilators.

"Main viewer, Kooraht."

The display changed from tactical to that of the Galv ship. Golden beams cascaded from the vessel, covering every inch of the Firestar Confederation warship.

"Sir, they're only transmitting audio, no video."

"Well, open the communication. Let's see if there are ready to surrender."

The crew inclined their heads to the right, their acknowledgment of humor.

"CREW OF THE FIRESTAR CONFEDERATION SHIP, YOU ARE TRANSPORTING A WAR CRIMINAL, Emissary de'tantel. PREPARE TO RELINQUISH HER TO THE GALV. WE WILL TAKE THIS AS A SIGN OF PEACE AND COOPERATION BETWEEN OUR WORLDS."

"Kooraht, notify the Galv that I was injured during their unprovoked attack and I'm in route to medbay.

Pilot, transfer your station over to engineering, as your services are no longer required."

"Sir? Who is going to pilot the slipstream horizon? Engineering isn't qualified."

"Jonqueen," the Captain said, catching the pilot off guard by using his formal name, "how many campaigns have we been on together?"

"Captain, I believe this is our fourth. Why do you ask?"

"Simply to say, you have been the best pilot I have ever served with. And to advise, we will not slipstream again. Maybe Valcianna will have use for us in her realm and we can serve to her glory. But we no longer need a pilot."

"Captain, I am still confused. As part of the bridge crew, I am trained to handle navigation, communication, and can serve as a weapons officer."

"Jonqueen, I have a more important duty for you. One that you must not fail."

"Captain, I have never, and will never fail you!" Jonqueen bristled, his gray hands on his hips, his black, almond-shaped eyes pinched to narrow slits.

The Captain smiled. "I know that, pilot. But this will be the most daunting of any task yet. I need you to guarantee that you will not fail…"

Jonqueen growled, "Captain, I have never failed…"

"… to protect the life of the Emissary de'tantel, with your life if need be."

Jonqueen inwardly gasped. "You would deny me the chance to serve you in battle to protect that… creature?"

"Jonqueen, our worlds—The Firestar Confederacy *and* The Shovain Star Empire require this of you. If she is not returned to Shovain, the armistice will end, and we will be back to fighting the Shovain *and* the Galv. The Galv will destroy both our civilizations."

Jonqueen stood before his captain, staring back defiantly. He nodded quickly. "Yes, sir." He dropped his glare and stared at the deck. "How am I to accomplish this?"

"Prep and power my shuttle, slipstream directly to Shovain. It will be a difficult passage in such a small vessel." The Captain stood, walked to his pilot, and placed his captain's insignia on Jonqueen's shoulders. "I wish I could give you a better ship. Treat her well. Now board my shuttle and wait for further instruction."

"Sir, the Emissary's contingent will not fit in the shuttle, and she *will not* leave them behind. How do I convince the Emissary to leave her attendants?"

"By any means possible. Even if it means physically grabbing her and tossing her in the shuttle."

Jonqueen leaned closer. "Captain, to lay a hand on the Emissary is a death penalty offense on both worlds. They will execute me at once upon our arrival on Shovain."

"Jonqeen, if you stay, you are surely dead, as is the Emissary. Your survival, and that of the Emissary, depends on you not only getting off this ship but arriving safely at Shovain." The Captain stepped forward, placing his gray-skinned forehead against the pilot's. He spoke too quietly for anyone to hear. "You are my only male heir, and I am more than proud of you. They will sing songs about you in Valcianna. I just don't want to go there *with* you. Protect the Emissary, as I know you can."

Jonqueen continued the contact with his father. "And of her attendants?"

"They knew the danger; and are prepared. Of this, the Emissary does not know. Do not divulge any of this until you are safely underway."

Jonqueen stepped back. "It will be done, father."

New warning alarms screeched to life as ceiling tiles fell and bulkheads groaned.

"Captain, grappling beams are increasing in strength. The Galv are trying to crack the hull," Anorak reported from his engineering station.

"Acknowledged. Looks like they're getting impatient. Kooraht, open communications with the Galv, advise I'm on my way back to the bridge, that they've damaged us worse than expected. Explain that it has taken time for me to pick my way through the rubble."

"Aye, sir."

"Soldier Griv'dr, target the grappling beam emitter and prepare to hit them with everything we have." The Captain turned toward the engineering station. "Transfer everything you have to the forward shields. I'm going to see if we can make them blink."

"Jonqueen, you must leave now. My shuttle is powering as we speak. I'm going to give you as much protection as I can, but it will not last long." P'tonich motioned to the soldier manning the NavCom board. "Continue communications with the Galv, advise them we have agreed to their terms and will transfer the Emissary by life pod. But they must release their grappling beam. We can't launch the pod with the beams in place."

"Aye, sir."

Captain P'tonich heard the bulkhead door to the bridge open, then close. *Hopefully, the P'tonich name would live on.* "Engineer, status of the life pods?"

"Sir, everything is arranged as requested. Just waiting for your word to launch."

"Very good. Status of the grappling beams?"

"They have lowered the containment strength, but still have enough coverage to hold us in place."

"That will not do. Kooraht, alert the Galv that their unprovoked attack will lengthen the hostilities between our worlds. We will release the Emissary as requested, only after all containment beams have powered down. Failure to do so will cause the destruction of both vessels."

"*WE WILL NOT RELEASE YOUR SHIP UNTIL YOUR TARGETING OF OUR VESSEL ENDS. IF THE EMISSARY IS NOT RELEASED IN 120 SECONDS, WE WILL DESTROY YOUR ship.*"

"Griv'dr, did you paint the location of the grappling beam emitters?"

"Aye, sir. I should be able to hit most with line-of-sight firing solutions."

"Very good," P'tonich energized the display on the side of his command seat. He confirmed that the life pods are charged and standing by. "Disengage targeting and keep sharp."

"Captain, they have terminated the containment beams. The Galv are requesting we transfer the Emissary." Kooraht announced.

"Thank you. I am ejecting pod one." He released the first lifeboat. The small rescue pod's engine ignited, slowly propelling the pod toward the Galv ship.

"Captain, the Emissary's pod is away. Should reach the Galv vessel in approximately eight minutes."

"Acknowledged. Navigation back us away, slowly. Let's see if we can get out of the grappling range." He switched over to direct-contact communications. "Jonqueen, have you convinced the Emissary it is time to leave?"

The display on the Captain's panel warmed, then focused on a small humanoid bound tightly in shimmering robes. It also showed Jonqueen's and a cadet's armor, smoking and sizzling. "Sir, she was less than accommodating. I had to stun her before she burned through our armor."

P'tonich nodded to the right, and his lips parted slightly, almost a laugh. This being, barely two-thirds their height and weight, could kill them by burning through their armor with its touch. "That is fine. Confine her in the shuttle and prepare to launch."

"Yes, sir. We should be ready for slipstream travel momentarily."

Chapter Two

Jonqueen programmed in slipstream vectors as the sound of escape pods being ejected continued. The Saint sat patiently in the copilot chair, staring intently at the forward viewscreen as the pods powered away. She removed her hood, allowing long, black hair to fall to her shoulders. The woman loosened the shimmering ceremonial robes, then reached forward with pale, ivory hands to adjust the visual feed on the forward display. Her dark, crystal-blue eyes followed the pod as its small engine ignited, driving it away from their vessel.

"Why are we launching all our escape pods *toward* the Galv warship? This makes no sense."

"It will momentarily."

"Well, it doesn't make sense now." She leaned forward, watching as a containment beam snared a pod, pulling it toward the massive ship. Leaning back, she let her gaze fall on the soldier. "My people, they are in the pod, yes?"

"They are," Jonqeen confirmed as he continued to program way-points and vectors.

"But why? The Galv has no need for them. It's me they…" she paused, hands covering her mouth. On the screen, the first pods vanished in a flash of green light. The Galv platform then rocked their ship with cannon fire. The Saint turned toward the soldier, tears in her eyes, her fist clenched. "You used us… them!"

A deep rumble trembled through the decking as the Star Crucible's sublight engines fired. The view on the monitor showed the Galv battle platform fading to the right, followed by a flash that whited out the camera.

"We did not!" Growled Jonqeen. The shuttle's lights dimmed as he directed power to the thrusters. His fingers danced over the engine control panel. "It was your Regent Teshvan Mar. He was aware, for this mission to succeed, we were required to get you back to Shovain at all costs. Your attendants came up with this plan should the Galv catch us. Each pod has a quantum-nova warhead. Hopefully, we can destroy the Galv before they destroy us."

A heavy cannon barrage followed another blast of white light. The hanger deck illumination flickered.

The shuttle shook as increased weapons' fire crashed against the Star Crucible's hull. The Saint sat in the copilot seat, harness secured and ready. "Have you ever piloted a shuttle through a slip before?" she asked.

"No." He concentrated on the shaking display panel while priming the slipstream generators.

"Are you sure you can?"

"Yes. Not that it matters whether I have performed this operation before. Either we do, or we do not. If we stay, we will die."

Smoke and flame erupted from the port-side wall as a Galv missile tore through the Star Crucible's hull and exploded against the shuttle, knocking it sideways and setting off damage alarms.

"Can you plot a slip?" Jonqueen shouted over the warning klaxons.

"Yes, it's been a while. But I can get us far enough away to make a course correction."

"Then do it. I have to repair the port stabilizer." Jonqueen unbuckled, then sprinted to the hatch. "No matter what happens to me, you launch the moment the Captain tells you. Get clear, then find your way home."

The Saint nodded as she transferred the controls for the slipstream projector to her console. Jonqueen broke the hatch open and grabbed a repair pack, then exited the shuttle as atmosphere vented into space. Several lengths of the shuttle's hull plating were pierced and buckled. Using magnetic couplers, he pulled the plates back into alignment. Another explosion rocked the hangar bay, dislodging him from the shuttle. He grabbed the edge of the hatch, holding on by one hand as the vacuum tried to drag him through the hangar breach.

His com chimed. "Soldier, are you safe?"

"No!" He hissed, his grip fading. Another chime sounded in his earpiece, the Captain's signal to launch.

"Stay there, I'm coming for you!"

"You must forget me and launch immediately!"

"I can't pilot this craft to Shovain without you."

The soldier felt the Star Crucible's engines increase in pitch as the ship slewed to starboard as it began its twisting, corkscrewing attack run. The ship shuttered as the Galv fired on them. "Emissary, you must launch! The Captain will engage the primary drive against the Galv ship anytime now." He shouted through the commlink. Through his earpiece, Jonqueen heard the command to fire all weapons, to launch every last missile at the Galv. "Emissary, did you hear me? We are about to die, and you must be off the ship!"

His shoulder erupted in agony as his armor began to smoke. The Saint dragged him up the side of the shuttle and through the hatch. When he turned around, the Saint was flat on her back, a cargo sling wrapped around her waist, the controller in her left hand. The Saint was gasping for breath, face white from lack of oxygen and the brutal cold of the decompressing bay.

The soldier palmed the hatch closure, lifted the Saint by her robes, and dropped her in the copilot's seat. "Strap in!" When she did not move, he stretched the harness over her shoulders, burning his hands on her skin.

A section of the forward screen changed to show the bridge. The Captain was glaring at him. "Why haven't you launched? We have no more time." His father ordered, then fell as an explosion blackened the view screens on the bridge. Smoke poured from multiple locations. "Get out now!" the Captain coughed and stood. Silver blood trickled down the side of his head. "Jonqueen, you have made me very proud. Now protect the Emissary." The screen darkened.

Jonqueen took a deep breath, then slammed his fist on the hanger bay release. The shuttled floated free, oriented itself with the opening. He fired its engines and the bay exploded in flames as a dozen meters of the Star Crucible's hull melted away.

Jonqeen pushed the sublight engines past the warning stops, channeling all available power to the drives. Alarms wailed as automated alerts warned of catastrophic damage to the engine core. The soldier silenced the warnings, then pushed the engines to 30 percent beyond the maximum. Smoke seeped from the power conduits as bone-rattling vibrations worked their way up from the engine bay.

"Are you mad?" shouted the Saint over the pounding. "The drives are overheating! We'll be dead in space if you don't pull back!"

"Pay attention!" He shot back, powering her view screen, now providing an aft view of the ship. The *Star Crucible* was breaking up and on a collision course with the Galv warship. Ahead of their former vessel, miniature stars were erupting in waves of white energy. "When the core ruptures on the Crucible, she will take out the Galv. The shock wave will be upon us in minutes. We must put as much distance between us as possible." He turned back to the engine diagnostics, his fingers dancing and tapping. The shuttle smoothed out, but the klaxons continued. "And there is this," He said, once again changing her display to match his. Crimson streaks of light burst from the Galv battle platform.

"Boarding crafts." Gasped the Saint.

"Correct. They are short range but are very hard to kill. We could fight off one or two, but I'm counting eight. I am hoping the shock wave will take a few out."

"Why can't we just slipstream out of here?" The Saint stared hard at her monitor, watching the withering cannon fire between the ships.

"I cannot get a slipstream lock due to the amount of energy released from the quantum warhead detonations." More warning lights bloomed to life on the console. The ships' schematics were quickly turning from yellow to red as power conduits approached critical levels.

A proximity alarm blared. The soldier jerked his head to the forward display in time to see a Galv fighter slicing toward them; its simple dagger shape silhouetted on his display. "Can you fight?"

"I have never…"

"You have now!" The console before the Saint opened as a single firing grip, and a targeting helmet appeared. "Put the tactical display over your eye. Every time the targeting array flares green, pull the trigger, and track him."

The Saint pulled on the targeting hood and gripped the trigger in both hands. The screen inside the hood warmed, showing a dizzying view of space outside the shuttle. A red icon pulsed, then flashed out of sight as the shuttle staggered from weapons fire.

"Destroy the Galv craft!" Jonqueen ordered.

The Saint twisted and turned her head, trying to find the attacking vessel on the 360-degree view screen. "He's gone, disappeared."

"Find him quickly." Jonqueen barked as his hands tapped madly on the command displays.

"I'm trying! I'm not trained for this," the Saint replied through a clenched jaw. Her head snapped from side to side, trying to locate the marauder.

Green streaks splashed against the starboard shields. The lights flickered before returning. The soldier threw the shuttle into a series of random twists and turns.

"Brace yourself and get ready." Jonqueen cursed under his breath, then cut the engine. The Galv fighter flashed past, then slowed directly ahead of them. "Now destroy him!"

The firing reticle glowed green, and the Saint pulled the trigger, tracking the Galv fighter as it attempted to dive under the shuttle. Flames erupted from its engines; then the ship exploded in a fireball that was extinguished quickly in the cold vacuum of space.

The Saint threw the hood off and sagged. "I've never taken a life before, even one as evil as the Galv."

"You did well." The soldier replied in a calm voice. "And you will have additional attempts to do so before we are safe." He glanced at his display and growled. The boarding crafts had closed the gap when Jonqueen slowed the shuttle and took evasive action.

"I can't. It's against all I stand for."

"You better stand for more than that, as we have eight boarding crafts intent on destroying us. They are closing too rapidly for us to escape. You will have to fight."

"Then you fight. I'll have no part of it."

The soldier stared at her, his annoyance showing in rows of jagged teeth. "It is amazing your species has lasted as long as it has. Fine, you pilot, I will kill." He retracted the weapon's control, transferring it to his side. "I hope you have piloted a slipstream, or the last deaths will be ours when the Galv pulverizes this ship."

"I have received slipstream navigation training in a simulator. I'm sure I can handle this."

The soldier snorted. "I hope your training was sufficient, as we will not have a 'simulated' death. See if you can get a string lock. And it does not matter where. I will try to keep them off us as long as possible."

The Saint didn't respond. Her hands danced over the slipstream drive controls, running algorithms, trying to find any spacial strings crisscrossing the sector. The display continued to flash a negative response, with no locks available. The proximity alarm sounded. She glanced up to see the oval shape of a Galv boarding craft closing.

"Soldier!" the engines whined as the Galv locked on with a grappling beam.

"Please keep searching for an exit vector, I have this." Seconds later, crimson streaks of cannon fire blasted the bow of the boarding craft, the grappling beam ceased, and the shuttle shot forward. The Galv veered away while the soldier held the cannon fire on the boarding craft's engine until the core ruptured. It bloomed orange, then vanished.

"We have another Galv vessel on an intersect course from above." The Saint said, pointing at her screen. "He's locking grappling beams…." The ship slowed again.

"Do not panic. Push the nose over and give the shuttle all the power you can. Cut life support if need be."

The bulkheads groaned as the Saint pushed the nose over. The soldier swung the cannon barrel around, changed the emitters from narrow beam to wide-focus, and targeted the Galv pilot. He pressed the firing stud. The viewports on the Galv boarding ship flared red, then imploded. The containment beam vanished as the craft veered off.

Their shuttle once again shot free. "Aren't you going to destroy his craft?" The Saint asked as their shuttle picked up speed.

"No, it is already dead. We need to conserve power. Where are the other boarding crafts?"

"They are still closing. Estimate they will catch us in…." The Emissary never finished her statement as the space around them burst silver-red, blinding her. She raised an arm over her eyes and turned away.

"The Galv battle platform core has detonated." Jonqueen growled over the alarms. "We must enter slip before the shock wave catches us."

"Trying to find a lock. Normal-space is completely distorted. Spacial strings aren't detectable."

"Shock wave in ninety seconds… increasing ship integrity, rerouting power from all systems. We might survive, but no guarantees the drives will." Jonqueen advised. Unbuckling his harness, the soldier staggered toward the engine bay as smoke billowed from the compartment.

"Wave still closing… what are you doing?" The Saint said over her shoulder as she searched for escape vectors.

"I am reading compression errors with the slipstream power matrix. If I do not repair it now, it might rupture upon reversion to normal space. It would trap us wherever we exit." He pulled panels from the floor near the rear of the shuttle—acrid smoke billowed from the hatch, filling the cabin with a greasy haze.

"Blast wave in forty seconds… how bad is it?"

The soldier closed the hatch and sealed it. "Terminal. We need to find a long spacial string because this is going to be a single transit." He returned to his seat, buckled in, then brought up his targeting scanner.

"Blast wave in twenty seconds."

"We have company. Find any string you can and engage the slip. A Galv vessel survived the detonation and is closing." Jonqeen slid the targeting hood over his head, then gripped the firing stud. "Drop engine power and bring him to us."

"Soldier, the shock wave is on top of us." The Saint argued.

"Just do it."

The Saint took a deep breath, then drew the throttle back, allowing the Galv vessel to close. "Hold steady, here they come."

"I have a lock! Energizing slipstream now." the lights dimmed as the shuttle opened a rip in space.

"Where is the terminus?" Jonqueen asked, still targeting the Galv vessel.

"Unknown, just trying to get ahead of the wave." The Saint pushed the engine throttles forward and drove through the slip.

Chapter Three

"Are you sure you are able to pilot through the slip?" The soldier hissed through a clenched jaw as the small craft yawed and rolled. He silenced the warning klaxons but couldn't stop the lights from flashing.

"I am qualified. Though my training did not include a ship this small."

"I believe that once we get beyond the distortions from the battle zone, the strings will untangle." The soldier said as he held fast to the arms of his seat.

"Let's hope so. We need a bit more speed." She held the steering yoke firmly in both hands as she followed the wormhole through slipstream.

The soldier slowly turned her way. "Why?"

"Apparently, remnants of the shock wave followed us in. It's gaining on us. I believe it will eventually overtake us. I don't know how much energy it will contain, but it appears deadly."

The soldier changed his display to show the aft view of the craft. It portrayed the wormhole as a long, winding amber tunnel. Closing on the shuttle was a churning cloud of debris. The soldier hissed. "Embedded in the cloud are the remains of the ships destroyed in the blast. The wormhole is channeling it forward, compressing the cloud. When it catches up to the shuttle, it will chew through us. Start looking for transit points, cross strings, anything."

"I'm trying. I don't know if it's the subspace distortions or damage to our star maps, but I haven't found an inhabitable world yet." She relaxed her concentration to risk a quick glance at Jonqueen. "Maybe a blue world will be our savior." She smiled slightly and then went back to concentrating.

The soldier scoffed. "A blue world—a tale to frighten children." He adjusted his display to concentrate on the broiling debris cloud. "Behind is a much more terrifying story." The cloud continued to tumble, expand, and contract. Explosions of red and silver light burst from it as trapped gasses detonated, increasing the speed of the wave.

"Anything on the star maps?"

"No, the void we are crossing is quite massive. I'm unable to get a lock on *anything*. There are no way-points or string vectors. On the positive side, the strings are smoothing out."

"Very well, do what you can while I monitor the wave." The soldier sat with his gloved hands clasped under his chin as data scrolled across his terminal. "The cloud is accelerating. How, I do not know. But I estimated we now have much less than an hour before it overruns us."

The shuttle buckled as a tremor shot through the deck. Hull breach warnings flashed. The soldier cursed under his breath as he swiped across his display board.

"What's happening?" The Saint shouted over the sounds of escaping atmosphere and alarms. She fought the steering yokes to keep the craft on the slipstream guide.

"We're losing slipstream containment and are facing a forced exit if I can't stabilize the slipstream. We are also slowing, the shockwave is closing, estimate the

debris field will contact us in….” The soldiers' hands
tapped madly on his display panel as a new explosion
ejected flames and burning conduit from the slipstream
bay. The lights in the shuttle flickered.

The Saint flipped up the cover on her control panel
and a palm-sized yellow pad appeared. Before the
soldier could stop her, she slapped the pad, and the
shuttle burst through the slipstream wall and back into
normal space.

The shuttle was tumbling, atmosphere venting from
multiple hull fractures. Smoke poured from the engine
bay as emergency warnings howled incessantly. The
soldier muted the alarms, unbuckled, and found himself
free-floating in the cabin—the artificial gravity offlinc.
His ears rang, and his chest hurt from the sudden
deceleration into normal space. The Saint hung limp in
her harness, blood leaking through her robes. A broken
flight-control yoke floated slowly around her.

The soldier pulled a med scanner from his belt and
waved it over the unconscious Emissary. “Broken ribs,
concussion, lacerations, minor smoke inhalation.” He
studied the scanner's report and sighed. “You will live.”
He swam through the cabin, pushing away console
shards and pooling bubbles of drive coolant. Finding
the hull leaks was easy: smoke drifted toward them,
forming whirlpools in the air. Jonqueen sealed the first
crack with his armor's nano-technology.. Within an
hour, he had sealed the atmospheric leaks. Entering the
fire-scorched engine bay, he freed blackened modules,
and replacing them with cannibalize parts from other
systems. He backed out of the bay and re-powered the

computer. Seconds later, as the artificial gravity initialized, scorched parts and balls of floating coolant rained to the deck.

Jonqueen returned to his seat to re-energize the engine core. Red lines showing damaged components flashed on the display boards, only a few systems in yellow, and none in green. He brought the thrusters online and stopped the spin. Stepping to the Saint, he put on ceramic-lined gloves and gently pulled away her blood-stained robes. Underneath her clothing, he discovered a crystal shard from a display panel embedded in her side, just below her ribs. The Saint's eyes opened but remained unfocused.

"You are wounded but will survive. Your worst injury is an impalement by a sliver of the console. I am going to remove it and seal the injury. But I have nothing for the pain. Do you understand?"

She nodded.

The soldier applied pressure and removed the glass dagger. The Saint tensed but remained conscious. "That was the painless part. I now have to cauterize the wound using the nanites from my armor." He held his palm over the wound. Black strings of nanites spilled out and flowed into the injury. Wisps of smoke rose as the nanites cauterized the wound. The Saint groaned, and passed out. The soldier sealed her robes, smiled, and gently patted her shoulder. She had lasted longer than some of the strongest warriors he had witnessed being patched up on the battlefield.

The sensor console beeped. Jonqueen brought up the display; it was the proximity warning again. A vessel was on a collision course. Adjusting the scanners, he narrowed the search. Two thousand meters out drifted a lifeless Galv ship. But not a boarding craft: a long-range armored transport. He ran the scanners over every inch of the vessel. The engines were cold, life support not functioning. Several hull breaches were purging the contents of the ship.

"Hope you died in pain." The soldier cursed and keyed in the engine's restart protocols. He then turned his attention to repairing the communications grid and long-range sensors. He cycled through the command bands, picking up nothing but cold solar static. To inspect the wrecked sensor array, a spacewalk would be necessary. But he would wait until the Saint regained consciousness.

The consoles slowly came to life as the soldier bypassed and repaired damaged nodes.

The Saint stirred and woke. "Where are we?" she managed.

"Unknown. Long-range scanners are down, along with communications. Only system operating is short-range scans. Engines are currently online, life support is minimal, and weapons are not operational."

"Is there any good news?"

"We have abundant fuel for the sublight engines."

"Slipstream?"

"Not possible. If we could find a planet within range of our fuel supply, one that had the requisite materials, I might be able to manufacture replacement parts." He spun his chair to look at her. "Why did you exit the slip when you did?"

She allowed a weak smile to crease her pale lips. "You'll think me mad, but just before the wave caught us, I glanced up at the display and we were crossing the plane of a blue world. I hit the slipstream abort panel, and we exited here."

The soldier stepped to the forward viewport and stared out into empty, dark space. "I, for one, hope it exists, despite the horror stories. It might be our only chance to survive." He crossed to the rear of the cabin and opened a locker. Pulling out an evac suit, the soldier turned to the Saint. "I have to repair the scanning array atop the ship. I should not be long. How is your pain?"

She took in a deep breath and tried to stand. "Manageable. Thank you. Do you need any assistance?"

"No. Please continue the sensor sweeps. There is a Galv armored transport two thousand meters to port. It is drifting and appears derelict. If it shows any signs of life, let me know, then shut everything down."

The Saint nodded gingerly.

The soldier sealed his evacuation suit and stepped through the airlock.

The Saint was slumped in her chair when the soldier returned. His worry was replaced with relief when he noticed the Emissary's chest slowly rising and falling, a light snore whistling from her lips. He moved to the communications panel and charged the scanning array. To his surprise, the board fully energized. His first sensor sweeps detected no planets in close range. "Maybe the blue world is out here and maybe it is not." He said to himself before firing the sublight engines. He aimed the ship toward a weak yellow star at the far edge of his scan.

With navigation, communication, and long-range scanners back online, Jonqueen returned to the scorched slipstream engine compartment. He opened the hatch and descended into the drive bay. The smoke was gone, but coolant pooled on the floor, and the acrid odor of fused and melted components was overpowering. What the exploding conduits hadn't damaged or destroyed, the fire had. Even if he had the materials from a dozen sets of body armor, he could do nothing. It would take a full-fledged space dock to tear down and rebuild the drive. When the Saint called him, he was severing the last of the power conduits to the drive and rerouting to the sublight engines.

She turned when he exited the slipstream bay. "We have a signal, very weak, and not of natural origin."

"Shovain or Firestar? It is not the Galv, is it?"

"Unknown. As I said, it's very weak and intermittent. I've set the NavCom to follow and decipher."

"Direction?"

"Straight ahead."

"Very well. I am increasing power to the engines. Might want to make yourself comfortable. This is going to be a long voyage."

The Saint nodded and stretched, wincing from the wound beneath her ribs. "There's only one stateroom onboard. You look like you could use some rest. I'll keep watch on the NavCom."

"No, you are the Emissary de'tantel. I was tasked with bringing you home. And as a soldier of the Firestar Confederacy, I need not rest. It is my duty to protect you and deliver you. When I require rest, I will let you know. Besides, you are injured. You need time to recuperate."

She stared up at him, moved to pat him on the arm, then thought better of it. "Thank you, sol…" The Saint sighed. "I'm tired of calling you by your assignment. What is your name?"

The soldier stared down at her before answering. "If we were in the Firestar Confederacy, I would be incensed at your request. But since we are not, my given name is Jonqueen P'tonich."

"Jonqueen, from the ancient text meaning *guardian of the hunted*. How prophetic."

"You have read the ancient text? I was not aware that any Shovain had read or could comprehend the ancient scrolls."

"There is much we don't know about each other. Maybe this journey to the blue world will help us understand each other better. Perhaps all this is predestined."

Jonqueen studied the Saint, his eyes narrowed. He took a deep breath and his expression softened. "Emissary, your name. What do they call you on your world?"

She slowly turned, smiled, and shook her head. "Let's not give up all our mysteries just yet. In time, Jonqueen, guardian of the hunted. In time."

The soldier snorted and let the corner of his mouth turn up just a millimeter. Sitting back down in the command chair, he stretched the displays out across the remains of the panel and started searching for a place to repair the shuttle. Even if it was on a horror called the Blue World.

Chapter Four

A speaker in the ceiling of the small stateroom hummed to life. "Emissary, if you would, please join me at the NavCom." The speaker cut out with a click. She pushed the bedclothes off and slid from the berth. The pain this time was much sharper than before, biting into her gut. *Oh, I hope this is just part of the FireStar healing treatment.* She glanced at the chronograph on her wrist. *I've been asleep for almost an entire solar day!* Limping, she made her way to the shuttle's small command deck.

"How are your injuries?" Jonqueen asked without taking his gaze off the instruments.

"I think worse than before. I fear there are more shards of the panel inside me."

The soldier nodded. "Possibly. The nanites will track and consume them. That could be the additional pain you are feeling. The treatment is designed for my physiology but will work with most beings."

"You wanted to show me something?"

"I do." He transferred the long-range scanner view to the main screen. At first, the image was a blurry starscape. "The image will clear momentarily. I have spent the last nineteen hours reviewing scans of this system and have two very interesting facts I want to share with you. One, I think I know where and when we are."

"Really, that's good news!"

"No, it is not. I have accessed the limited amount of information we have on the current star alignments. We are in the *Devoured Vortex*."

"I've never known the Firestar Confederacy to have a sense of humor," the Saint teased. "That's a bigger child's tale than that of the Blue World."

"Regardless, the description fits. No life, no inhabitable worlds, nothing but a weak, dying star."

"So, when we fail so show up on Shovain, unless they know which direction to look for us, we are marooned."

"That is correct. But there is more to it than that. As I said, I know where we are, but uncertain of *when* we are."

"When we are? What are you talking about?" The woman turned his way, eyes wide.

"I have compared the position of the stars with the shuttle's available maps. Taking into account celestial drift, my best guess is that we have traveled back approximately five thousand solar cycles."

"That is not possible!" The Emissary said as she slumped into the co-pilot seat.

"I hypothesize as when we opened the slipstream, the Galv engine core exploded, warping the spacial. Not only did we open a wormhole through space, but also time. That can be the only explanation why the pressure wave continued to build and accelerate. We should have been able to outrun it. But with the compression of time *and* space, it was squeezing the wormhole from behind and forcing all the energy forward."

The Saint stared blankly out of the forward viewport. "So, there is no possibility of rescue." She said, her voice barely a whisper. "The Galv has won after all. Our people will continue to fight each other and die. The Galv will then obliterate what is left." She closed her eyes. "There is a very good chance we might end up being the last of our kind."

Jonqueen didn't reply but nodded in agreement.

"So, where do we go from here?"

"I have set the NavCom toward the star on the display." Tapping on his panel, he changed the focus to a detailed view of the system surrounding the star. "There is one planet orbiting close enough to support life as we understand it. Unfortunately, I have detected no transmissions, which can mean three things: either there is no life, or what is there is too primitive to be of any help. Or there is a society advanced enough to know we are here and are shielding their communications from us."

The Saint traced the projected orbits of the planets around the sun. "How long before we are in range to know more?"

"At our current speed, we should be able to refine our scans in twelve days."

"We have enough fuel?"

Jonqueen nodded. "Fuel is not an issue. We could run at maximum burn for fifty-eight solar days. Food is our pressing issue. Our emergency supplies will last less than nine days. The ship was being re-stocked when the Galv attacked. I can instruct the nanites in my armor to convert some of the material to a protein I can ingest. This will stretch the food resources. If we must travel over twelve days, we will need to find an edible food sources on another planet. And that might prove difficult."

The Saint nodded. "Very well. I guess all we can do is sit back and wait."

Several uneventful solar days passed. Jonqueen was sleeping when The Saint called him. "Please join me at the NavCom. We are receiving transmissions. They're faint and might be nothing more than background radiation, but I don't think so."

The soldier slowly climbed from the berth he and The Saint had been sharing. His mind felt sluggish, and his legs were heavy. The nanites have been reconfiguring his armor for the past five days, turning it into a paste he could eat. He wouldn't starve to death until he ran out of armor, but the material was tasteless and lacked the energy he required to remain sharp. He toggled the com in the cabin. "On my way." He stretched, then tightened his armor for the third time. Soon it would be too loose to be effective.

The Saint turned to him when he reached the shuttle's small command deck. "You look weary."

"I am," He said without elaborating. "Can you playback the transmissions you received?"

She retrieved the data files and replayed them.

Jonqueen leaned forward, resting his hands on his thighs. After several minutes of rapt attention to the signals, he swiped his hands across the board. The view changed to the black emptiness of space. He leaned back and sighed.

"Well," asked the Saint. "Are those transmissions or not?"

Jonqueen turned her way and nodded. "They are. According to the ship's computer, there is a relatively advanced civilization four days' travel from our position. Not anywhere near our technological level. But they are developed and have rudimentary scanning devices. As for what kind of beings these are, I do not know. Some communications might contain video content, but I have not been able to decode the signal. I will continue to work on it while you rest."

"Rest? I can't rest now, not this close to …something." She sat in the co-pilot chair, crossed her legs, and entered commands into the computer to generate a model of the system they were approaching. "You spend your life amongst the stars. I live in one small community on Shovain. All I have experienced are simulators and holo-vids." She leaned forward. "Despite the perilous position we find ourselves in, I find this fascinating. How long before we can determine what type of species we might encounter?"

"Within forty-five solar hours, we should be close enough for detailed scans of their world. We will then know if the planet is wet, dry, or near death. I'm working to decipher several of the transmission bands. The signal is unlike anything I have ever encountered."

"So, it's very advanced, then?"

"No, incredibly basic, almost like a child's babble." He tapped hurriedly on the panel. "But for the life of me, I cannot find an algorithm that can decode and display it."

"I'm sure you'll figure it out. I have faith in you."

"Why? We are marooned, and are likely to starve to death."

"Because, in the time we have spent together, you haven't failed. And I have a hard time believing that a simple child's babble will stump you for long."

He tilted his head in acceptance of her statements.

"Now, figure out that data, and let's see who our saviors are to be."

"You think they can save us?" Jonqueen asked her directly.

She smiled at him and said nothing more.

Jonqueen cursed under his breath. "Another aggravating trait of your species."

The soldier continued to investigate the weak signals emanating from deep in the distant solar system. All the algorithms aboard the shuttle failed to decrypt and understand the signals. And to make matters worse, The Saint's words haunted him. *How could such a primitive world produce a communication he could not crack? Babies babble.* He leaned back in the seat and stared at the ceiling. "Emissary, do you still have the Firestar Confederacy's communications data cube?"

The Saint sat up slowly, took a deep breath and rubbed sleep from her eyes. "Yes, I was instructed to keep it close by at all times. Why do you ask?"

"May I please hold it?"

She stared at Jonqueen, eyes questioning. "I am not supposed to not let it leave my person. Without the device, we will not have the ability to communicate."

"That is true, but your comment of 'child's babble' has me thinking: could your device transcribe the signal into a language we—I, you—can understand? That is its basic function."

"We won't be able to communicate if I hand it over, or at least I won't be able to understand you."

"You are correct. But if this works, I can build an interpretation key that will transcribe whatever this signal is into our two languages."

"And if it doesn't, it could damage the cube, and we won't be able to communicate at all."

"Unfortunately, that is also true." He held out his hand. "The comboard in this vessel will translate my words so that we can communicate during the time I'm reconfiguring the cube."

The Saint dropped the glowing orange, pendant-sized device in his hand. He placed one palm on the data board, the other over the cube. A mist of nanites descended on the device, changing its shape and color. Moments later, he held it up. It was now more diamond shape and grayish-green.

"Now, let us check the babble." The ship repeated his words in a monotone, metallic voice. He placed the translator in an opening on the comboard. The diamond began to glow and pulse as data streams spilled from it. The color of the cube morphed from green to amber, and finally, a deep red. It flashed several times, then darkened.

"Did it work?" The Saint asked, rising slightly from her chair.

"I believe it has," the soldier said through the ship's speakers. "The ship is now decompressing all the data it has gathered and is building a computer matrix to translate the broadcasts. We should know what to expect in the next few hours." He retrieved the translator and again held his hand over the crystal. A second cloud of nanites swarmed the diamond-shaped device, changing it back to its original design.

"I have enhanced the auditory abilities of the crystal. It should be able to translate the speech of the aliens we will encounter." He handed it to the Saint, dropping it in her hand before their fingers touched. She replaced it in the pouch she wore on her side, winced, and held her head.

"Emissary, are you ill?"

"No, Jonqueen. Whatever you did to the crystal, it… feels strange, not in synch with my interface. I'm experiencing a touch of nausea."

"I am sorry; the interface might be more sensitive now than before. It might take a few hours before the communication matrix in the cube and your subdermal interface are fully synched."

The soldier studied the data from spilling from the comboard, quietly nodding. "It is working better than I had expected. Whatever this species is, their world is ablaze with communications. I have seen nothing like this before. The sheer volume of data flowing from the planet is staggering." His fingers slid across the display panel, dancing and tapping commands. "I am having the computer coalesce the information into various categories." He shook his head again. "I have also detected several bands of communications that I feel are military." His hand continued to fly across the comboard board. "One issue we are experiencing is their communications are as free-flowing as any I have ever encountered. It also includes basic encryption algorithms that are not the easiest to penetrate."

The Saint turned his way and watched the soldier's black eyes narrow, and his angular face tighten. "You are quite enjoying this, aren't you?"

He paused, sat back, stretched his arms, and clenched his fists. "This race is either unparalleled in their primitive brilliant ways or absolutely insane."

"Why so?"

"They transmit every aspect of their existence. I am detecting communications that can best be described as their attempts at music, art and," He sat up straight, his eyes narrowing again, his breath quickening, "war." Ashamed of his lack of composure, he regained his calm.

"War? Are you sure? Do they pose a danger to us?"

"Not currently. I feel certain that we are far beyond their abilities to detect." He replaced the data streams with a closer view of the solar system. "I'm only detecting communications from one of the small worlds in the habitational zone around the system's primary star. Scans on the outer worlds have shown the to be void of any life. We will soon be close enough for me to refine the data."

"So, more waiting."

"Yes," he answered quietly. "Much more waiting."

They were approaching the outer planets, and the quality of the data streams was increasing exponentially. The scans confirmed only one inhabited world. Jonqueen's terminal chimed, advising the computer had compiled the data.

"Emissary, are you awake?"

The Saint stretched, yawned, and then pushed up in her seat. "I am now. Do we know more?"

The soldier nodded slowly. "We do. My fascination with this race has increased exponentially." He turned to her. "They are a world at war. I am detecting trace amounts of high explosive residue in their upper atmosphere. I am not sure to what scale the fighting is, but I am certain that the populace is a warrior breed."

Jonqueen paused as additional data streamed from the console. "While you slept, I instructed the computer to present a composite image of the dominate specie. The shipboard AI has gone one step forward: it has found two images that it believes to be the male and female."

"Have you viewed it yet?"

"No, I thought it would be more interesting to see the images together."

"I agree. Please put it on the forward display." The Sainted brought her robes in tight and pulled them close to her face. "I am excited and terrified at the same time. I will never forget the time I encountered a Leftrokian as a child. I still have nightmares." The Saint shuddered and drew her robes even tighter.

"They are an… interesting species. Benign, but horrifying in appearance." The front view screen changed from displaying the data feed to cold black starlight; then, the species appeared on the screen. The soldier sat back hard, and the Saint gasped. The image was more troubling than the Leftrokian could ever be.

"This can't be," whispered the Saint as she held her hands against her face.

Chapter Five

The screen was slowly rotating, a three-dimensional picture of a dark-haired, blue-eyed female on display. Next to the woman, a male slowly turned. His brown hair, dark eyes, and olive skin peered back at the Saint and Soldier.

"Are you sure the compute's rendition is correct and that these are accurate depictions of the inhabitants of this world?"

"I am. And I am as shocked as you are. They appear to be Shovain." He sat back and watched the images rotate. "Are there any ancient records from your world of lost colonies, separatists leaving for the stars?"

"None that I am aware of. But, there are legends, stories of a fierce Shovain tribe that was incredibly powerful and wise. They were led by a female chieftain whose hair blazed like a supernova. The scrolls tell of her unwavering bravery."

"And what happened to this tribe?"

The Emissary laughed and shrugged sheepishly. "They are just stories, ancient tales told to children when there were afraid. They legend seemed to originate during one of the darkest periods on Shovain existence, when we were still fighting each other, destroying our civilization."

"But no records of lost colonies or separatist?"

The Saint shook her head. "Explorers have searched all the habitable worlds in the Shovain system, and dozens more that can't sustain Shovain life. Despite all

the rumors and whispers of lost transports, we have
found no remains of our ancient ancestors on any
planet."

"Fascinating. And yet, here they are."

"Yes, here they are." The Saint said nodding.

They sat in silence as the shuttle continued toward
the small, weak sun. The male and female images slowly
revolving.

The soldier terminated the images and brought up
the ship's diagnostics. "We should be in the planet's
orbit within thirteen hours. I am continuing sensor
sweeps of the outer worlds for defensive weapons or
vessels. But from what I have observed, I feel we are in
no danger."

Jonqueen entered commands into the shuttle's
computer.

"I have additional data on the planet," Jonqueen said
after a moment. "Oxygen, nitrogen atmosphere, very
similar to your home planet. Its inhabitants identify this
world as Earth," barely taking his eyes off the
information being displayed by the computer, the
soldier turned to the Saint, "and it has a slightly higher
ambient temperature and gravitational field than
Shovain."

"Can they detect us?"

"No. The outbound scans I have intercepted are
crude. We should be able to remain hidden until
landfall, if we choose to land."

"Is there anything else I need to know about the
planet?"

"Yes," Jonqueen answered. "There is this." The
screen changed from the scans to the world they were

approaching. "Our destination." Jonqueen zoomed in on the planet, it slowly rotated on the main viewer. "Your species on a blue planet."

The Saint walked over to the main screen and stared at the image. "Have you ever seen a planet like this?"

"Never."

"How can anything be alive on it?"

"It apparently has a breathable atmosphere, abundant plant life, and blue oceans. It defies all that our scientists have taught us to believe. We might be able to breathe the air, but the food will surely be toxic."

"How long until we arrive?" The Saint shifted in her seat.

"If we push the engines, eight hours." The soldier replied.

"Any thoughts as to the inhabitants? Will we be able to communicate, or will they attack us?"

"My nanites are learning the languages on the planet, will transmit the speech patterns to your data cube. Communication should not be an issue. But with the amount of high-explosive residue in the atmosphere, we can assume they are hostile."

The Saint settled back in her chair as the blue planet spun on the screen. It was strange to see a world she had been taught since childhood to fear, slowly approaching. And to have a species that mirrored her own was too bizarre to comprehend. They would have to wait half a solar day to know for sure.

"Is there anything you need me to do to prepare for landing?"

"Not immediately. Once we reach a geosynchronous orbit, I will need you to watch for missile or attack craft.

We should be able to handle anything they send at us, but we have already received several surprises. Once we thoroughly scan this planet, I will find a place to land where we will not be discovered. Then we will figure out what next to do."

"Do you need rest? You've been on deck for several solar days now, you must be weary. Plus, you haven't eaten. Rest, so you will be at your best."

The soldier turned and let the corner of his mouth tick up. "I appreciate your concern, but I am fine. My nanites are very efficient at keeping me sufficiently nourished." He turned back to the control board, made a course correction, and then turned back. "You are more than welcome to eat or sleep. I fear that our days of luxury are soon to end."

"I've slept enough. I'm tired of sleeping and doing nothing. I think I'll keep you company."

"Very well."

Jonqueen brought the shuttle from the moon's shadow and fired the thrusters, navigating behind a long, spindly satellite containing several of the planet's inhabitants. "Brave beings, I will give them that." He throttled down the thrusters and drifted past the station.

"I'm monitoring communications. They have not seen us." The Emissary said.

"I have blacked the hull. They will not see us unless we crash into them. Their sensors might pick up a random heat signature, but they will not know where it emanated."

The soldier changed the image from the space station to an arid section of the planet. "I have been scanning the Northern hemisphere. There is ample desert to land, though I am uncertain if there is a sufficient technological base for us to repair the slip drive."

As the shuttled descended toward the blue planet, soft vibrations rippled through the deck plates. "Encountering the first layers of their atmosphere, slightly heavier than your world. I'm adjusting our gravity to match. You will start feeling heavy soon."

The Saint stared out the shuttle's windows, watching the blue world fill the transparent portal. "It's so very… alien." She said as they flew over the Atlantic Ocean. "I've never seen seas of this color. It looks lifeless."

"Anything but. These seas are teaming with life, once again, most likely toxic to us, but very much alive."

Red streaks of plasma flickered around the edge of the viewports as the shuttle rocked slightly, the descent becoming rougher. "I am trying to keep our approach on the light side of the planet as much as possible to prevent our entry from being noticed. At night we would resemble a meteor."

The world swerved slightly; the shuttle rocking. "That was interesting. What just happened?"

"Unsure,"Jonqueen said. "Possibly atmospheric conditions we cannot detect, adjusting our course toward the open deserts. It will take an orbit or two to keep us in the light and not attract attention. If you will, please stow our gear, secure any loose items. We are about to encounter increased atmospheric pressure; the descent will not be smooth."

The Saint nodded in agreement, unbuckled, and crossed the deck. She reached the small sleeping quarters when the shuttle veered again, and an explosion rippled through the craft. Alarm bells wailed as the shuttle rolled.

"What happened?" She shouted over the sound of alarms and vibrations.

"Unsure! Starboard thruster bank has exploded… trying to compensate." The shuttled rolled to the left when another explosion knocked the Saint to the floor. "Main engine bay explosion, leaking coolant and fuel." Smoke seeped into the cabin from the aft bay.

"Could this be prior damage from the slip?" The Saint yelled over the alarms and shuddering craft.

"I doubt it." His hands danced on the board. He cursed under his breath. "I need you to buckle up and arm weapons!"

"I didn't think they could see us!"

"They cannot, but the Galv can." He hissed, fighting a shuttle that was quickly losing its ability to fly. "They have followed us and concealed themselves from my scans. I should have destroyed their craft when we first exited the slipstream."

The Saint powered the weapons grid. The firing yoke materialized out of the console. She pulled the hood on and scanned the skies. "Don't see them!"

"Be prepared, I'm about to come about!"

Jonqueen engaged the atmospheric brakes, throwing the Saint forward. The shuttle pitched violently, and an oval flat-gray vessel shot past. Bringing the power back on, they pursued the Galv transport. The sighting reticle flashed red; the Saint pulled the trigger. Flashes of charged protons streaked from under the bow, stitching a destructive trail up the rear of the transport. She held

the firing stud until the Galv rolled away, climbing for
the edge of space.

The soldier rolled the damaged shuttle away from the
fleeing craft, pushing the nose over. Hot plasma gases
no longer licked at the edge of the cockpit, but hungrily
tried to devour it. A side panel burst into flames, smoke
beginning to fill the craft.

The Saint pulled the hood off and turned to the
soldier. "We must go after them!"

"That is not an option. We have lost most of the
starboard thrusters, and the sublight engines have
suffered extensive damage. We will do well to survive
this landing, much less pursue the Galv vehicle." He
glanced her way, then back to the controls. "You did
well. The Galv suffered significant damage to their
drives. They may not have the power to escape this
planet's gravity. Let's just hope they burn up in the
atmosphere."

"I'm monitoring local communications, picking up
reports of a major fireball shooting across the sky. I
assume that is us?"

The soldier nodded.

"Civilian transmissions don't seem to be interested in
us, but…" she paused and closed her eyes, "we might
have attracted the attention of military assets. They are
dispatching," she paused again, "interceptor aircraft."

The soldier snorted. "They will be no match, even in
our damaged state."

"We can't fire on them. You must get us down
before they reach us."

Jonqueen sneered. "As you will." He banked hard to
starboard, the shuttle groaning and creaking.

"You're not going for the desert?"

"I no longer feel we can reach the western deserts without being detected. There is a quarry within our glide-slope. We should be able to land and remain hidden. Making a second orbit is no longer possible."

The shuttle plummeted toward the Eastern horizon, smoke and flames trailing in its wake. The ground quickly closed as Jonqueen steered the damaged craft toward the quarry. Fighter jets screamed overhead. "Brace yourself. The repulsors cannot arrest our descent completely. Contact with the ground in thirty seconds."

Pulling her harness tight, the Saint braced for impact. Collision alerts competed with Klaxons broadcasting fire and smoke warnings. The shuttle careened through a hundred feet of trees before slamming into the quarry floor. The lights went out in the shuttle, and darkness swarmed in.

Chapter Six

Sam loved watching his radio-controlled plane fly. It was a scale model of a WWII P-51 fighter. It had been his father's, and now it was his. He watched it climb toward the clouds, the miniature, raspy engine howling as he pushed the throttle forward. He guided it through a series of spirals, brought the nose over, and let it back toward the grassy field. Sam deftly worked the controls, bringing the small aircraft out of its spin and parallel to the ground. It flew past at over eighty miles per hour. He tracked it as it flew from his left to right, then pulled back up on the yoke to send it racing back toward the sky.

His father used to fly it with him when he was in astronaut flight school. That was ten years ago, before his father's plane was lost in a search-and-rescue mission off the coast of Florida for a downed 'copter. A fishing boat later rescued the helicopter's crew. No such luck for Crawford Shepherd. The bird he was piloting crashed into the sea and sank in several hundred feet of water.

The small engine began to cough and sputter. Sam brought the little plane back to a near-perfect landing on the grassy field by the high school. It bounced twice before rolling to a stop twenty feet away, the prop no longer spinning. Opening the trunk to his father's fire engine red 1970 Camaro Z28, Sam pulled out a small can of fuel. He was walking over to the plane when a football smacked him in the back of his head. He dropped the can and turned to see Ronnie Howell laughing and strutting his way. Trailing him were Brandon Newhard and Fletcher Jones.

Crap, not now, Sam thought as he picked up the ball.

"Yo, flyboy, how 'bout tossing us back the ball?" Ronnie yelled to him.

Sam took the ball and threw it back, but far over the boy's head. "My bad, man."

"Uncool, flyboy. Very uncool." Fletcher snapped, then trotted after the ball. He picked it up, underhanded it to Ronnie, who cocked his arm, then drilled the small plane where it sat on the ground. The plane flipped over and landed upside down. The trio laughed.

Sam ran over, picked up the ball, and punted it as far as possible. "If you broke it, you're paying for it!"

Ronnie charged and shoved Sam hard in the chest, knocking him flat on his back. "Oh yeah, you think so? You're lucky I don't stomp it flat!" He growled, raising his foot to crush the plane.

A shrill whistle followed by a booming voice made him pause. "Ronnie, if you don't get your butt on the field by the time I get there, you'll be running laps for the next week!" Coach Barns shouted as he came up behind the boys. He grabbed Fletcher and Brandon by the neck and pitched them forward. "That goes for you two morons as well. Get your butts on that practice field, or you're running laps with your girlfriend. Now get!"

Fletcher and Brandon gave Sam a wide berth but spit at him as they passed.

"Enough!" screamed Barns. "You two are running laps until practice is over."

With his mirrored sunglasses perched on his balding head, Coach Barns walked over to Sam and helped him to his feet. "Son, you all right."

Sam brushed himself off and nodded. "Yeah, I'm good. I just hope they didn't hurt the P51."

"How's your chest?

"My chest?"

"I know about your heart condition."

Sam stared at him. "I'm fine." He picked up the plane, ran his eyes over it, and let out a long breath when he realized the football had done no damage. "How did you know about my heart?"

Coach smiled. "Part of the job, son. You haven't taken PE since you've been in school. So, I figured there must be a reason."

"Yeah, it's a congenital defect. Mom's afraid that if I get too overheated, I could have a heart attack. It sucks, but there's nothing I can do about it."

"There's still a lot you can do." The coach said as he placed a thick, muscular hand on Sam's shoulder.

Sam nodded, "Yeah, that's what mom keeps telling me." He shrugged. "I'm still trying to figure out what I want to do."

"Still want to be an astronaut like your dad?"

"Technically, dad was never an astronaut, just in the training program, but yeah, that's what I want to do." Sam rapped on his chest. "But with this issue, I'm pretty much earthbound."

Coach gave Sam's shoulder a fatherly squeeze. "Well, son, maybe you can work for NASA and search the stars from good ol' terra firma."

Sam nodded slightly. "Yes, sir, that might work. Won't be the same rush as launching into space, but they give you a nice shirt with a cool patch."

Coach Barns chuckled, then patted him on the back. "It'll work out son, might not be what you want, but it'll all work out." The coach pointed at a group of boys wrestling another kid to the ground. "Alrighty, son, gotta rustle up my knuckleheads before they get into trouble. Take care, Sam."

"You too, coach."

Coach Barns jogged across the field, blowing loud blasts with his whistle to gather up the football team. Sam carefully picked up his plane and fuel can, then walked to a more secluded section of the park to fly. Once refueled, he launched it back into the sky. With the plane airborne again, twisting and turning as it streaked skyward, he forgot about the football players, his damaged heart and the world around him.

Pulling back on the sticks, he piloted the P51 into another climbing, corkscrewing ascent on the clouds. He flew the plane through a series of barrel rolls before pushing the nose over and back toward the ground. Once again, his thumbs managed the controls instinctively, pulling the plane from its demise ten feet off the grass and climbing toward the pines at the end of the field. The aircraft was flying over the trees when the plane…exploded. The orange flash blinded him for a moment. When he turned back, he saw smoke and pieces of his plane falling from the cloudless sky.

Sam stared disbelieving at the plane's falling, smoldering remains, his hands still working the dead controls of the doomed fighter. Anger pulsed in his head. He dropped the controls, clenched his fist, and sprinted for the tree line toward the figures exiting the woods.

"You've gone too far this time!" He screamed, anger blurring his vision. His charge slowed when he saw the large, flat-gray weapon barrel pointing at him. The person holding it was not a football player or anyone. Correction, *anything* he had seen before.

Sam stuttered-stepped to a stop, turned, and ran toward his car several hundred feet away. His heart was pounding in his head and his breath coming in ragged gasps. His saliva tasted coppery. He reached the car and ran around to the driver's side. He dug in his pocket for the key when the creature raised its weapon and fired.

His teeth clacked shut, nearly biting off the tip of his tongue. He crashed against the side of his car and dropped to his knees. The pain in his head was incapacitating. Just opening his eyes made tears flow. Sam staggered to his fee and slid along his car, clutching his temples. Now it wasn't just his head, but his back, chest, and legs were on fire. He collapsed to the ground. *Oh, God, I'm having a heart attack.* He rocked to his knees, fighting to keep from vomiting. *Mom, I've got to call mom. She doesn't know where I am.* Sam pulled his phone from his pocket and stared at it. The display was black, shattered. He pushed himself into a sitting position. The breathing was easier, but his eyes still burned, the woods and grass watery. A shadow passed over him; then cool hands were holding his face. The world still wavered, but a woman knelt before him, studying him, concern etched across her intense sapphire blue eyes. She was talking to him, but he couldn't understand what she was saying.

Her words were like static and wind, crunching dry leaves and snowfall.

Not a heart attack; I've had a stroke. "I can't understand you," Sam croaked.

The woman glanced up, and he followed her eyes. The creature from the woods towered above him. It wore black armor and boots that seemed to shimmer. The creature's armor ran up his neck to his angular face. Its skin was grayish, its eyes much too large, and obsidian black. He pointed at Sam with long fingers that ended in talons and spoke. Unlike the woman, his voice was all thunder and grinding sand; oceans crashing and rusting metal.

Sam wanted to rise, to run, but his legs wouldn't comply. His heart pounded in his ears. The woman turned suddenly to him and gently stroked the left side of his neck. The pain vanished, and his heart slowed.

"Who… what are you?" Sam whimpered.

The woman cupped his face in her hands, easing it from side to side. "Help… us," she whispered, her voice resembling snowfall.

"Help you? How… I mean, what do you need?"

The tall alien pointed at Sam, then to the woods. His voice boomed again, harsh, guttural.

"Please?" the woman asked. She glanced from the alien to Sam. "All will be explained."

Sam backed up against the fender of his Camaro and stood. "Okay, get in." Keeping his back to the vehicle and facing the strangers, he slid along the side, pulled the door open, and climbed in. The pair stood outside the Chevy, staring at him. "Get in," he said once more. The pair stared at the door.

Sighing, Sam reached over and pushed the passenger door open. The woman stared at her companion, then spoke in the same, soft voice, but the words were unintelligible. "Do you want a ride or not?"

The woman walked around the car slid in cautiously, her comrade standing outside the vehicle, growling questions at her. She responded in her soft, sing-song voice resembling wings in flight.

Sam fired the engine, then put the transmission in the drive. "If you want a ride, get in the car!" His anger was building, heart pounding.

The man stooped and stared into the Camaro. The flat ridge on his face that could be a nose and nostrils flared. He spun around, firing his weapon at the tree line.

"What are you doing…?" Sam stopped shouting as two beings appeared along the edge of the woods. Unlike the two beside him, these creatures were opaque, partially transparent. Their forms were flickering, fading, and then coalescing. Long, tube-like weapons crossed their chest. The beings started running toward them, their limbs gobbling up the distance. The tall alien fired again, hitting one ghost. It sparkled, vanished, and then reformed a hundred feet to the right of where it had been. The being fired again, and the remaining ghost fizzled, then disappeared.

The woman turned to him, eyes wide. Terror etched across her face. "Please, help us!" she cried in her whisper voice.

Sam stared at the remaining ghost. It reformed completely and closed. "Get him in the car!"

She spoke again, her sing-song voice rising in pitch. Her partner climbed clumsily into the back seat.

Sam floored the accelerator and spun the wheel, driving away from the creatures and down the dirt road lining the football fields. A tree beside his car exploded as he drove past. The soldier held his weapon outside the vehicle, returning fire.

They picked up speed, pushing past sixty on the narrow dirt road. A ghost appeared just ahead and off the road to the right. Sam swerved to the left, away from the being, and across a grassy parking area. Several explosions of dirt and gravel struck the ground ahead of him. Sam swerved again, this time driving back toward the dirt road. The road straightened, headed past the sports fields and further into the forest. "What are those things?" Sam shouted over the wind and engine noise.

"They are the Galv," answered the soldier in his gravely, rusted voice. "They are after the Emissary and will do everything in their power to kill her. It is my job to prevent that."

More geysers of exploding dirt pockmarked the road ahead of the Camaro. Sam swerved around them, pushing harder on the accelerator. The Camaro howled, spitting rocks and sand behind it. They crested a small hill and nearly went airborne. At the foot of the bridge stood two alien soldiers, weapons ready. The first one fired, hitting the Camaro straight on. The engine coughed and sputtered. The second creature blasted a hole in the roadbed. Sam jerked the wheel to the left and toward the tree line as the first soldier stepped forward and fired broadside at them.

Flashes of light exploded in the trees, and Sam's vision faded.

Night had fallen, and the air was considerably cooler when Sam woke. An owl hooted nearby, answered by the call of a whippoorwill. Sam stretched and felt the steering wheel dig into his chest. He was in his car, not sleeping comfortably in his bed. He instinctively reached for the ignition. The keys were there, but the engine failed to turn over. Sam opened the door, stepped out, and stared at the dark sky. The moon was straight overhead, the stars out in wild abundance. Turning a slow circle, he discovered the car was deep in the woods and surrounded by tall pines.

"What in the world?" he muttered. Running time back in his head, he had no recollection of driving here. The last he remembered was flying the plane, talking to the coach—then waking in the car: that and a bizarre dream of aliens, of being shot at. Still unsure where he was, he followed the car's path through the brush and out to the road that swept past the school and deep into the Camden National Preserve.

Sam pulled his phone from his pocket. It was dead; the screen reduced to glass splinters. "Awe, really?" Rubbing his face with his hands, he started walking. He was at least a mile from the school, and the school was four miles from home. An hour later, he reached the main road leading to town and home. A clock on the Charlestown Bank and Trust advertised low checking fees and the time—two-thirty a.m. The walk home was at least another hour. He'd be home by three-thirty. "Mom is going to be pissed."

Two miles from home, a pair of headlights crossed all lanes of traffic, raced up to him, then screeched to a stop. "Sam, where in the hell have you been?" his mother scolded him through the passenger-side window.

Sam shrugged and scratched his head. "Mom, I'm not sure."

"Don't give me that crap," she shouted, reached over and unlocked the door. "Now get in."

Sam jogged over to the car, glanced back toward the woods, then climbed in reluctantly.

"I have spent the last six hours combing this city for you!" She checked her mirrors, put the car in gear, and squealed the tires as she took a quick U-turn. "Half a dozen people reported seeing you driving like a manic past the school and down the forest service road." She swung around a slow-moving pickup truck, then glanced at him. "Where's your car?"

Sam leaned back hard in the seat, took a breath, and turned to his mom. "It's in the woods. Deep in the woods. I don't know how I got there."

They pulled up to a stoplight. Sam's mom leaned over and sniffed him. "Have you been drinking… or doing drugs?"

"Mom, no, never!" Sam said, raising his hands and leaning back in the seat. "You know that." The light turned green, and his mother drove through the intersection. "I know this sounds like a joke, but I really don't know where I've been for the last eight hours, how my car got way, and I mean way off the road. Or, how this happened." He pulled out his phone. The display was dead, glass pulverized.

"I did as I do every Tuesday afternoon. Went down to the practice fields, took the P-51 and flew it. Had another run in with that asshole Ronnie Howell…"

"Watch your language." Sam's mother's eye's were narrowed and red-streaked. "You're in enough trouble."

"Well, he is." Sam growled. "You know it, I know it. The whole dang school knows it." He took a moment to clear his mind before continuing. "Anyway, he and his band of jerks show up, taunted me, tried to smash the Mustang with a football… same old crap. Luckily, Coach Barnes came by, told them to layoff or run laps." Sam slumped in the seat, his head against the headrest. "I talked to coach for a bit, and then…" he held his hands palms-up before letting them fall into his lap. "I woke up in the car. It won't crank, and my phone is smashed."

Sam's mom stared straight ahead as she drove down the dark streets, most of the traffic lights staying green. After several miles, she glanced his way while keeping her eyes on the road. "I'll have Uncle Kevin check on your car tomorrow and see if he can get it cranked." She turned off the main road onto a narrow two-lane black-top leading to their house. "And tomorrow, when you get home from school, I want you to go through all of this with me again."

Chapter Seven

The trees are burning; the ground is exploding, and hell-on-earth is chasing him through the woods. He tries to speed away, but his car, now pedal-driven instead of V8 powered, is sluggish, barely moving. The woman beside him is bleeding heavily; her robes are stained crimson. She sobs, moaning that she has failed. Failed at what? Who is she?

Another tree explodes, setting more of the woods on fire. Sam quits pedaling, stops the car, jumps out, and runs to the passenger side. He pulls her from the car, is surprised by how light the woman is. A ghost materializes ahead of him, pulls a smooth tube from its side, and shoots the woman, the blast turning her to ash. Sam struggles to hold her together as she crumbles and filters through his fingers.

Sam woke sitting bolt upright in bed, screaming until his throat hurt. Sweat poured from his face. His door flew open, and his mom raced to his side. She held him by the shoulders, shaking him, her eyes wide with fear.

"Sam, what in the world is wrong?" His mom hugged him tight as he trembled and sobbed.

"Mom," he whispered. "She's in danger. They're trying to kill her." Sam slumped against his mom.

"Sam, who's in danger? What are you talking about?"

"The Emissary. Her bodyguard can't save her. The Galv, they're close. They…" He sagged unconscious.

"Sam, c'mon, wake up! You're just having a nightmare." She rocked him hard. Sam's head lolled as his eyes rolled up in his head. A shadow fell over them. Sam's mom turned to see her daughter framed in the doorway.

"Mom, what's going on? What's wrong with Sam?" she asked, voice breaking.

"I don't know. He's burning up. Run to the kitchen and get me a wet cloth and thermometer."

Sharon returned moments later and handed the thermometer to her mom as she placed a wet cloth on her brother's forehead.

"Sam, I need you to open your mouth so I can take your temperature." The teen moaned, barely responding. His mom pried his mouth open and slid the digital gauge under his tongue. When it beeped, she read the display with a gasp. "Oh, son, it's 104. What's going on?" She pulled the covers back, and tried to get him to sit up. "Sharon, get him a shirt. I'm taking him to the hospital."

Ten minutes later, they mostly carried Sam to his mom's van. They buckled him in and drove straight to the emergency room, violating speed limit signs as if they were suggestions. At the hospital, an orderly put him on a gurney, and pushed him inside.

A tall, weary doctor in a wrinkled white coat examined Sam, checked his eyes, took his blood pressure, and listened to his heart. "How long has he been like this?"

"Not long. He woke up screaming in the middle of the night. I thought he was having a nightmare, but then he fainted and hasn't regained consciousness." Sam's mom ran a hand through her shoulder-length red hair.

"Any history of drug use?" The doctor felt Sam's neck, then the sides of his throat.

"Sam? Are you kidding? Won't even take aspirin," Sharon answered quickly.

"Alcohol?" With his fingers on Sam's wrist, the doctor pressed on, checking his pulse as he stared at his watch.

"No. Nothing. Not even energy drinks."

The physician put a hand behind Sam's back. "Help me sit him up. I want to listen to his lungs." Together, they pulled the boy into the sitting position. "Take his shirt off."

The shirt was nearly to Sam's shoulders when the doctor dropped the stethoscope out of his ears. "What in the world," he muttered

A series of angry red circles dotted Sam's back, each the size of a silver dollar. "Does he have any allergies?"

"Pollen… nothing that would do this." His mother put her hand on one of the rings. "They look like burns."

"If I didn't know better, I'd say they are electrical burns." He glanced over Sam's shoulder to his mother. "Where has he been recently?"

"That's another mystery. He didn't come home after school, so I checked with all his friends, anyone that knew him. Nobody had a clue where he was. I found him about two o'clock this morning walking down the highway. He said he woke up in his car near the high school practice fields but doesn't know how he got there."

"Hmm," the doctor said as he rubbed his eyes. "For now, I'm going to dress those welts, then admit him."

He laid Sam down on the gurney. "I'll order a full spectrum of tests, a complete blood workup. If we find anything, I'll let you know immediately." The doctor finished making notes, dropped his pen in the pocket of his white coat, and stood.

Sam's mom yawned, then gave the car keys to Sharon. "I'm staying here tonight. Why don't you go on home and I'll call you later."

Sharon hugged her mom, then ran a hand through Sam's disheveled brown hair. "Please call me as soon as they tell you something. I've never heard anyone in my life scream like he did. It gives me chills to think about it."

The doctor finished writing notes. "You can stretch out in the waiting room. I'll ask a nurse to find a blanket for you."

Helen rubbed her face. "Thanks. It's been a long night."

After the doctor removed Sam's shirt, dressed his welts, and had a hospital gown put on him, an orderly wheeled Sam out of the emergency room. Helen followed the man to the second floor, then commandeered a couch by Sam's room.

She woke to an empty, quiet building, the sun just peeking over the tops of the trees. The halls were still dim as she entered Sam's room.

Helen gently rapped on his door. "Good morning, Sam," she called quietly, then pushed the door open, then stopped in her tracks. Sam was leaning forward, staring at a blank television, eyes wide open, not blinking. "Are you okay?"

Sam slowly turned her way but kept his eyes on the dead monitor. "Shhh, the Emissary is trying to tell me something. But I can't understand her."

"Honey, the TV's off. There's nothing on." Helen stepped back out of the room, motioned for a nurse to come quickly, then stepped back in.

"I know the TV's off, but I can see the Emissary. She's hurt, bad. And her bodyguard." he paused and licked his lips. "I think he's dying." He turned away, his eyes on the blank screen. "Mom, the Galv, they're following them, they—the Emissary and the," he paused again to stare at the television screen. His head cocked as if he was listening. "He's a soldier, not a bodyguard. He can't run much longer. If I don't help, the Galv will kill them both."

Helen hurried across the floor and touched her son's shoulder. "Sam, what do they need you to do?"

The trance broke. Sam turned his attention fully to her. "They need me to help get them off the planet."

The door creaked as a nurse pushed it open. "Sam, how are you this morning?" She had a small clipboard in her hand.

Same looked from his mom to the nurse. "I need to go. Now." He slid his legs off the bed.

"Where, Sam? Where do you need to go?" Helen paused, trying to push her son against the pillows.

"I need to go home. They're coming. The Galv are close…." He briefly tried to force his way past his mom, then dropped back into the bed.

Helen pulled the covers back over her son, then turned to the nurse. "Have you ever seen anything like this before?"

The nurse shook her head. "No, never. Blood pressure was up last night, and he had a low-grade fever. But as for the hallucinations, I have no clue. I'm sorry."

Helen shook her head and moved to stand by the windows. "This is just so bizarre."

"The doctor can prescribe your son a mild sedative. Let him sleep off whatever is troubling him. Hopefully, he'll be better by this afternoon," the nurse said with a warm smile. "Maybe it's just a wild prank."

"Oh, puh-lease. If this is a prank, I'm selling his car to teach him a lesson!" They laughed, and the nurse excused herself from the room. Helen moved to watch her son, now sleeping peacefully. She ran her fingers through his collar length hair.

Two hours later, she spoke with Coach Barns, who confirmed there had been some shenanigans at the practice fields, but nothing more than 'boys being boys.' He agreed Sam was upset, and that they had talked, but didn't see anything that would have him acting the way he was. Helen listened patiently, then thanked him for his time. Barns said if he remembered anything else, he would call her back. She then called her uncle.

"Good Morning, Kevin."

"Good Morning, Helen. How's the boy?"

"Physically, he seems to be fine. But there's something going on in his head that has me worried."

"Such as?"

"I found him wandering down the highway last night, said he woke up in his car, that he was parked deep in the woods. Sam has no clue how he got there."

"Well, that's exactly where I found it. Way off the road. I can't believe he drove that far in."

"If he's wrecked the car, he'll beat himself up over it."

"The car seems okay, though the battery is toast.. It was melted down to a pile of goo. As was most of the wiring. Whatever he did, it completely fried the car's electrical components. And there's smoke damage to the paint."

"Huh," Helen said quietly into the phone. "That's interesting."

"Interesting? How so?"

"Sam woke up in the middle of the night screaming, saying that he was being chased, that the woods were on fire."

There was silence on the other end; after a moment, Kevin continued. *"Now that you mention it, the woods around his car were scorched and half a dozen trees blackened. Sam's car had round patches on the body where the paint was blistered."*

This time, it was Helen's turn to be quiet. "Kevin, were the burn marks about two inches in diameter?"

"Yeah, how did you know?"

"Sam has the same marks on his back."

"Now that's very weird. What does Sam have to say?"

"Not much, actually. He's either been asleep or talking crazy."

"Well, keep me informed. I'm towing his car back to the house. I believe we can fix the wiring easily enough, but the paints another story. Car will have to be sanded and repainted. I'll put a new battery and wires in the trunk. Sam can start on it when he feels better."

"Thanks, Kevin, we owe you one." She set the phone down and turned to gaze at her son. "What in the world did you get involved in, boy?" She returned to the windows, watching cars pull in and out of the hospital, some leaving with good news, some with bad. She sighed heavily, exhausting all the air from her lungs, then dropped into the over-stuffed chair by the windows.

Helen was dozing when her phone rang. "Hello?" She breathed, not wanting to wake her son.

"Ms. Shepherd? This is Coach Barnes again. Is this a good time to talk?"

She yawned, nodding that it was a good time, then stifled a laugh, knowing he couldn't see her nod. "Coach, yes, this is actually a good time. I was napping and didn't want to end up sleeping all day." She stepped out of the room. "Did you think of something else?"

"No, ma'am, it's what I found on the practice field." There was silence for a moment, then the sound of something sliding on a counter or table. *"The plane your son was flying, was it red and blue, the wings having feathers painted on them?"*

Helen thought back for a moment. She's seen Sam fly that plane a dozen times, and before that, her husband piloted it. But she had never really paid that close attention to it. "I think so, why, did Sam leave it behind?"

"No, I found pieces of it, or what's left of it. There was a little of the wings and tail section. It looked as if it'd been blown apart."

"The plane was Sam's father's. He would have protected it with his life! When he wakes, I'm getting to the bottom of this." She paused and rubbed her face with her palms. "Thanks for calling me back. If you find anything else, let me know." The coach agreed and ended the connection. Helen stood by the door to his room, staring at paperwork that meant nothing to her, wondering how things had turned upside down.

The morning faded into the afternoon. Helen slept fitfully in a chair by Sam's bed. A soft touch on her hand awakened her. She opened her eyes to find Sam staring at her. This time, his eyes were clear.

"Sam, are you okay? How do you feel?"

"Okay, I guess." He leaned against the windows. "Why am I in the hospital? Were we in an accident?"

"No, far from it. You were sick last night, very sick." She reached up to hold his hand. "We brought you in," she glanced at her watch, "almost twelve hours ago."

Sam stared at her wide-eyed. "Seriously?"

"Yes, seriously!" A small laugh escaped her. "What's the last thing you remember?"

He pushed off the wall, his eyes drifting unfocused across the room. "Waking up in my car, walking home, you picking me up, then going to bed." He pursed his lips as he stared at the ceiling. "That's it."

"Do you remember any of the dreams you were having?"

Sam shook his head.

"You woke up in the middle of the night burning up and screaming. You were crying uncontrollably about the Emissary, saying she was bleeding out, that the bodyguard couldn't help."

"That's crazy, mom."

"This morning you were staring at the TV—which wasn't on—saying the Emissary was talking to you. You said the Galt were closing."

Sam shook his head again. "Not *Galt*, mom, they're the Galv."

Helen stared at Sam, gripping his hand firmly.

"Mom, that kinda hurts!" Sam pulled his hand loose and massaged his knuckles. "Didn't know you were that strong." Helen didn't respond; she just stared straight at him. "What?"

"You just corrected me. I said 'Galt' and you said, 'No, mom, the Galv.'"

"I did?" Sam crossed his arms over his chest. "That's weird. I don't even remember saying any of that."

"Sam, that's also what you said last night, and this morning. That the 'Galt or Galv' were after the Emissary and you had to protect her."

Sam shook his head emphatically. "Mom, I swear, I don't know what you're talking about. All I know is yesterday I was flying the Mustang, having a great time until that jerk Ronnie showed up. I spoke to coach about him and… that's about it. That is until I woke up in the car and you gave me a ride home."

Sam sat down on the edge of the bed, his hair still matted to one side of his head.

"Sam, did you share a drink, a… brownie," she smiled at him, "with anyone?"

"You think someone drugged me?" Sam laughed hard. "Oh, sure, real conspiracy stuff there. Some jerk wanted to see the most boring kid in school wig-out." He rolled his eyes. "No, I didn't eat any wacky brownies or drink after some kid in school."

Helen laughed. "Just making sure."

"Uh, how long do I have to stay here?"

"Probably not long. If all your tests are clear, they'll discharge you."

An hour later, the nurse came by with a stack of papers advising that the bloodwork looked good, and if he's not feeling any discomfort, they would release him.

The nurse took the clipboard, then handed her a card with the hospital's contacts. "If anything changes, or he has any further episodes, please bring him back in." Helen put the card in her pocket. "Also, Doctor Karlsten couldn't figure out what in the world those rings were on his back. He said it could have been something as simple as hives or an allergic reaction to medication. Doctor Karlsten said if they return, to remember what was going on previously, and we might be able to figure it out."

"Thanks for all your help," Helen hugged the nurse. "C'mon boy, your sister's downstairs waiting on us." They walked through the halls to the elevator, finally reaching the lobby where Sharon waited.

Impatiently tapping her toes while playing with her phone, Sharon said without looking up, "are you going to live?"

"Apparently so. Sorry to disappoint you." Sam replied, smiling.

"So, what was it?" Sharon asked, sliding her purse onto her shoulder

"Doctors don't know," Helen shrugged slightly. "Might never know." They exited the building into the bright, late afternoon sunlight.

Sharon drove the family's minivan while Helen sat in the passenger seat. Once on the highway, she asked the kids if they were hungry.

"Starved!" Sharon said with enthusiasm.

"Sam, what about you?"

When he didn't respond, Helen glanced over her shoulder. Sam was staring at a large display sign attached to a grocery store. "Sam?"

"Mom, do you see that?" Sam pointed toward the display advertising local specials.

Helen glanced at the store, then back to Sam. "What, their sale on ground beef and steak? Yeah, it's not that great of a deal. That's why we don't shop there."

Sam shook his head slowly. "No, there's a woman's face in the center. She's staring at me." He swallowed hard. "I can almost hear her. She looks terrified."

"Pull over!" Helen said sharply to Sharon, who swerved across a lane of traffic and pulled off the road. "Sam, do you see her now?"

He nodded.

"Is she still talking to you?"

He nodded again. "But I can't understand what she's saying. Her words are staticy." Sam took a deep breath, then turned toward his mother. "Mom, you can't see her?"

"No," Helen said evenly. "Sharon, turn around, head back to the hospital."

"Mom, no!" Sam blurted. "Take me home. They're coming."

"Sam, you're seeing things." Helen countered quietly, fighting to keep the panic down.

He shook his head. "I don't know how I know this but take me home. She's coming and needs my help."

Sharon glanced back and forth between her mom and brother.

"Drive home, Sharon, but don't stop unless I tell you to." Helen clasped her hands as if praying. "Sam, I sure hope you know what you're talking about.

Sam leaned back, letting a long breath out. "Thanks, mom. I know you don't believe me... I don't believe myself much at the moment, but this is what I need to do."

Sharon pulled the van into traffic and continued the half-hour drive home. Sam remained glued to the windows, starting at every display. After a few minutes, he sighed heavily, then stretched out in his seat. "Mom, don't worry, I'm just tired."

The rest of the drive was quiet. Sam dozed in the back of the van, the radio tuned to a soft-rock station. As they approached the small brick house, Helen motioned for her daughter to pull into the drive. Sam's car was parked beside the driveway, near the road. The blistered paint and smoke smudges were easy to see. She woke Sam. "We're home, sleepy-head! Any more other-worldly visions?"

He smiled sheepishly. "No, mom. No visions, not even in the radio dial."

"That's good. Now let's go inside and fix lunch. Your uncle dragged your car home for you. He's supposed to have left parts in the trunk."

"I'll call and thank him later, gonna first see how much damage I did." He unbuckled, opened the door, and walked over to his car. Ribbons of blistered paint ranged down the side. One turn signal was distorted as if hit by jets of flame. "Did I fall asleep in a forest fire?"

His mother and sister went inside the house, leaving him alone with his father's first pride and joy. He shook his head as he morosely walked around the sports car. The paint was ruined. Some blisters were down to the metal. He brushed his hand over the scorch marks on the passenger-side fender. The paint dissolved as if it was dust. Sam stared at the sky and shook his head. He opened the hood to inspect the engine. The battery was blackened and turned inside out. "What in the hell could do that?"

The spark plug wires drooped lifelessly from the distributor. When he fingered one, it crumbled to ash. As did the remaining seven.

He glanced into the car. The interior looked fine, with no sign of the calamity affecting the outside. He was about to open the trunk when he noticed a silver-gray smear on the inside passenger door. He leaned in and touched it. It was tacky, almost fluid. The streak seemed to congeal on his hand, refusing to be spread. It resembled mercury.

Sam wiped the stain on his pants and opened the trunk. As promised, a new battery, spark plug wires, and several spools of various gauge wiring were waiting for him. He grabbed the spools and closed the trunk. He was busy removing the dead spark plug wires when a rock hit the side of his car. Sam jumped back to see Ronnie Howell and friends sauntering down the roads.

"What's up, flyboy?" Ronnie threw another small rock that bounced off the roof. His friends laughed and made weeping motions with their hands.

"Stop hitting my car with rocks," Sam calmly said as he closed the hood.

"Watcha going to do about it, flyboy?" Ronnie closed on Sam, and chest bumped him. He was a good three inches taller and forty pounds heavier than Sam. Months of harsh summer football practice had left Ronnie with thick biceps and a mean attitude.

"Try it again and find out." Sam countered, shoving the other boy back.

Ronnie slowly kneeled and picked up a rock. He held it over a fender and let it drop. It clanged off the car and fell into the engine compartment. "Oops, don't know how that happened." He stared at Sam, eyes challenging.

"Hmph, kinda what I thought." Ronnie's friends laughed again. He bent over, grabbed a fist-sized rock, and aimed at the windshield. He stepped forward to throw it when Sam's right hand flashed forward, grabbed him by the throat, and lifted him to his toes.

"I told you to stop throwing rocks at my car." Sam's words were barely audible. His face was neutral, but his eyes were flat, dark.

Ronnie tried to respond but only gurgled. He punched Sam twice in the ear without effect. Ronnie's friends backed away.

"Sam," Helen screamed. "Let go of him!" She ran across the yard, waving her arms. "Sam, you're killing him!" Helen pushed between the boys, finally breaking her son's grip. Ronnie fell on his back, gasping, dark bruising already forming on his throat.

Sam stared down at his mother, emotionless. "I told him to stop throwing rocks at my car. He wouldn't listen."

"Y'all go on, get out of her." Helen shouted. The boys lifted Ronnie to his feet, then pushed him down the road.

"This ain't over, flyboy!" Croaked Ronnie as he gasped for breath. "Tomorrow after school, meet me at the practice field!" He spit on the ground. "And don't bring your mom. Don't want anyone saving your ass."

Sam didn't react to the boys' retreat. He stood with his hands on his hips, thumbs through his belt loops.

Helen turned around to face her son. "Sam, what's going on with you?"

Sam glanced at his mom, and stared through her, his expression blank. He blinked and life returned to his eyes. "I'm sorry mom, what did you say?"

"You choked that boy, you almost killed him!" Helen said, eyes frantic.

"What are you talking about?"

Helen pointed down the road, where Ronnie and his friends slowly walked away. "That boy, Ronnie, you were choking him. He couldn't breathe."

Sam shook his head. "Mom, all I remember was working on my car, then you yelling at me." He stared at the teens. "If I was choking him, I'm sure there was a good reason for it."

Helen smiled briefly, then let it fall. "It's not the choking that bothers me. I mean it does." She ran a hand through her hair. "It's the not remembering what you're doing that has me concerned."

Sam shrugged. "Don't know what I can tell you."

"Well, let's go inside. I'm exhausted, and it's been a hard twenty-four hours. Your uncle said he would be glad to help you with the car. But for now, let's just relax," she paused when a faraway expression overtook Sam. Helen grabbed him by the shoulders and shook him.

"Sam, you're doing it again!" Her voice edged up in pitch. "What in the hell is going on with you?"

"Mom," Sam swallowed hard and whispered. "Look." He pointed weakly across the street toward an empty lot of brush and saplings. "Do you see them?"

Helen turned toward the lot, stepping in front of Sam. "Son, I don't," she paused as the air across the street rippled, appearing to melt. A woman stepped through the mirage, followed by a limping, tall, gangly man. The woman was holding an arm across her chest.

"What in the world?" Helen murmured, backing up and dragging Sam with her. "Get in the house, call 911." Sam barely moved. "Now, Sam, do what I told you."

The strangers quickly crossed the field, now standing in the middle of the road. "I am sorry. We don't mean to frighten you." The woman whispered, her voice like the crinkling of paper.

"Who are you?" Sam asked.

Helen stood between Sam and the Saint. "Can you understand them?"

"Yeah, it's hard, but I can." Sam tried to move around his mom, but she pulled him back by a sleeve.

"Huh uh, Sam." Helen shook her head. "You're not going anywhere."

"They're hurt. They need our help." He whispered.

Facing the woman, Helen pointed. "I don't know who you are, but if you cross the street, I'm calling the police." She pushed Sam toward the house. He stumbled and almost fell. "Get in the house and lock the door. Don't argue with me."

The Saint seemed to barely move but closed the distance between them almost instantly. "Sam, the Galv, they are close. They will find us soon. Please, we need your help." The Saint's voice was softer, fading. The soldier beside her was limping. "Jonqueen is badly injured and may die."

Swallowing hard, Sam asked, "Who are you?" Biting his lip, he turned from the woman, toward his front door. When he turned back, the Saint closed the distance again, now standing before him. She smiled weakly, then touched the back of his hand. His knees buckled, and he collapsed. Helen tried to grab him, but only slowed his fall.

"What did you do?" She lunged forward and grabbed the Saint by her robes.

"All will be well," the Saint whispered as she motioned for the soldier to stand down. She ran a fingertip along Helen's temple. Helen crumpled beside her son.

Chapter Eight

Helen stared at the ceiling, watching the fan spin slowly, the blades in no hurry to rotate. The light in the den was muted, the blinds closed. She took a deep breath and tried to remember her dream. Were there… strangers? Was the air… watery? Did the strangers come through the water? Weird. She glanced at the wall clock and froze. A woman sat across from her wearing long, flowing, shimmering gowns, the colors constantly changing. Behind her stood a tall, thin man dressed in black, his face hidden by the haze of light pushing through the blinds.

"We mean you no harm Helen Shepherd, mother of Sam."

Helen tried to sit up but toppled over.

"The disorientation will pass. I am sorry. In your frightened state, my touch was overwhelming." The Saint paused as if uncertain, then dropped to a knee in one fluid movement. She tipped her head forward, raised her eyes and gazed at Helen. "It is with great honor I kneel before you."

"I can understand you," Helen said.

The Saint tilted her head slightly. A soft smile appeared on her ivory face.

"You aren't from around here."

The Saint's smile widened. "From a different time."

Helen sat up. She covered her eyes with both hands; the disorientation lessening. "Why do I have a sense that you mean that literally?"

"Once again, I apologize for the light sensitivity. It will pass."

"You didn't answer my question," Helen said, removing one hand from her face.

The young woman's eyes sparkled. "But you didn't ask one. You stated an opinion."

Keeping a grip on the arm of the couch, Helen leaned forward. She stared at the young woman who appeared to be in the midst of youth, but also ancient and wise. "Where are you from?"

"As you surmised, a different time."

"And planet?"

The Saint nodded. "You are as the old scrolls revealed. Wise, fearless."

Helen was about to address how nutty that answer was when Sam came into the den holding a tennis racket. "Sam, what's going on? Are you going to play tennis?"

Sam waved at his mom, then handed the racket to Jonqueen. "Will this work?"

The old man behind the Saint reached out with long gray fingers that ended in nails resembling talons. The man took the racket and waved his palm over it. His facial features wrinkled, making him appear even older. "It is very crude but will suffice."

Helen continued leaning forward, her elbows resting on her knees. "Sam, care to explain?"

"Mom, as you have probably guessed, they aren't from around here."

"Well, duh, that much is obvious." She looked over at the Saint. "My guess is Canadian." She turned to the soldier. "Best guess is some old East Block nation, a cold war soldier."

Sam laughed. "Not exactly. A little further off the beaten path." He motioned to the Saint. "Would you like to explain?"

The Saint smiled her enigmatic, soft smile and reached for Helen. "If you would, please hold a hand out, palm up."

Helen hesitated, "Sam?"

"Mom, it's okay."

Helen tentatively did as asked. The Saint took her hand and clasped it between her own. "What is the last thing you remember?"

"What?"

The Saint leaned forward, her dark blue eyes driving into Helen's. "What do you remember?"

"I… well, coming home from the hospital, pulling into the drive. Sam jumping out to check his car. Then…," She shrugged. "Did I pass out? Are you a nurse?"

The Emissary leaned her head toward Sam. "Please sit beside your mother and hold her."

Sam stepped across the room, then dropped beside his mom. "Mom, relax. This is—incredible."

"Sam, what in the world are you talking…"

The woman squeezed Helen's hand. Helen gasped, her back arched, as her eyes opened wide. She stared at the ceiling without blinking, her mouth trying to form words that would not come. In her mind, she saw streaks of starlight, planets with orange seas, and impossible sunrises over molten iron fields. She witnessed starships exploding and burning in space, incredibly beautiful beings and horrifying ones at the same time. She saw the Galv and felt their presence. Helen cried out and fell against her son.

The Saint sagged, letting go of Helen. She took several deep breaths, then pushed hair from her face. "Your mother, she is quite strong. Most beings I can project my dreams and experiences into easily. But your mother, her consciousness, it is well defined." The Saint leaned forward again, taking Helen's hand once more.

"Mother of Sam, I am sorry for the pain and fear I have filled you with. But it's the only way you would understand."

Helen was sobbing when she sat up. "So many dead. How—how do you handle it?"

The Emissary continued to hold Helen's hand. "With hope, it will all soon end. That's why it's imperative we complete our mission."

"Mom, are you okay?" Sam asked, still holding tight to his mother's arm.

She nodded, wiping the tears from her eyes. "I will be." She glanced around the room. "Where's Sharon?"

"Gathering up clothes for Emma."

"Who?"

Sam pointed gently at the Saint. "The Emissary de'tantel. Apparently, in their language, it means something like Saint of Life. Sharon came up with Emma. The Galv can track her through her clothing and the aura she gives off. Sharon has things she can wear. I'll get rid of the gowns to throw the Galv off her trail."

"The Galv, you mentioned them last night. Who are they?"

"They are a pestilence in the universe," the soldier offered, his voice rough. "They exist only to destroy worlds."

Helen turned to Jonqueen. Now that she could see him clearly, she shrank back. "You're obviously a soldier, a commando of some sort. Can you stop them?"

"No. I can only delay them. If we do not find a way off this planet, they will eventually hunt us down and eliminate us. And once they figure a way to communicate with their kind, they will arrive on massive ships to strip your world of all its resources. You will be powerless to stop them."

The room was quiet after Jonqueen spoke, the whirl of the ceiling fan the only sound interrupting the silence.

Helen spoke first. "I remember seeing you two come across the field; you were hurt. Is there anything we can do to help?"

"Mom, that's what the tennis racket is for. Apparently, his armor is based on some type of nanotechnology. He can repair and heal himself if he can get to their ship."

"And how does the tennis racket fit in?"

"It's the carbon fiber one I bought last year. It's not exactly what he needs, but his nanites can eat it, I think, and start repairing his body and armor."

"Seriously?" Helen asked, now paying close attention to Jonqueen.

"Barely." Jonqueen answered. "There is some acceptable material in this I can use, but not much."

Helen watched in amazement as a gray cloud drifted from his hand, gradually settling over the racket. It slowly dissolved, the material drifting up into his arms. The strings sagged with the loss of tension. "You have a spacecraft?" she asked, then shook her head and laughed. "Of course you do. How could you have gotten here without one?"

"It is hidden in a deep ravine close to here," Emma answered, her voice again soft as snow. "But we must hurry. We set a self-destruct on it to engage if we don't return." Noticing the shocked expressions on Sam and his family, she continued with a laugh. "I am sorry, poor choice of words. There will be no explosion. Jonqueen's nanites will dissolve the ship down to its basic molecular building blocks. There is no danger to your world or environment. Your scientist might detect a negligible increase in background radiation, but that too will dissipate within days. All that will remain will be a dusty patch of grass where we landed."

"Mom, I think I know where they landed. It's behind the practice fields, near the old sand mines. I'll drive them there."

"Be careful, Sam," Helen said, pulling the van key from her pocket.

"I will, don't worry so much." He leaned over and kissed her gently on the cheek.

"She is right to worry," Jonqueen said harshly. "The Galv are aware of our presence here. We need to leave this place immediately."

Sam glanced at Emma. "I know it's not a star cruiser, but we have a new CD player and a collection of music I'm sure you've never heard before."

"One moment Sam Shepherd. It's imperative that I change out of these robes." She took the clothes Sharon held for her, inspecting a pair of stone-washed jeans at arm's length. She raised an eyebrow. "It has been many, many ages since the women of my world have worn trousers. I must record this image to show my colleagues when I return." She performed the same action with a faded pink and yellow tee shirt. "Now, this," she rubbed the shirt against her cheek, "is extraordinary fabric. We do not have this on my world." Emma held it to her face and breathed deeply. "May I have it?"

Sharon laughed hard. "That old cotton tee shirt? Please, take it. I have many more." Sharon pointed toward the closed bathroom door. "You can change in there."

Jonqueen followed her. "You will need to hurry. I can sense the Galv. They are close."

Pausing, Emma took a deep breath. She glanced around the room as if seeing through the walls. "I too, feel them. I'll be quick." She shut the door. Moments later, she stepped out resembling any high school girl around the country.

"Wow," Sam said, walking toward her. "I would never guess you were from a bazillion miles from here."

Emma inclined her head slightly to the right, smiled, and blushed. "What a beautiful thing to say."

"We must leave—now." barked Jonqueen.

Sam led them to the van, opened the door, and jumped in. Jonqueen stood at the passenger door, staring into the vehicle. "Your transportation appears fragile. How will you protect the Emissary?"

"The van's perfectly safe. But you need to ride in the back. The dark windows will hide you, keep you from scaring children." Sam pushed the passenger door open. Jonqueen held it for the Saint. She climbed in, her eyes sweeping the dash, looking nervous. "Trust me, we're fine." After a moment's deliberation, Jonqueen opened the side door and climbed in, taking the seat behind Emma. "Now, you guys need to buckle up." When Emma again looked unsure, he reached over, grabbed the seat belt, and brought it across her waist and into the lock.

Jonqueen followed his example, glowering at the restraint. "This hardly seems sufficient protection against the Galv."

"Against the Galv, it probably isn't," Sam said sharply. "But against local traffic, it's fine." Sliding the key in the ignition, Sam started the van and backed out of the driveway. He put the van in drive, then headed toward the school.

His passengers rode quietly, neither speaking. Jonqueen stared straight ahead as if he was a mannequin. Emma gazed out the window, watching the traffic slide past. After a few minutes, she relaxed and leaned back in her seat.

"I've traveled between worlds, across galaxies, and apparently through the fabric of time itself. I've seen beings that would give you nightmares and worlds I could never describe. But this," Emma swept her hands across the front of the van, pointing down the highway and at pedestrians on the sidewalk, "is the most fascinating, exciting adventure I have ever participated in. It's just all so wonderfully chaotic."

Stopping at the next light, Sam turned to her. "And you find chaos fascinating?"

She nodded vigorously. "Yes. My life is completely scripted, planned; my every move is meticulously detailed. From my birth to my death, all is pre-ordained."

"Your death is planned?" Sam asked, shocked. "Seriously?"

"Yes, Sam. Barring an accident that ends my life, when my time of usefulness has concluded, I will be honored, then euthanized."

"That's… horrible," Sam said with a shudder.

"It's the way of my world, Sam Shepherd."

"And the same for Jonqueen?"

She glanced back at her protector, who still hadn't moved, and laughed. "No, his life is similar to yours. His race borders on being nomadic, traveling from world to world. Fighting to survive."

The light turned green, and Sam drove through the intersection. "Hand me your robes. I know how to pull the Galv off your trail for a while."

Emma held the clothing to her chest, looking pensive.

"You said it was how the Galv track you. There's a truck up ahead with Wyoming plates. I'll toss them in the back. Hopefully, their next stop will be hundreds of miles from here."

Emma took a deep breath, nodding slowly. "They've been worn by Shovain emissaries for eons. To lose them will cause much turmoil."

"How much turmoil will it cause if the Galv kills you?"

"Considerable," Jonqueen said, surprising them both. "You know what he says is correct."

Emma stared out the passenger window, still holding onto the robes.

"Hey, maybe with your equipment we can track the truck down when it's safe to do so and get your robes back."

The Saint slowly turned to face him. "Sam Shepard, ever the optimist you are." Emma took a deep breath and handed him the bundle of shimmering silk robes.

Sam gently accepted the bundle. "I'm sorry, I really am." He pulled up short of the truck and tossed the bundle into the bed. The driver never noticed. At the next light, the truck turned left toward the interstate. Two lights later, Sam veered off the highway toward the town limits.

"One thing I'm not clear on: how do you plan to get off the planet and return home?"

"If the damage to my shuttle isn't terminal, there is a remote chance I can repair it with materials from this world. If not, the Galv still have a ship in orbit. Once I commandeer it, I should be able to piece together a serviceable star-drive. It might be a single use, but enough to reach the edges of your solar system and broadcast a signal home."

"What of the Galv here? Will they continue to search?"

"No. When we commandeer their vessel, I will eliminate those on board. Their avatars will fade and vanish."

Sam drove down the service road leading past the football practice fields. Emma hadn't spoken since he tossed her robes into the bed of the pickup truck. They crossed the bridge where he had awakened in the car. "How much further?"

"We are close," answered Jonqueen. The road climbed again. "This meadow," Jonqueen pointed out the right side of the van, "if your vehicle can traverse it, this is where we need to go."

Sam slowed and drove cautiously through a shallow ditch and into the field, the ground covered with thigh-high weeds and bushes; small saplings pushed their way through the hard packaged, abandoned farmland. He drove another half-mile, weaving around ever-larger pines and oaks. The far edge of the ravine loomed ahead.

"You can stop here," Jonqueen ordered. "We will not be long."

"What, you're not going to show me your ship? Are you serious?"

Jonqueen pushed the door open and walked around to the driver's side. "This is an Imperial vessel. I have executed soldiers for breathing on it. You will not approach it."

Sam bolted out of the van. "And this is Earth where you have no power over anyone!" He moved to stand between Jonqueen and the path to the craft. "And there's no way you're going to stop me from seeing your ship. Not after all you guys have done to me," he argued.

Jonqueen turned to step around him when Sam grabbed his elbow.

"No way, man. I'm coming." Sam saw wisps of black smoke coming from his hand. Jonqueen groaned, jerked his arm back, and stumbled away. "What was that?"

Emma ran past him to Jonqueen's side. "How bad are you hurt?"

The soldier's eyes narrowed in pain, his sharp, gunmetal gray teeth barred. "I have been hurt worse." He pulled a swatch of plastic-like cloth from the inside of this armored coat and pressed it on his elbow. The material turned ash gray, then melted into his sleeve.

Emma spun around to face Sam; her eyes blazing. "You are to never touch him again! Is that clear?"

"What'd I do?" Sam asked, confused. "I mean, sure, I guess. But why? All I tried to do was keep him from walking away. I didn't even grab his arm hard."

Taking a deep breath, Emma regained her composure. "It is not your fault, Sam. As formidable as Jonqueen is, we—you and I—are toxic to his species. Our touch is enough to dissolve his armor, then his skin, and then his bones. Your touch is similar to you being exposed to acid."

"How was I to know? That old battleax looks like he could chew through a chain-link fence as if was butter."

"There is no way you could know. That is why I try to stay completely covered. It is to protect him from accidental contact."

Sam stared at the woman, who was as exotic as she was simple.

"Emma, are you human?"

"In what way to you mean?" she countered.

Sam laughed and threw his hands up. "What do you mean 'in what way'? There's only one way. Either you are, or you aren't. He," Sam pointed to Jonqueen, "definitely is not."

"No, Sam, he is definitely not human. His specie is called Kznas'ik. They resemble us in form, but are very different, and very ancient. They predate the Shovain—my people—by hundreds of thousands of years. The Kznas'ik traveled between the stars when your ancestors were discovering fire."

"We must continue," Jonqueen interrupted with a growl, still holding his injured arm. "You may come as well." He walked past Sam and set a quick pace through the brush.

Emma ran up to him, gliding in her effortless way. Sam jogged to catch up.

"You haven't answered my question. Are you human, from Earth?"

"It is difficult to explain," she said without breaking stride.

"Not really. Just a simple yes or no answer would be great."

"Sam, please, I'm afraid the answer will upset you."

"I'm pretty tough, try me."

"Jonqueen, I will catch up momentarily." The soldier did not respond. He just continued to push through the thickening brush. "Sam, the simple answer is 'yes'; we are essentially human. At least, that is my assumption."

"Essentially?"

Emma sighed, then gripped his hand faster than he could react. Flashes of lightning exploded inside his mind. Swirls of color and dizzying displays of light took his breath away. When she let go, he sagged against her. She gently lowered him to the ground. Emma then kneeled before him. "Sam, what you just experienced is how we communicate on my world, in my time. Our species has evolved far ahead of your own. Yes, we are, on a basic level, human, at least we appear to be. But we are to you, as you are to Neanderthal man. Born of the same elements, but vastly different."

Sam's eyes grew hard. "You think we're just primates? That's how you see us?"

"No, absolutely not! The ancient scrolls tell of your strength, fearlessness, and creativity."

Sam wiped away the angry tears that slipped from his eyes, ashamed at letting his emotions rattle him. "So, we're overachieving baboons."

Emma held his face in her hands. "Oh, Sam, you still don't understand. We view your time as near perfect! We can never have what you have. Yes, our species has branched out, but who is to say for the better? If billions of lives weren't at stake, I'd send Jonqueen home and remain here. But I must return to my world, my time."

Sam smiled and sniffed back the last of his emotions. "Just out of curiosity, how many years separate us?"

Emma shrugged. "We can't be sure, but Jonqueen estimates it is over five thousand."

Chapter Nine

A shadow blocked the sun. When Sam looked up, Jonqueen stood over him, pointing toward the road. "Do you know these humans?"

Sam stood and stared in the direction Jonqueen was pointing. A trio of teenagers walked toward them, Ronnie Howell leading the way. "Crap, not now." He stood, wiped his face dry, and glanced over at Emma. "Go with Jonqueen to your ship. I'll handle this."

"Sam," Emma said, stalling. "There's three of them. I can feel their hatred toward you. It's palpable. This is more than you can handle. I'm afraid they intend to hurt you."

Sam smiled and nodded slightly. "Yep, you're probably right. Now you two disappear. This is a fight that's been long in coming, and I'm tired of running." He started walking toward Ronnie while looking back at Emma and Jonqueen. "They don't need to know about you. Go to your ship and do what you can."

Emma and Jonqueen remained standing.

"Go on now." Sam stopped, pulled the keys from his pocket, and tossed them to the soldier. "If you can pilot across space and time, you can handle a Dodge minivan." He jogged toward the other boys without looking back.

Jonqueen watched Sam leave, then said to Emma. "Those humans will most likely inflict destructive harm on him. He has neither the aptitude nor the ability to defeat them, nor protect himself."

"Initially, I believed that myself. I now feel we have underestimated him." Emma watched Sam close in on the other boys, her hands clenched tightly over her chest.

"His reaction earlier today was an anomaly. We enhanced his strength and bravado from your contact. I fear it has subsided. He no longer has the speed or strength your touch provided. This encounter will be short, and possibly deadly for your Sam of the blue world."

Emma nodded, then turned to face Jonqueen. "You are correct in one aspect. This will not be a long fight. But you are incorrect about the outcome. Sam has what he needs to win this battle but will not use it. Pay attention, soldier. You are about to learn an incredible battle lesson."

Jonqueen glared at Emma but did not contradict her. He stood with his hands cradling a newly formed weapon.

"So, what did your nanites create for you?"

"Just a precaution in case this interaction does not go as planned." He raised the long, black tube, his thumb hovering over a gold trigger. "It should subdue the humans without causing injury."

"Jonqueen…"

"But it will be painful." The corner of his gray lips twitched.

"… you care about the boy."

"He has proven to be a curiosity, at best."

"That's what you said about me!" Emma laughed.

"There's hope for you yet." Careful not to touch the soldier, she motioned toward the ship. "While he is

preoccupied, let us return to your shuttle and salvage
what we…." She stopped and spun around, sensing the
impact as Sam was hit from behind and crumpled to the
ground.

"Sam!" She ran in his direction.

The boys turned as one to the shout.

"So, boy, what'd you do, bring your sister to help?"
Ronnie stood over Sam and kicked dirt in his face.
"What's the matter? Couldn't get mommy to come hold
your hand?" He spat on the fallen teen.

One of Ronnie's friends dropped a clump of grass
and mud on Sam's head. "Now, didn't I tell you I was
going to get you, boy? Ain't no coach or mama out here
this time." He stomped at Sam but missed when Sam
rolled to the side.

"Stop it!" screamed Emma.

Ronnie glanced her way. "What do we have here?
Puke-boy got himself a girlfriend? Y'all entertain
yourself while I check this out." Ronnie started for
Emma when Sam grabbed his foot and tripped him.
Ronnie fell hard on his stomach. Sam scrambled across
him, pinning him down with a knee to the spine, then
wrapped an arm around the boy's throat and squeezed.

"This is between me and you!"

Ronnie rolled over to his side, but Sam clung to his
choke-hold.

"Keep fighting and I'll choke you out!" Ronnie
squirmed, and Sam pulled tighter. "Give it up or I'll
break your freakin' neck," he grunted.

Ronnie quit fighting.

"Now tell your friends to back off!"

The boys moved without being told, backing a safe distance away. "Now, me and you are going to talk. We're going to clear the air once and for all." Sam let go of Ronnie and scrambled away. Ronnie rolled to his knees, gasping for breath, his face red and sweating.

"I'm going to mess you up," he wheezed.

"And I'm going to let you, but first we're gonna have a little chat."

"Screw you, flyboy. First thing I'm going to do is break your nose." Ronnie staggered to his feet, the red draining from his face.

"If that will make you feel better, go ahead. But this time no cheap shots." Sam backed up a few steps. "Here, I'll even close my eyes, make it easy for you." He shut his eyes, waiting for the explosion of pain from Ronnie's heavy fist crushing his face. After a few moments, he opened his eyes, relieved he still could. "Good, let's talk." Sam glanced over Ronnie's shoulder; Emma and the soldier were disappearing into the woods, walking toward the shuttle.

"So, what in the hell do you want to talk about?" Ronnie snarled.

"Why do you hate me so much? I mean, what did I ever do to you?"

Ronnie leaned forward and spoke in a voice barely over a hiss. "Lived, that's what you did."

Sam's brow shot up. "Lived, what do you mean?"

"What I mean is, when your old man died, you should have withered up and blown away. But you didn't. You lived."

Sam scratched his head, held his hands, palms up, and stared at the sky. "What in the world was I supposed to do…" then he knew. "Oh man, you're blaming me for your life?" The heat built in his blood. He had never in his life wanted to strike someone, to hurt them, as he did now. Sam took a deep breath, held it, then let it out slowly. "Ronnie, before my dad died, you were my *best* friend. Don't you remember?" Unclenching his fist, he showed Ronnie the white line running across his palm. "Remember this? You have a matching scar. We watched some cheesy black-and-white Indian movie and tried to imitate them and become blood brothers."

"Yeah, well, that was before your dad ruined my life!" Ronnie screamed in Sam's face.

"By dying? Is that what you're saying? My dad dying in a plane crash, a flight he wasn't supposed to be on. And that has ruined your life?" Sam stepped a few feet away, his blood pulsing in his veins. He ground his teeth, trying to keep his composure. "The only reason he was on that rescue plane was because your dad was too drunk to get out of bed. My dad covered for yours." Sam was shaking, anger turning white hot.

"If your dad hadn't been such an *upstanding man,* he wouldn't have been on that flight." Ronnie spat in response. "And my dad wouldn't have spent the last five years drinking his life away." Ronnie was shouting, his words echoing off the sides of the ravine. "Now he's locked up and my mom's a wreck. At least you still have your mom and sister. I ain't got nothing." Ronnie turned away, throwing shadow punches wildly at the air as tears of anger flowed.

Sam rubbed his face hard and took a couple of deep breaths, smothering the fury building inside him.

"Ronnie, I hate that life screwed you over. I do. But if I could talk to my dad, or touch him just once, even if was through prison bars, I would jump at the chance." His anger was gone, his adrenaline spent. "I'm sorry your life is so wrecked. You were my *best* friend growing up. I've never had as good a friend since. Maybe one day we can have a beer together and talk all this out." He glanced at his old friend. "Not today, but, y'know, soon-ish."

Ronnie stared at the ground without reacting, his hands no longer clenched. A flash of amber light startled the boys. Ronnie glanced up as if he was going to speak when a shaft of amber blasted him off his feet. He landed on his back, the front of his shirt smoking. A trio of amber beams hit the surrounding ground, sending geysers of dirt skyward and setting a dead pine sapling ablaze.

Sam felt more than heard Emma screaming, 'Galv!' He pivoted toward the van and sprinted hard, reaching it just as Jonqueen and Emma were diving inside. Jonqueen threw the keys on the dash. Sam snatched them up and stabbed them into the ignition. He twisted it forward, bringing the vehicle to life.

"How did they find us?" Sam yelled as he drove across the tree-lined meadow. A Galv soldier appeared directly in front of the van. Sam gunned the engine and drove through the being before it could raise its weapon. The van sputtered and coughed after passing through the transference beam. The Galv soldier offered slight resistance, rocking the van as if a cross-wind hit them. Sam glanced in the rearview mirror, watching as the Galv tried to reform before bursting into a light show of sparkling tracers.

"Did I kill it?" Sam asked over the racing engine. He swerved around a small knot of trees too large to drive over. An amber ray hit a tree, exploding it into splinters.

"No," barked Jonqueen. "You disabled it for the time being, but it will return."

Sam drove wildly across the patchy field, dodging shallow depressions and creating dust clouds.. He slammed on the brakes and threw the van into a slide.

"What are you doing?" Jonqueen growled in a pitch so low the van's glass vibrated.

"I can't leave Ronnie," he said and turned to Jonqueen. "Remember, pull this lever to 'D'. Skinny pedal is the accelerator, the wide one makes it stop. Now get the Emissary out of here."

"You are putting billions at risk for one that would not have waited a second for you." Jonqueen growled, showing a mouth of sharp teeth.

"But I'm not him!" Sam unbuckled and jumped from the van. "If you want to save billions, you better shut up and drive." Sam glanced over his shoulder as Jonqueen struggled into the driver's seat, put the vehicle in drive, and floored the engine. He sped over several saplings, smashing the grill but not stop the van. The remaining pair of Galv fired on the van; one hit the passenger side rear quarter panel. The side windows exploded as the energy beam blackened the rear hatch. Jonqueen made the roadbed and turned sharply, nearly flipping the van. He straightened up and sped out of sight.

The Galv paused as if someone had pressed a reset button and became motionless. Sam stooped low, darting between trees, thickets of briars, and kudzu. Ronnie was still lying on his back in a tangle of blackberry vines, his shirt no longer smoking.

The alien soldiers flickered, growing faint. Sam crawled to Ronnie, grabbed him by the wrists, and pulled him through the brush and tangles of vines. He kept a wary eye on the slowly dissolving Galv as he dragged his friend to the edge of the tree line.

Ronnie moaned, and Sam cupped the boy's mouth, whispered, "Shhhh," and pulled him another fifty feet into the woods. He dropped to his knees, then rolled over to his back, his heart pounding from the exertion, his breath coming in ragged gulps.

Ronnie's eyes fluttered open. His lips moved, but no words came out.

Sam struggled to his knees and spoke in a whisper, "You were shot, and the folks that shot you are about fifty yards from here." Ronnie's eyes opened wide with fear. "You're fine, not hurt bad. Not with a bullet, but some kind of energy weapon." Ronnie's eyes went from fear to confusion. "Maybe a long-range taser," Sam lied. "I'll explain later. Just don't speak. When you can walk, we'll get the hell out of here. But for now, be quiet."

Ronnie's eyes closed.

Sam crawled back to the edge of the trees and lay flat on his stomach. The Galv still hadn't moved, but their forms were solidifying. "Crap, this can't be good." The soldiers initially moved haphazardly, jerking and twitching. Then their movements became more fluid. Sam thought they resembled a cross between an armored caveman and…pigs. It was their stocky form and snout-like face. A rusted-silverish helmet with matching shield covered their eyes and ran down the back and sides of their neck. Additional armor continued from their blocky shoulders to their feet.

The soldiers walked a slow circle, as if measuring a small grid. Then, on cue, the two paused before turning toward the woods. Their forms fully materialized, and they began marching toward the tree line.

Sam ran low between the trees, keeping to the shadows. Ronnie was sitting up when he reached him. "C'mon, we gotta go." Sam grabbed him by the shoulder and helped him stand.

"What's going on? What happened to my shirt?" Ronnie slurred and stumbled.

"I'll tell you later. But we need to get out of here. Now." Sam glanced over his shoulder. The Galv were quickly crossing the field and would soon enter the woods. Pushing Ronnie, Sam urged him to run.

Tripping and staggering, Ronnie crashed through the brush, then bounced off a small tree. He lost his balance and fell. "Ronnie, c'mon, man, get it together! We have to get the hell out of here." Sam felt the air around him tingle, then dived to the ground, pushing Ronnie flat. A tree ten feet away exploded, debris raining down around them.

"What was that?" Ronnie cried, scrambling back to his feet.

"I don't know." Sam lied again. "Just run. Run!"

Sam grabbed his childhood friend by the arm, pushing him forward and forcing him deeper into the woods. More streaks of amber light blasted trees around them, showering the boys with fiery embers. Ronnie finally shook off the earlier stunning and kept up with

Sam. The Galv fell behind and eventually quit firing. The boys reached a small creek, splashed through it, climbed the steep bank on the other side, then dropped onto their stomachs.

"Who's shooting at us?" Ronnie whispered, his face streaked with sap and ash.

Sam crawled through the brush, all the way to the creek bank and held his breath. He listened for the sound of limbs cracking and heavy footsteps. He counted to sixty, raised up on his knees, and peeked across the creek. The woods were silent again.

"They are… well, aliens."

"Illegal aliens, as in Mexicans?"

Sam laughed quickly, more from exhaustion and fear than anything else. "Not quite. I'm talking aliens as in… aliens." Ronnie just stared at him. "As in little green men, as in not from this solar system. Are you following me?"

"Yeah, right. Ha ha, very funny, Shepherd. Seriously, what was all that back there, fireworks?" Ronnie said as he brushed dirt and debris from his hair and face. When he glanced back up, Sam was staring at him. "You're serious, aren't you?"

Sam nodded.

"Where are they from?"

"I don't know. All I know is that they are from another universe, another time."

Ronnie's eyes pinched almost closed. He crossed his arms over his chest. "Really?" He laughed. "You almost had me, Shepherd. Funny." He walked away, paused, and turned back. "So, what do they want?" He held his hands up. "Wait, let me guess. They want you to 'take

them to your leader'!" He laughed again; this time
harder. "Is that it?"

"No. They are here to kill the two beings I was with
when you decided to beat the crap out of me."

"That hot girl and old man were aliens? They looked
human to me."

"The girl, she's human-ish. Mostly human. Like
humans 2.0. The other person resembles us but isn't
human at all."

Ronnie laughed again, then stopped. "You're dead
serious. You're not screwing with me, are you?"

"Dude, we had trees exploding around us,
transparent pig-men stomping through the woods. What
did you think was going on?"

Ronnie shuffled his feet, stirring up a small cloud of
dust. "I thought someone slipped something in my
Coke." He pulled at the tattered remains of his shirt.
"Thought you were part of it. Cut up my shirt to freak
me out." He took his shirt off and hung it on a bush.
"But I've never seen you mess with drugs."

"C'mon, let's get out of here before they return."

"Do you think they will?"

"Yeah. Surprised they haven't." Sam hurried along
the creek bank, watching the far trees. "Where did you
park?" he asked when Ronnie jogged beside him.

"Trucks at the bridge."

"Good. I need you to drive me home." Sam broke
into a run, dancing around trees and over fallen logs.
The wind was now picking up, rustling the leaves.
Through the swaying pines, Sam could see the bridge
about a hundred yards away. He slowed to a quick walk,
sweeping the tall pines, looking for the silent Galv.

Motioning with his hand, he made Ronnie pause. "Stay here. I'm going to take a look."

Parked down the road was Ronnie's lifted Ford F-150. Sitting on the tailgate, waited Ronnie's friends. They each had a drink in their hand, their feet swinging back and forth. Sam edged beside the road, staring first to the right, then left. "Looks clear. Let's get out of here."

They exited the woods soundlessly. Julius Green, tall, stocky, about two-hundred pounds, and Ronnie's current best friend turned toward them, his eyes narrowing. "What the hell is this?" he said, pointing at Sam. "Where's your shirt, and what in the hell was all that noise? Sounded like a bulldozer crushing trees."

"I ain't got time to explain." Pulling the keys from his pocket, Ronnie squeezed the FOB, unlocking the doors. "Get in and let's get out of here."

"What about him?" Julius cast his thumb at Sam. "Don't tell me y'all are all buddy-buddy now."

"No. Now shut up and get in."

The boys climbed in, leaving Sam the bed of the truck. When Ronnie told them to make room, Sam cut him off. "I'm fine. Drop me off at my house." He scrambled into the bed and leaned back against the truck's cab. Ronnie floored the accelerator, the big tires shot twin rooster tails behind the Ford. They climbed the hill toward the practice fields, reaching the highway within minutes. Sam relaxed and smiled. *Man, would I love to be a fly on the wall inside the cab.*

Sam watched the traffic stream by as they drove through town. The drone of the tires made him drowsy. He was about to nod off when he felt the truck turn hard right and down an old asphalt road in need of repaving. He glanced up as Ronnie pulled over in front of his house. Sam threw a leg over the bed and jumped clear. Ronnie climbed from the cab, shut the door, and met him at the rear bumper. He stared over Sam's shoulder and down the road.

"Hey man, what you said back there," His throat bobbed as he collected his thoughts. "About my dad." He stopped again and leaned against the truck's bed, staring at Sam's small, neat house. "You're right. My old man's thirty minutes down the road, and I haven't seen him in over a year." Ronnie turned away, his voice dropping in volume. "I miss him, man." He wiped his eyes with the heel of his palm. "I ain't got no sister I can talk to. Just me and mom, and she's usually busy with some function or another."

"It's cool, man." Sam reached up and knocked Ronnie's shoulder with a fist tap. "I appreciate the ride, but I've gotta go. Got things to do."

Ronnie pointed at the house. "Your aliens?"

"Yep."

"What'cha got to do for them?"

"Get them off the planet before the Galv hunt them down and kills them."

"Sounds like a walk in the park." Ronnie grinned. "Hey, if you need anything, hit me back. I'll do what I can."

"Will do."

"Well… okay then." Ronnie walked over to the driver's door, opened it, then stopped. He glanced over at Sam. "Be careful, man."

"You know it."

Ronnie climbed in and roared off down the street.

Chapter Ten

Jonqueen stood in the living room, watching Ronnie drive away. "The youth appears unscathed."

"I told you there's more to him than you gave him credit for." Emma joined him at the window. "And it seems he has come to an accordance with his enemy."

Jonqueen nodded. "That was unexpected." He closed the curtains. "We must question him on the Galv, how far they pursued him, how many he saw."

"Do you think they are tracking him?"

"I would consider it a possibility. With your close contact with him, there might be residual trace particles on him from your touch. If they see him as a threat, he could be in grave danger."

The door opened, and Sam strolled in, smiling.

"Son, everything okay?" Helen asked. "Emma told me about the run-in with Ronnie."

"We're good, mom. Maybe not to the level we were as kids, but…" he shrugged.

"Well, it's a start." Helen finished for him. She walked over to her son and hugged him. "I'm glad."

"Sam Shepherd," Jonqueen said in his rusted, gravelly voice. "The Galv, did they pursue you?"

Sam pushed free of his mom. "Yeah, but not immediately. I grabbed Ronnie and dragged him into the woods. When I turned around, the Galv were motionless and had almost faded away."

"How long did the transference beam fade?"

"Not that long, maybe five minutes. Then it came on strong, real strong." He glanced from Jonqueen to Emma. "I think they *fully* materialized. They were pushing the grass down, and bending saplings."

"Did they continue to pursue?"

"Oh yeah, big-time. Must have followed us at least three-quarters of a mile through the woods. And these weren't the stun shots from earlier. This time they were blasting trees apart. We eventually lost them and hid until they completely faded. Then Ronnie drove me home."

Emma and Jonqueen stared hard at each other.

"I take it this is bad news?" Sam asked, his eyes flicking between the two.

Emma tried on a brave smile, but it faltered. "The worst. We feel they have assigned you a threat index. Not only do they want to terminate me and Jonqueen, but now your life is in danger."

"Me? I'm in danger?" Sam said as his eyes widened; he took a step back, hands clasped on top of his head. "Crap. Never thought they'd come after me. What about your ship? Were you able to salvage anything?"

"Very little." Jonqueen replied in his harsh, guttural countenance. "The Galv completely fused the slipstream drive. When they appeared in the woods, the self-destruct was expedited. I could only salvage a short-range comboard and enough nanite matter to repair my armor and build a few new weapons. Before the ship disintegrated, I downloaded the most up-to-date star charts."

"So, is it total loss?"

"The ship, yes," Jonqueen replied. Then his eyes narrowed, and his long fists clenched. "But from what you report, all is not lost."

"I don't follow."

"I'm sorry, Jonqueen, but I too am confused," Emma said, agreeing with Sam. "We have no way off the planet and no way home."

Jonqueen's lips split in a minuscule imitation of a smile. "Their actions convince me of two things. One, they are trying to eliminate us and anyone that can assist. Two, they are concerned that someone will slip past them. For them to fully materialize and hunt you, Sam Shepherd, this means their vessel is still in operational condition, and probably has a functioning star-drive."

"Jonqueen," Emma asked, showing a flicker of optimism, "can you pilot their craft?"

"I am not sure, but I believe so. Maybe not as efficiently as the Galv, but I should be able to reconfigure their drive matrix into one I can operate."

"Maybe I'm missing something, but how are you going to get to their ship? I assume it is in orbit?" Sam asked.

"Yes, most likely in a geosynchronous orbit above this area."

"Back to my question: how do you plan on getting onboard? We have no way to get you there."

Jonqueen pressed his palms together in front of his face and stared over the top of his fingers in an eerily human-like movement. "I am unsure. However, during our approach, I scanned all your communications, both military and civilian. I know that a civilian aerospace facility has a launch planned several days from now. Their intention is to demonstrate a new engine prototype that is untested, and as of now, unknown of on your planet. They hope it can propel the vessel to your moon and back within two of your days. I also know that this flight, if taken, will result in the destruction of the craft."

Helen crossed her arms over her chest and stared at Jonqueen. "How in the world can you know that?"

Jonqueen slowly turned to face Sam's mother, his gray lips pinched tight. "As I stated previously, I had ample time to study the communications broadcasted from this world. I find it amazing no other beings have traced these signals back to this planet and enslaved you." Jonqueen paused, then focused again. "By analyzing these transmissions, I determined where the signals initiated. Then it was easy to circumvent all security protocols and view the schematics of the ship and drive."

"Just like that," Helen snapped her fingers, "you were able to decipher the blueprints and decide that the ship wouldn't fly."

Jonqueen leaned down, stared hard at Helen, then imitated her action and snapped his thin, gray fingers. When he did, a gray cloud of nanites sprung from his fingertips and hovered in the air before retreating into his skin. "Yes. To be completely accurate, I did not say it would fail. I said it would not succeed if you measure success by the safe return of the craft and pilots. The vessel will break free of the planet's gravity and reach lunar orbit. And it will do so in the time planned. But the stresses on the craft will cause it to break apart when it attempts to return home. The engine design—incredibly primitive by my world's standards—is quite advanced for your time."

Sam leaned against the wall, arms folded across his chest. "I'm usually on top of anything to do with new launches but haven't heard of anything of late. Who's launching?"

Jonqueen faced Sam. "Solar Xploration, from their private facility on your South-Eastern coast."

"Solar Xploration?" Sam blurted out. "Are you sure? My dad used to fly with one of the founders. The man was dad's best friend."

"Yes, I am certain."

"Mom, are you still in contact with Mr. Dellion?"

Helen nodded slowly, then held up a hand. "It's been a while, probably a couple of years, since I've talked with him."

"Can you dig up his number? We need to speak to him."

"Sam," Helen cautioned, keeping her eyes on Jonqueen, "if you plan on calling him and telling him you have space aliens in your house that need to borrow a rocket, he'll think you're crazy."

"Mom, we've got to do something." Sam pressed as he pushed off the wall, stepped over to the window, and pulled the drapes back. "If the Galv find them—us— we're in big trouble."

"Sam, this isn't like borrowing your neighbor's car. You're asking to borrow a billion-dollar car." Helen joined Sam by the window and put an arm around his shoulder. "I'll make the call, but don't be disappointed if he shoots your idea down."

"He won't shoot us down, well, not after he meets Jonqueen and Emma. Proof that there's extraterrestrial life out there," Sam pointed toward the sky, "will convince him to help us."

"If he doesn't think we're nutty as a fruitcake." Helen laughed. "This has got to be the craziest thing you've ever gotten us into, Sam." She looked at Emma. "And you're okay with us using you to get through to Thomas?"

Emma nodded. "Yes, Helen, mother of Sam. It is very important that Jonqueen and I return home. I feel we need to leave soon. I'm not sure of our position in time, but if my world is waiting on our return, and the same time has passed between both existences, they might soon declare us dead. If that happens, the wars will continue and the Galv will destroy both our civilizations."

"I understand. I also know that if we reveal you two, and we can't get you off this world, every scientist on Earth will examine and prod you. I don't want you guys to become zoo exhibits."

Jonqueen's eyes narrowed, and his lips pulled tight against his sharp teeth. "I would never allow that to happen." His voice dropped to a growl deep enough to vibrate the walls.

Helen reached out to touch him, then withdrew when he flinched. "I know you won't, Jonqueen. I'm not going to let it happen either." She pulled her phone from her pocket. "I'll try to get in touch with Thomas."

"So," Sam said, turning to face Jonqueen, "you think this engine design will work?"

Jonqueen was slow to answer, the snarl still on his face. "If the schematics I reviewed are correct, the craft should generate the required speed to reach your moon and return within two of your days. I also believe that with a few modifications, this vessel might reach point-one percent of light-speed."

"Will it be enough for you guys to reach the Galv vehicle?"

"Yes. I feel certain the Galv have positioned their ship far enough out to shield it from view. I believe we can commandeer the launch vehicle after it escapes your atmosphere and then intercept the Galv craft."

"How will you defend yourself if you are detected?"

"We cannot. If the Galv monitor the launch—which I am sure they will—it will be up to you to guide us in."

Sam's eyes flew wide. "You want me in the launch vessel?"

Emma smiled and shook her head. "No, Sam Shepherd. You will not be launching with us. The risk that we will be discovered and destroyed is too high for your young life. What Jonqueen means is that you will remotely pilot us in from the launch site. The Galv, while not psychic, have the unique ability to detect when they are being surveyed or scanned. And they have our brain wave patterns in their database. If they see the launch vehicle drifting their way, they might concentrate their scans on us. Though not brilliant, they might anticipate our actions."

"But if they see an Earth vessel approaching, won't they just destroy you on sight?"

"No," Jonqueen said. "They will look upon the craft as nothing more than debris, of no concern." He took a deep breath. The thin slits for nostrils flared. "Once we are within their firing arc—where their weapons cannot target us—I will engage the engines and crash into their vessel. I have already constructed the template for an umbilical that will connect the crafts and allow me to board and destroy any Galv I encounter."

"Still, don't you think they will take notice of an Earth launch veers off course and toward them?"

"Their arrogance is great. They will view the launch as a primitive attempt at space flight and not give further thought. The Galv are secure in the fact that your planet cannot detect them. I will assist the technicians we will work with in locating the Galv."

"And then I remotely pilot you to their ship?"

"That is correct. I will construct a control panel that you will utilize in concert with the launch facility. Once we reach a predetermined position, I will assume control."

"Sounds easy enough," Sam replied and shook his head. "All we have to do is convince Mr. Dellion to loan us his billion-dollar baby, then step aside while you crash it. Piece of cake."

Jonqueen cocked his head and stared down at Sam. "Yes," he snapped his fingers again, sending another cloud of nanites in orbit around his hand. "Piece of cake."

Sam and Helen stared at the alien, shocked. Emma laughed hard, dropping her face into her hands. "Why, Jonqueen, you joke! I think it's time to get you back home to your dour family." She laughed harder. Jonqueen tilted his head her way and curled the edges of his gray lips.

Realizing that the tall, gangly alien had just cracked a joke, Helen joined in. "Will wonders never cease!" She fought the giggles and shook her head. "Okay, he's going to think I'm drunk or a lunatic. How do I convince him we have not one but two alien races on the planet?"

"The launch site has a powerful radio scanning antenna," Jonqueen replied. "When you establish communications with him, I will provide the coordinates and a frequency to which the antenna can be aimed. Once he has the modulation programmed, I will provide him a second set of coordinates for him to fire their high-band laser array. The array will charge the scattering field the Galv use to prevent detection. Their ship will then glow briefly, allowing your country's defense satellites to detect it. The satellites will have to be in position to record the image, as this will only work once. The ship will be visible for less than eight seconds."

"How do you know all this?" Sam asked

Jonqueen glared down at him, his eyes narrowing. "Because I do. If you continue to question everything I say, the Galv will surely find us before we can escape this planet."

Sam stepped back with his hands up by his shoulders. "Just asking! Sheesh, maybe he needs to be on decaf."

"Sam, please don't take it personal. Jonqueen isn't accustomed to being questioned, especially by youth." Emma glanced his way. "And you must trust him. If he says it is so, then it is."

"Mom," Sharon asked from the kitchen. "What is *that?*"

Sam, Emma, and Helen raced to the kitchen and stared out the window. Sharon pulled back the curtains. The kitchen windows faced the backyard and sparse woods that edged up to a pasture. At the far side of the pasture, the brush sparkled and swayed.

Sharon pointed to a shimmering form coalescing into a stocky figure. "Is that a Galv?"

The form crossed slowly through a farmer's pasture; the vegetation falling to the side as it passed. The being's shape intensified at two hundred.

"Jonqueen!" called Emma, her voice rising in panic. "We have a Galv soldier, almost completely materialized, at the rear of this dwelling."

"And we have two more approaching from the front." He rasped, his voice like tangled barbwire. "Does this building have any other exits?"

"Only the front and back door, plus the garage." Helen answered.

"Then we will have to fight our way out of here."

The Galv crossed the field behind the house, sending the cows running, nearly trampling their calves. The soldier reached a second electrified fence and passed through it. Sparks jumped and sizzled from the wires as the Galv made contact. Its form flickered, faded, and reformed after it passed.

"What the hell happened to it?" Helen whispered.

"The electrical current coursing through the containment fence disrupted the transference field." Jonqueen leaned closer to the window, speaking in a quiet, less biting tone. "I am surprised that an energy source as primitive as the one used on this planet would have such an effect on the Galv." The alien soldier struggled to pass through the electric fence, it's form shuddering. "This structure, does it use the same power source?"

"Yes, sure. Everyone in this city, and I would guess the country, uses the same electricity."

Jonqueen backed from the window; his eyes focused hard on the walls, his lips drawn tight against his sharp teeth. "If that is the case, we have a way to disrupt the Galv until they adapt." He lifted his nose and sniffed the air. "The power conduits, they are within the walls?"

"Yes, why?"

The soldier continued to walk through the house, following close to the wall. "Is it a trait of your species to constantly ask questions regardless of the situation?"

"Sorry, a bad habit."

"Maybe your species should have your healers tend to it before it destroys you as a race," Jonqueen said. He walked to an intersection of walls and held his hand slightly before the surface, then swiped down the front. His nanites consumed the drywall, exposing the wiring within. Jonqueen grabbed a thick cable and pulled it from the wall, the insulation melting. In a fountain of sparks, the wire broke in half. Working quickly with his nanites, Jonqueen created a small oval dish resembling a satellite receiver. He connected the wire to the base of the long tube he kept in his coat, then the antenna dish to the narrow tube. The dish began to glow and pulse.

"When the Galv breach the perimeter of this structure, I will use this device to generate an energy field. It should sufficiently disrupt their transference beam and allow us to escape."

"Jonqueen, will it disable all of them?"

Dropping the dish down to his side, Jonqueen did something entirely human. He signed. "Unknown. The primitive power source within this dwelling creates unpredictable power spikes with my equipment. If the weapon handles the discharge without exploding, I am confident we can disable the Galv."

"And if it explodes?" Helen asked.

"Let us hope it does not." Jonqueen answered flatly.

Sam raced to the kitchen from the living room. "They're moving faster. They're halfway across the yard. Where do we need to be?"

"They are coming for me first, then the Saint." Jonqueen glanced around the room. He pointed to a door at the end of a hallway, off the living room. "Where does that lead?"

"That's the garage. It's full of junk, not much room to hide," Sam answered.

"We will not be hiding. Go there and prepare to fight." He lifted his face to the ceiling and slowly turned. "They know where I am. I will hold them off as long as I can, but you must make sure the Emissary gets out of here at all costs." Jonqueen walked to the front window and pressed the array against the glass. The flat-black cylinder and dish penetrated the pane without breaking it. A pistol grip formed at the base of the tube. He squeezed the grip, and a trio of scarlet bolts of light flashed from the barrel, hitting the Galv soldier in the chest. The alien stumbled, fizzled, and then strengthened. "Go! Now!"

Jonqueen aimed his weapon at the second soldier in the front yard. The pitch from his weapon increased in volume until it was earsplitting. This time, the beam was a solid red streak. It hit the soldier and flared. The soldier stopped moving, then exploded in a starburst of light. Jonqueen then turned his weapon on the first soldier who had closed within one-hundred feet of the home.

Sharon grabbed Emma by the hand and stumbled as Emma's life force swarmed her. Sam pushed both women, directing them toward the garage. He took a quick peek over his shoulder as Jonqueen fired again with his tubular weapon. The scarlet bolts slammed again into the Galv before passing through and setting the grass on fire. Explosions rocked the house. "They have breached the structure!" Jonqueen shouted, his voice shook the walls and shattered the windows.

Sam forced the women down the hall, then glanced over his shoulder. Jonqueen pulled the dish from the window and aimed it toward the kitchen. The dish hummed and vibrated. The walls rattled, and the floor trembled. Sam pulled the garage door open the same instant a pressure wave slammed them through the opening and out of the house. The rafters screamed as the atmospheric pressure increased. The air thickened, became too dense to breathe, then the world turned black.

Chapter Eleven

When Sam opened his eyes, there was no sound. Moments later, he detected a hushed static. Sam pushed to his knees and saw the Camaro in the middle of the yard, the bright afternoon sun glaring off the scorched paint. He stared at it, wondering why this bothered him. Then his head cleared, and he realized the garage door was gone, blown across the yard, and wrapped around a tree.

Then the roar of pain hit. His eyes, head, and entire body felt like he'd been thrown down a flight of stairs. Struggling to his feet, he saw red splotches on the ground. His right pant leg was dark and wet near mid-thigh. Running his hand down his leg, he collapsed to one knee when his hand brushed a shard of metal jutting from his jeans.

Movement to his left caught his attention. A pink running shoe was moving slowly under an avalanche of boxes. His sister wore pink shoes. "Sharon!" He tried to shout, his voice weak. Sam hobbled over to where she lay buried.

"Mom!" Sam screamed. "Help me!"

The world was returning to focus; the deafness fading. Sam could hear his sister's moans and jets of water spewing from broken waterlines. The pain in his leg was approaching blackout proportions. Sam grabbed debris with both hands and threw it to the side.

"Sam," Helen hoarsely whispered as she picked her way through the destroyed garage. "Are you okay?"

Sam turned to see his mother limping toward him. "Mom, where's Emma?"

"I don't know." Helen helped pull a large plastic tote filled with winter clothes off her daughter. "Sweetie, are you okay?"

Sharon nodded, then shook her head and brushed insulation off her face. "My knee hurts," she moaned. "I can't bend my leg." Tears etched clear trails down her dust-coated cheeks. "The pain is really bad." She reached up, and Sam carefully lifted his sister. He slipped an arm around her waist and carried her out of the ruined garage.

"Mom, did Emma get blown out of the garage with you?" Sam asked over his shoulder.

"She must have, but I haven't seen her since the house exploded."

Sam blinked. "The house exploded?" He gingerly helped his sister to the ground.

"It must have, look." Helen pointed at the roof, or what remained of it. Most of the decking was gone, all the windows shattered, and the kitchen completely leveled. "I'm going to check on Jonqueen, see if you can find Emma." Stumbling through the remains of the garage, Helen found a heavy pair of neoprene rubber gloves and pulled them on.

Sam limped across the yard, unable to put much weight on his right leg. "Where can she be?"

Sharon shrugged, then pointed to the field across the street. "There!"

Emma was backing into the woods as a Galv soldier closed on her.

Ignoring the pain in his leg, Sam spun around, stared past his car, and into the field. Emma was backing through the bramble, a flickering being closing on her. "Emma!" Sam shouted, then grabbed a shovel and used it for a crutch as he limped across the yard. His leg bled freely. He could feel it soaking his jeans, trickling into his socks. He ignored the pain and pushed into a lopsided run.

Sam crossed the road as Emma disappeared into the woods. He ran harder, the metal sliver ripping into his thigh. "Emma!"

The soldier entered the wood line.

Sam traversed the ditch lining the woods, entering the field, and stumbled through the scrub. Emma was a dozen yards ahead, the Galv drawing near, saplings and briars now slowing it down. Emma danced through the trees as a low-pitched vibration built-in volume. The Galv raised its weapon and fired. A tree to Emma's left exploded into splinters.

Sam passed a pile of illegally dumped bricks, picked up a chunk of mortar, and threw it as hard as he could at the Galv Soldier. The brick shard landed beside the alien. The Galv paused, turned his way, then continued its pursuit of Emma. Sam grabbed two more fist-sized chunks and ran, gritting through the pain. The alien soldier was now only forty feet ahead. He threw the brick full force, stumbling from the movement. The chuck of masonry hit the soldier in the back, just below its thick neck. The Galv stopped and turned his way, its weapon rising.

Sam threw again. This time, the brick shard hit the soldier in its face. The brick penetrated the transference beam, then fell behind the soldier. The alien rocked and became momentarily solid as the weapon slipped from its claw-like hand. Sam blocked out most of the pain and charged.

There was a quick flash of light as the Galv Soldier fully integrated, no longer partially transparent, turned to face Sam as he swung the shovel. The blade hit the alien's thick, squat neck, knocking it back. Sam pivoted and resumed his attack before the soldier could regain its balance. This time, he stabbed the shovel into the midsection of the alien. The transference beam was partially disrupted, and sparks danced off the metal blade.

Sam retreated and cocked the shovel over his shoulder.

The alien thrust a meaty arm forward and connected with Sam's face, knocking him backwards. The soldier swung again, catching Sam in his stomach and tossing him in the air like a rag doll. Sam landed in a cloud of dust. It raised the short barrel weapon it carried and pointed it toward the teenager.

A scream behind the Galv made it turn. Sam looked up to see Emma race from the woods, jump on the soldier's back, and wrap her arms around its neck, trying to bring it down.

The Galv soldier shrugged her off as if she was weightless, turned from Sam, and stomped after Emma. Sam struggled to his feet, grabbed the shovel, and threw it like a javelin at the soldier. The shovel glanced off the alien as it fired its weapon. A flash of energy sizzled from the barrel, leaving a small crater where Emma had previously stood.

Sam picked up the shovel and swung it as he closed. The blade caught the soldier across the front of its flat face, staggering it. Sam was bringing it around for another slash when the alien twirled faster than Sam could move, stepped inside his reach, and grabbed him by the throat. The alien's three talon-like fingers squeezed, cutting off his air. It took the shovel from him and tossed it across the field. As his vision dimmed, Sam saw a flash of red.

"Leave my kids alone!" Helen screamed, lunging with a hand-held taser. The soldier pivoted toward her as she pressed the emitter against its chest and hit the firing stud. Instantly, the alien stopped moving and vibrated. The weapon dropped from its hand as its form wavered.

Sam scrambled away, limping into the trees for cover.

The tasers emitters shot waves of electricity coursing the length of the alien's body. Its form pulsed wildly. Helen pushed harder, shoving the taser into the convulsing form, now only semi-solid.

"Helen Shepherd, get clear!" Emma shouted.

Helen sprinted way, leaving the taser in the spasming alien. Flames and streaks of blueish-white light jetted from the convulsing form. A scream of static poured from the soldier as a gray flash of light exploded skyward in an ashen column.

A rain of transparent gray embers dropped from the sky.

"Did we kill it?" Helen asked after pulling her hands from her ears.

"I believe you did," Emma replied, slowly crossing the gray-stained grass. "It was trying to return to its ship, but that device you attacked it with distorted the transference beam. The ship couldn't recover the soldier." Emma pushed the fused ground around with her foot, then reached down, grabbed a stick, and stirred the dirt. "This is all that remains."

Sam limped over, his right pants leg now drenched with blood. "Mom," He collapsed against her. "You saved us."

"It's what mamas do." She reached past Sam, motioning for Emma to come forward. "Come on, I have enough arms for you, too!"

The Saint stared at her momentarily, then stepped into the extended embrace. After standing stiffly, she leaned forward and wrapped her arms around Helen and Sam.

Helen gently pushed back from Sam and took Emma in her arms. "Honey, what's wrong? You're crying."

Emma brushed the tears from her face and managed a weak smile. "I'm sorry, crying is unheard of on my home world. I've never seen it in public and have only done so one other time."

"Why are you crying now?"

Emma gave Helen a last squeeze, then stepped back to compose herself. She used her hand to wipe the remaining tears from her eyes. Her jaw clenched and released. "If we had crashed on a survey mission, or were just in transit, I would have sent Jonqueen home alone and remained here."

"Are you serious?" Sam exclaimed. "When you can go anywhere in the universe, you'd stay on this little 'ol primitive world. That's crazy!"

Emma worked up a smile. "No, Sam Shepard. You do not realize, even with all our advanced technology and interplanetary ships, our world is emotionally cold. There is virtually no laughter, no tears. And as strange as this might sound, there is little danger. As I said earlier, in the time I live, you are brought into being to complete a task or fill a position. You are retired, euthanized when you can no longer function or are no longer needed.

"Since I have been here, I've been subjected to emotions that are researched and theorized. Your society is closer to Jonqueen's than my own, even though your species are very dissimilar."

"Jonqueen!" Helen said with a gasp. "We need to check on him! I was so worried about the both of you. I ran off without looking to see if he's okay." She turned to run when Emma grabbed her wrist.

"The old soldier is alive. He's seriously hurt, but his nanites are attending to his wounds." She let go, smiling. "I have spent considerable time with that individual and when he's hurt, the best thing you can do is let him be." She allowed a soft laugh. "If you think he's obstinate now, you should see him repairing battle damage. A most unpleasant being, I assure you."

"How do you know?" Sam asked while looking toward their destroyed home.

"It's the nanites. Same way we can now communicate but couldn't when we met. They form a mental link between species. I can detect him from many of your miles away. I can also tell if he's injured and how bad."

"Do we have the nanites inside us right now?"

Emma nodded. "Yes, a tiny amount."

"Can you tell where we are, and all that stuff?"

Emma shook her head. "No, only Jonqueen. Originally, it was so he could know where I was at all times. But something changed that allowed me to detect him as well. We think the nanites rewrote their own programming, but don't know how."

Helen patted Sam on the shoulder. "We need to get that leg looked at and check on Sharon." She ran her hand through her hair, pulling it tight against her head, then stared at the destruction to her home. "This is going to be hard to explain to the insurance company." Slipping an arm around her son's waist, she helped him limp home. Sharon was waiting for them on the house's front steps, her head in her hands. She leaned back and glanced up at her mother.

"Mom, what are we going to do?"

"I don't know, sweetie." She walked up to Sharon and hugged her. "But let's check on Jonqueen, see if there's anything we can do to help."

The door opened, and a very dusty Jonqueen staggered out. Streams of silver blood dribbled through the torn sections of his armor. He leaned against the side of the house. "The damage to this structure was unintended. The power source is raw and unpredictable; my nanites had a difficult time controlling the power feed." He paused, breathing hard. "If it is any consolation, I believe I have destroyed, if not seriously

degraded, the fighting capabilities of the Galv soldiers."
Jonqueen collapsed and slid down the brick wall.

"Helen Shepherd, your son and daughter are in need
of your healers," Jonqueen said. "My nanites are nearly
depleted. I have repaired as much damage as I can to
my core. But I need more time to restore myself. I
require a place I will not be disturbed." He took several
deep, ragged breaths. "I also fear our battle with the
Galv will result in unwarranted attention with the
security personnel in this vicinity. We need to leave this
place."

Helen nodded. She glanced at her van. The right
passenger-side quarter panel was twisted and scorched,
and the windows shattered. "Sam, how long do you
think it will take to get your Camaro working?"

Sam shrugged. "I have no clue. I haven't had time to
check out the damage since it was towed home. I don't
even know where my keys are."

"Maybe I can be of assistance," Jonqueen offered in
a weak voice.

"Jonqueen, you are in no condition to do anything."
Emma kneeled beside him. "Sam Shepherd will figure
something out; of that I am sure."

The sound of an approaching vehicle caused them to
turn. A raised, black Ford F150 pulled into the
driveway, rolled up to the van, and stopped. Emma
moved to stand in front of Jonqueen, blocking him
from view. Sam turned, a grin spreading across his face.
The driver's door opened, and a teenage boy in jeans
and boots jumped out.

"You know, when I got home, my mom asked me
how my morning was, and I told her about the same as

always, except I ran into you, and we, you know, buried the hatchet and all that." Ronnie walked around to the front of his truck, paused, and stared at the ruined house. "I was about to tell her we actually came to blows, then some gray dudes showed up, shot me in the chest, and that you saved my life by dragging me off into the woods." Ronnie took his ball cap off and pointed to the house. "Then I heard this sound, this… groaning, high-pitched whine, and I knew where it was coming from. Somehow I *knew* those gray dudes…."

"They're called the Galv; they're from outside our galaxy," Sam corrected.

"… the Galv, from outside out our galaxy? Right," Ronnie continued without raising an eyebrow. "Like I said, I *knew* they were here, don't know how I knew. And apparently I was right." Ronnie swept his eyes over the destruction and whistled. "I hope y'all won."

"We definitely won the battle, but the war is far from over," Sam confirmed as he hobbled up to the truck.

"You guys all right?" Ronnie asked, glancing from Sam and his bloody leg to Sharon. He then noticed Emma. "Sam, who's that?"

"That's Emma, she's from," Sam paused, considered telling the truth, then decided against it, "out of state. She's visiting with us for a few days."

"Man, she's hot!" Ronnie whispered. "I mean, her eyes, are those contacts? It's like she doesn't have pupils, just dark marbles for eyes."

"I know, they're kinda freaky. I think they're contacts," Sam lied, then nodded toward the ruined van. "Hey, would you mind driving me and Sharon to the hospital? We didn't want to call 911 and have to explain this." Sam waved his hand toward the destroyed house. "They'd probably bring the cops, and the cops would want to investigate and all that. Anyway, I've got a slice of metal in my leg," Sam pulled the sticky jeans away from his skin, "and I think Sharon has a sprained knee. Also," Sam pointed to the van, the rear quarter panel melted and crumpled, "the van got wrecked today. I'll try to not bleed too much in your truck."

Ronnie stared at the van. "Gray dudes do that?"

"Yep."

"Wow, good thing they didn't hit us in the woods. Sure thing, man."

Ronnie walked over to Sharon, helped her off the ground, then half-carried her to his truck. Sam pulled the door open, lifted his sister in, and climbed in beside her. Ronnie turned to look out the rear window, put the pickup in reverse, and backed out of the drive. "You sure those guys aren't Russians? Iranians?" He backed into the street, straightened the wheel, and then put the truck in drive.

Sam shook his head. "No, that would be much easier to deal with." As the truck picked up speed, Sam stared out the side mirror. The remains of his house were slowly shrinking in the glass. "You can't repeat anything I'm about to tell you."

"Wouldn't matter if he did," Sharon said, cutting Sam off. "Who'd believe him?"

Sam smiled and nodded in agreement. "That is true, but what I'm about to tell you, you can't tell *anyone*. And that means your mom—no one."

"Cool, no problem." Ronnie said. "Cross my heart and hope to die." He made a motion of zipping his lips

closed, locking them, then tossing the key out the
window.

Sam stared at his friend for a moment, then told his
story. He began by starting with the incident at the
practice fields, the planned escape off the planet, and
ending with the fight across the street from his house.
The drive to the hospital took twenty minutes. Sam was
finishing the story when they drove up to the emergency
room door.

Ronnie jumped from the cab, jogged around, and
opened the passenger side door. Sam climbed gingerly
from the cab, followed by his sister. "So that girl at your
house, not a foreign exchange student?"

"No," Sam grunted, putting weight down on his
injured leg.

"And that creepy old man sitting behind her, no
relationship?"

"No. He is her protector."

Ronnie helped Sharon limp into the waiting room as
Sam went to the nurses' station to complete paperwork.
"Dang. If I hadn't seen those gray dudes, I wouldn't
believe it." Ronnie dropped into a hard, yellow plastic
chair. "So, what are y'all going to do now?"

Sharon shrugged and pointed toward Sam. "Mom
and Sam are going to call an old friend at Space
Xploration. They are going to try and borrow their
launch vehicle, and use it to send these guys back to
where they come from, and *when* they come from."

"Seriously?"

"That's what they claim."

Ronnie sat back in the chair and crossed his arms over his chest. He suddenly sat up quickly. "You said 'when they are from'? You mean to tell me they are from another time?"

Sharon nodded. "Yes, and completely unintentionally. From what I can understand of their conversations with mom and Sam is that they use some kind of 'worm hole' technology they call 'slip stream' to cross the galaxy. Apparently, a ship exploded when they entered their worm hole and the energy shot them through space and time. Anyway, that's their guess."

"If I get this straight, they are going to borrow a spaceship, then hijack those gray dudes ship to blast back across the galaxy."

"That's pretty much it." Sharon said nodding.

"You know what sucks?" Ronnie said as he stared at the ceiling. "This is the coolest thing I've ever heard of and I can't tell anyone 'cause they'd lock me up in the loony bin."

Sam and Sharon were seen, treated, and released three hours after they arrived. The ride home was quiet, no one speaking. Ronnie busied himself navigating traffic while Sam stared at his one long pants leg and one short. He signed, noticing the streetlights turning on as the sun retreated. "Ronnie, what made you come back?"

Ronnie slightly shrugged and switched on his headlights. Twice he started to talk, then stopped. "Y'know, I felt like crap when I got home. I've been so freakin' mad at you for years. I just wanted to pound you into oblivion every time I saw you, to smash the windows in your car." He checked his mirrors and fiddled with the radio. "But after running through the woods with those Galp dudes…."

"Galv," Sam corrected.

"Sorry, Galv… chasing us, blowing the trees to splinters, and realizing you had saved my butt, it all started feeling pretty stupid." He glanced at Sam and offered a shrug and weak smile. "All those years being angry after being such good friends as kids." Ronnie turned away as he passed a sputtering dump truck. "And you didn't do nothing. I'd known it all that time, and I think that made me even madder!" He laughed hard, then stopped.

"I went home and asked my mom how to contact my dad." Ronnie brushed a tear away with the back of his hand.

"Good for you, man. I know he'll be glad to see you." Sam reached over and gave Ronnie a quick squeeze on the shoulder.

Chapter Twelve

From blocks away, they could see flashes of light. Red and blue strobes pulsed through the trees, reflecting off the road and houses lining the street. Ronnie slowed, and Sam tapped the dash, then pointed down the road. "Keep going but drive slowly like you're rubber-necking." They stared out the window, Sam counting three fire trucks and four police cars. He dialed his mom's number. Helen answered on the first ring.

"Mom, how long have the cops been there?"

"Sam, don't stop, you guys keep driving." The phone went silent for a moment, then his mother's voice returned. *"Cops have been here a couple of hours. They also have an arson squad here; they're really picking through the debris. Apparently, someone, don't know who, called 911, said they heard an explosion and went to investigate. They thought we were all in the house. Cops aren't sure what happened, and the fire department is obviously baffled."*

"What did you tell them, and where's Emma and Jonqueen?"

"I told them we don't know what happened, that we were cleaning the garage when the house blew up. As for Emma and her friend, they seemed to detect—or at least Jonqueen did—that authorities were on the way. They ran back into the woods across the street."

"Okay, good. At least they're safe. Have you had a chance to call Dellion?"

"Oh yeah, I was on the phone with him with the first fire truck arrived. Needless to say, the call didn't go well." Helen

snorted. *"At first, he thought I was pulling some kind of silly joke on him. Then he thought I was drunk. Now he thinks I'm a crackpot."*

"How'd you leave it with him?"

"I said, 'how about I deliver you two living, breathing extraterrestrials? Would you believe me then?'"

"What did he say?"

"He hung up and refused to take my call."

"Well, that's what we'll have to do."

"That's what I figured you'd say. I told Emma and Jonqueen you'd have to drive them to Florida, but we'd first have to fix your car."

"I'll start on it tonight. If it's just the plugs, wires and fuses, I should be able to get it going by morning."

"No need. The thought of the internal combustion engine fascinated Jonqueen. He released a cloud of nanites on it and had it running in an hour." Helen quieted again. Sam could hear conversations in the background. The fire department was trying to get her attention. She spoke quickly. "Sam, stay with Ronnie until I call. I'm going to try to enter the house and see what clothes we can salvage."

"Okay, mom. I'll be waiting." Sam ended the call, then turned to Ronnie. "Can we chill at your house? Mom wants me to stay away until the cops leave."

"Yeah, no problem. My mom was asking about you anyway, wanted to see you… grill you for information." He turned up the radio. "Plan on having your brain picked," he laughed and pressed the accelerator down

The visit with Ronnie's mother was warm and friendly. She apologized to Sam for being distant since his father died and asked about his mom. She said she was glad he and Ronnie finally made up and never understood what happened between them. Ronnie's mom was getting into her brain-picking rhythm when his phone rang.

"Hey mom, everything okay now?"

"It is for now," Hellen replied. *"The police and fire department are gone, but the house is wrapped in yellow 'crime scene' tape. The fireman advised us not to go inside, that the house was unsafe."* She laughed. *"I wanted to tell him that being in the home four hours ago was even more unsafe. Me and Sharon are going to pick through the house and try to get us all some clothes."*

When Sam and Ronnie pulled up, Helen was in the garage with armloads of clothing and personal items.

"Ronnie," Helen said as she set a basket of clothes by the van. "Thanks so much for helping us with all of this. It was hard enough to explain how our house exploded without catching fire, or having a natural gas line." She laughed lightly, then stretched, twisting her back from side to side. "If you boys will give us a hand, we've put clothes, blankets, towels, etcetera in the garage. We need to put them in the van for now."

"Where's our guests?" Sam asked.

"Emma is helping Sharon, and Jonqueen is… well, I'm not sure where he is. But he's around."

Ronnie tapped Sam on the shoulder. "Hey, can I meet these guys? I mean, the only aliens I've ever met swam here." Ronnie cracked himself up, then laughed harder when Helen stared at him disapprovingly. "What? They're Cuban! They had to jump off the boat and swim to shore." He winked at Sam, who shook his head.

"C'mon, we'll start with Emma." Sam started toward the house, with Ronnie following close behind.

"Seriously? She has a human name? I thought it would be something strange and unpronounceable."

Sam turned. "I don't know what her true name is. Her title is *Emissary de'tantel*. It's some form of diplomatic title, that's all I know. So, we call her Emma. It's easier. She also seems to like it."

"Does she speak English?"

"I guess," Sam said, scratching his head. "I never really thought about it."

"Then how do you communicate?"

Sam stopped and shrugged. "When we met, I couldn't understand a thing she said. Then the next thing I knew, I could. I think she has to touch you first. It's weird. I don't know how to explain it."

Ronnie stared through the dark garage toward the roving beams of light emanating from inside the house. "What does she sound like?"

Sam shrugged again. "I don't know how to explain it. To me and my mom—I haven't asked Sharon—she sounded like wind through the trees, or the soft hush of falling snow. Almost like a quiet, comfortable static."

"That's weird as hell, you know that?" Ronnie said, staring at his friend.

"Hey, that's what it sounds like. I'll let you judge for yourself." Sam picked his way past fallen insulation and wallboard. He pushed through the door leading into the house and called for his sister. "Hey Sharon, are you with Emma? Ronnie's here and would like to meet her, if it's okay with her."

The lights in the room stopped moving, came together, and started toward them.

"Hold on, we'll meet you guys outside." Sharon called back.

The boys waited in the yard by Sam's car. Moments later, the light in the garage brightened as the girls made their way through the debris. Emma was now wearing a pair of clean jeans and a light-gray Nike tee shirt. She pulled her hair back from her face, showing off high cheekbones and ivory skin. Emma's eyes sparkled intensely under the flashlight's illumination.

"Man, she's… gorgeous! I can't believe she's not human." Ronnie whispered.

Sam turned his way but kept his eyes on the girls. "Well, she is human-ish, just a much more recent version of us. Remember, she's from thousands of years in the future."

The girls approached, and Ronnie stepped forward with his hand out. "Hi, I'm Ronnie."

Emma brought the light up to Ronnie's face. She hesitated, grabbed his hand, twisted it down, and pulled him forward. "You!" She hissed.

Ronnie cried out in pain as he dropped to his knees. Emma advanced on him, still holding his hand, and bending the wrist backward.

Sam and Sharon staggered; hands pressed against their ears as waves of heavy iron static pummeled them.

"Emma!" Sam croaked as he dropped to a knee. "What are you doing?"

"This one attacked you!" She screamed in her high static voice. "He is like the Galv. I will make him pay!"

"No!" Sam shouted as he staggered to his feet. "It's okay, we're good. We're not fighting anymore." He could feel waves of anger pulsing off the girl, slamming into him. Fighting the rage pouring off Emma, Sam stepped close enough to put his arms around her shoulders and pull her free of Ronnie. The connection was severed, and an explosion of raw energy coursed through him, whiting out his vision and knocking him flat on his back. He tried to crawl to his feet, fell over, and collapsed.

"Sam!" Emma cried. She dropped beside him, lifted his head, and brushed dirt from his face with her hands. "I'm sorry. This has never happened before."

Sam glanced up and stared into her eyes as they softened from intense fiery blue to the dark sapphire he was accustomed to. He made it to his knees when he felt the world go numb below him.

He was being rocked back and forth, a cool, wet cloth draped across his forehead.

"Sam, can you hear me?"

The voice was distant, on the very edge of his hearing. He tried to speak but found that he didn't have enough strength. He nodded feebly.

"Can you sit up for me?"

Sam tried to push down to lift his body, found that the air in the room weighed several tons, and quit trying. He shook his head slowly; the effort draining him.

"Okay, that's fine. Rest."

Sam felt covers being tucked against him, and the world stayed blank.

Sunlight filtered through the windows, hurting his eyes. Sam sat up slowly, his head swimming with the effort. The light fixture on the ceiling was not familiar. He rolled to his right, and a wall of posters came into focus. All the posters were for heavy metal bands, none he listened to. Rising to his elbows, he saw a dresser and a collection of sports trophies—football, baseball, basketball, and a few he didn't recognize. Sam forced himself to sit up, the effort taking his breath away. He glanced to his left. In an old, worn recliner was his mother. Pale light leaked through dusty blinds, barely illuminating her red hair.

"Mom," he whispered, his dry voice. He licked his lips. "Where are we?"

Helen sat up abruptly, threw the blanket off her lap, and stumbled over to the bed. "Sam, are you back with us again?"

"Mom…" he swallowed and grimaced. "What's going on?"

"We're at Ronnie's house. You're in his bed." She sat on the edge beside him and brushed his hair back with her fingers. "We don't know what happened. You tried to pull Emma away from Ronnie and," she shook her head. "Even Jonqueen is stumped. We think being on Earth, combined with all the stress she's under, that her psychic or extra-mental ability has been amped up. When you grabbed her, all the anger she felt toward Ronnie was channeled to you. For lack of a better description, you guys arced."

The door creaked open, and Emma quietly stepped through. Her face was wet, her hair hanging in tangled pulls. "Is he…" she began, her voice hitching.

Helen smiled and sat on the edge of the bed. "He's okay, sweetie. Whatever happened between the two of you really knocked him for a loop."

Emma hurried across the room without seeming to move. She hesitated by the edge of the bed, a smile trying to break through her concerned eyes.

A grin spread across Sam's face. "Remind me to never make you mad."

"Sam Shepherd, I never meant to hurt you." Her eyes dropped. "I didn't think I could." A tear slipped down her cheek.

Sam pushed the covers away, glad he was still in his jeans and hadn't been undressed by his mom. He stumbled around the end of the bed and sat gently beside her. He hesitated, then took her hand. "It's okay." He held her hand in both of his. A weak energy current pulsed between them. "You've been crying."

She nodded, her hair falling in front of her face. "It's a very… strange feeling. Painful and comforting at the same time. Not sure that I like it." She glanced up, her eyes opening as color warmed her cheeks. "I fear if I spend too much time here, I'll never want to go home."

"Honey, don't you have someone at home that would miss you? Parents, siblings? Anyone?" Helen asked.

Emma turned to face Helen. "Our world is not like yours. Our 'parents' are chosen for the best genetic variation and compatibility. I was educated from birth to fulfill a need. We have no family." Another tear slipped free.

"Don't you have friends? Co-workers?" Sam asked.

She brushed her hair from her face, holding it back with one hand. "I have colleagues I study and learn with. They would be considered friends, but not to the level you experience. All our training is to benefit the Shovain people."

"Wow, that's… depressing!" Sam blurted out with a laugh.

Emma stared at him, eyes wide with shock. A grin slowly formed on her face. "Yes, Sam, it is." She stood and regained her composure. "And I need to go home. The Shovain need this treaty with the Firestar Confederacy."

Sam nodded. "I know you do. I wish you didn't have to."

"As do I, Sam Shepherd."

Emma turned and walked out of the room without looking back. Sam moved to follow when his mom took him by the elbow. "Sam, I know that look on your face. You're going to try to talk her into staying."

Sam glanced at his mom and shook his head. "Nope, just the opposite. I was thinking of ways to keep her from staying. I know she wants to, wants this." Sam waved his hand around the room. "She wants our primitive back-water life." He walked again, then stopped. "But I will miss her like I've missed no one in my entire life."

"I know you will, honey." Helen pushed off the bed. "Your shoes and a change of clothes are in the car. You need to get dressed and head for Florida."

When Sam entered the kitchen, Ronnie sat with Sharon and his mom at the kitchen table. "What's up, sleeping beauty?” Ronnie said, grinning. He moved from the table to give Sam a spot.

“Morning,” Sam replied sheepishly.

“Help yourself,” Ronnie’s mom said to Sam. “Everyone else has already eaten. Your girlfriend acted like she’d never had bacon and eggs before in her life. She ate like there was no tomorrow!” Terrie Howell said happily. “Was good to see a girl eat like that.” She winked at Sharon, who then stood and grabbed a piece of buttered toast.

“Happy?” she said, laughing. “Now I’ve got to run an extra mile today.”

“Thanks, sleeping for twelve hours makes a boy hungry.” Sam said as he loaded a plate with eggs, bacon, and toast, then poured a glass of milk. “Speaking of Emma, where is she?”

Terrie nodded toward the bathroom, and whispered. “She apparently, uh, overdid it a bit. Not the best way to compliment by running off to the bathroom.” Terrie Howell said with a smile as she cleared the dishes.

“She’s not used to eating such a heavy southern breakfast.” Sam said between bites.

Terrie turned from the sink where she was rinsing off the breakfast plates. “Now, where is she from? And how’d she end up staying with you?”

“She’s from Canada,” Sharon said quickly. “She’s on a cultural exchange program. I’m supposed to go up there this summer and live with her family.”

“Really?” Terrie asked, now drying her hands. “Learn something new every day.”

A door down the hall opened, Emma stepped out and shuffled to the kitchen.

"Honey, you okay?" Terrie asked. "You look rather pale. My cooking didn't make you sick, did it?"

Emma allowed a weak smile as she shook her head slowly. "No, Ms. Howell," she replied, then stood behind Sam. "Your breakfast was wonderful. I'm just not accustomed to eating so much. I apologize if I was rude."

Terrie draped a damp drying towel on the edge over the sink, then walked up to Emma and hugged her. "Sweetie, if I could get more kids to eat like you, I'd be a happy woman!" She kissed Emma lightly on the top of her head. "Now, I hear you guys have to get going. You're heading to Florida?"

"Yes, ma'am," Sam answered. "Part of the cultural exchange." He cast a glance at Sharon, who winked.

"Well, next time you come through—and there better be a next time," Terrie emphasized, "you better come visit."

Emma smiled. "Yes, Ms. Howell, I will definitely come visit." Emma's cheeks flushed red.

Terrie reached out and gave her another hug. "These Canadians, they're so polite." She said, laughing. Terrie gave one last squeeze, then let go. "Sam, don't be a stranger. I so enjoyed talking with your mom again and watching you sleep." Everyone laughed.

"Yes ma'am, you'll be seeing more of us," Sam replied, standing. "But we gotta go."

Sharon, Ronnie, and Helen were waiting by the door.

"Helen, when y'all get back, remember, you can stay with us until your house is repaired."

Helen stepped forward and gave Terrie an emotional embrace, then stepped back. She wiped her eyes with the back of her hand. "Thanks, Terrie. For everything. I don't know how long I'll be gone. Me, Sharon, and my uncle are going to load up as much as we can salvage and store it at his house. I'll be staying with him for a while. I'm sure the boys will be fine on their trip, and if you need me, call me on this number." Helen pulled a small writing pad from her purse and wrote her number.

"If I need you, I'll definitely call." She walked over to her fridge and put the note under a magnet. "Y'all have fun!"

Sam and Helen waved goodbye, then stepped out the door. Helen tossed Sam the keys to his Camaro. Sam caught the keys in mid-flight. "Mom, did you drive it here?"

"Yes, I did. And you can thank Jonqueen when you see him. This car didn't run that good when your dad drove it."

"Awesome!" Sam said as he ran his hand over the roof. There was no sign of the damage inflicted by the Galv. "So, what's the plan?"

"You, Ronnie, Emma and Jonqueen are driving to Dellion's office to see if we can convince him to let us use his launch vehicle. Hopefully, when he meets Jonqueen, he'll be more than convinced."

"Let's hope so." Sam opened the driver's door, picked up an Atlanta Braves hat off the seat, and put it on. Ronnie and Sharon climbed in the back. Helen opened the passenger door and held it open.

"Sweetie, you can ride up front." Helen said to Emma as she pulled the seat forward, then climbed into the rear, squeezing in with Ronnie and Sharon.

Sam put the key in the ignition, then paused and turned toward Emma. "Ronnie's mom could understand you. Did you touch her, or whatever it is you do that helps us understand you?"

Emma momentarily put her hands over her face and shook her head. "Yes, and no," she said through her fingers.

Ronnie pulled forward, his elbows on the back of the bucket seats. "No, man, it was kinda funny. Mom was sleeping on the couch, and I had Emma touch her wrist. Mom came off the couch like she'd been shot out a cannon." He slapped the back of the seat. "It took her a few minutes to settle down, and when she did everything was cool, she could understand Emma. But for a few minutes, she was seriously wigged out." Ronnie laughed and fell back in the seat.

"Dude, that was cruel." Sam said, breaking into a big grin.

"Ah, she got over it quickly. Was surprised to find a house full of people, but it did her good. Haven't seen mom so thrilled and energetic in a while."

"That's good." Sam turned the key, and the engine roared to life, throatier than he recalled. "Alrighty then. If no one has any objections, let's go to Florida and borrow a spaceship." Sam dropped the car in reverse, twisted around to look out the rear window, and backed the car out of the driveway. He straightened the wheel, put the car in drive, and touched the gas. The car shot forward with a cloud of tire smoke and the angry squeal of rubber. Sam let off the gas and glanced over at Emma. "I don't know what Jonqueen did to my car, but I really like it!"

Chapter Thirteen

The drive from Ronnie's house to Sam's was an easy fifteen minutes of lightly used secondary roads. Sam tuned the radio to a local rock station and hummed along with the radio as he drove. He was in a great mood and glanced at Emma. She was leaning back in the bucket seat, hands folded in her lap, and her head turned toward the open window, letting the wind blow her dark hair around. Her eyes were half open.

"You seem comfortable."

Emma turned his way and nodded. "I still don't feel completely safe in your ground vehicle, but I am enjoying the experience immensely. In all my travels, I have never felt the wind in my hair and the sun on my face as I do now. My world is compartmentalized. There are no random breezes, no changes in the weather. The temperature is strictly controlled. We are almost forbidden to leave the confines of the city."

Sam cut his eyes to Emma, then back to the road. "Seriously? Why not?"

"Believe it or not, our world is not safe outside the habitation zones. There are ancient ruins overrun with wildlife that are hazardous to the population. Plus, there are still zones around the planet rife with nuclear and biological agents."

"Is this because of the wars you have been fighting?"

She nodded. "It is, and more." She faced Sam and gave him an almost feral smile. "Remember, Sam

Shepherd, millennia ago, we were still much like you are now. We fought, killed."

Sam whistled and shook his head. "You guys seem so enlightened. It's hard to believe you guys fought."

"Yet, it is true. We have a very dark past, as do most sentient beings. Fire and war are the crucibles that shape, or destroy species."

Emma turned away, her face once again to the open window. "I will miss the wind in my face. I can assure you of that, Sam Shepherd."

"Well, when you get home, have someone build you a car. You can roll down the windows and drive around the city."

She reached over and patted his arm. "I might just do that, Sam." She turned to the window, closed her eyes, and let the wind blow across her face.

Sam turned the radio off and drove along in silence, concentrating on the road and listening to the sound of the engine. Checking the rearview mirror, he noticed his passengers were all positioned similarly, leaning back with their eyes closed. No one moved until Sam pulled into their yard. He parked beside their van and shut the motor off. On cue, his passengers sat up, yawning. Black and yellow ribbons wrapped around the remains of the house and danced in the morning breeze.

"We're home," Sam said absently. He opened his door, then pulled his seat forward so Sharon and his mom could climb from the rear of the car. "Where's Jonqueen?"

Emma paused, glancing at the horizon as she slowly turned. She pointed toward the field across the street.

"He's there. I believe he is collecting the remains of the Galv."

"Why would he be doing that?"

"Jonqueen is more than a soldier. He is trained to do more than fight. He has a vast knowledge of advanced sciences and biology. His nanites equate to having millions of computers working along-side you. They interface directly with him, help him analyze everything he encounters. I assume he's cataloging the remains to find a weakness, anything we can use in our fight against them. Normally, they self-destruct before capture, leaving only trace molecules behind. In all probabilities, this is a significant discovery."

Emma started for the wood line, Sam at her side, Ronnie trailing behind. Helen stayed beside the car with Sharon. "Me and your sister are going to make one more run through the house to see if there is anything else we can salvage." She called after them.

The teens waved over their heads as Emma set a brisk pace across the road and into the field. Jonqueen was kneeling in the dirt, obscured by the brush. When they reached him, he was scraping clear debris shards into a bowl.

"We have a unique opportunity." He said without rising. "When the Galv soldier tried to self-destruct, the electrical current Helen Shepherd held against him disrupted the sequence." Jonqueen held a glass Pyrex baking container with clear, misshapen cubes resembling shattered windshield glass. They vibrated along the edges of the bowl, bouncing into each other and tumbling. Some locked together to form larger blocks, then split apart, crumpling into grains of gray sand. "There is still an active matrix between the remains. I believe I can create a weapon that will deactivate the matrix, allowing us to kill the Galv with greater ease."

Ronnie pushed through the brush, stopped, and bent over. "Hey, Sam, check this out. I think it's part of the gray dude's helmet." He reached down to pick it up. Jonqueen spun around, raising the black tube-like cylinder he carried. A ball of silver light shot out of the tube, hitting Ronnie in the chest and knocking him on his back.

"Do not approach it!" Jonqueen growled, his voice resembling gravel and lightning. Abandoning the bowl, he dashed over to where Ronnie had fallen and brought up his tube. He raised it high over his head as silver spikes jetted out. He brought the spikes down hard on the misshapen helmet, penetrating it. The helmet began to strobe and spark. Jonqueen pulled the pike out of the dome, collapsed the tube, then grabbed Ronnie by the back of his shirt, lifting him off the ground and thrusting him forward. "Run!"

Emma grabbed Sam's wrist as they sprinted in the opposite direction, dragging him with her.

"What's going…" was all he said before a deep drone, sounding like thousands of balloons rubbing together, filled the air. He and Emma were at the edge of the blacktop when a vibration turned the asphalt to marbles. The air split with the crackle of lightning, and they were thrown across the road, landing on their stomachs in his front yard.

With the air knocked from his lungs, Sam rolled to the ground, gasping for breath. "What was that?" he gasped.

Emma pushed herself to her feet, her clothes and hair coated with dirt and debris. "The Galv," she said before dropping to her knees and wincing. "When they lose their containment beam, their helmet—which is actually part of the Galv—disengages and falls to the side. It carries telemetry regarding the enemy strength, communications, and targeting coordinates. It's synched to their brainwaves. So even with the soldier neutralized, his mind can continue to communicate. It is also what you call a 'booby trap' meant to immobilize enemy forces." She climbed to her feet, reached down, and helped Sam stand. "We need to leave. They will know of the destruction of the unit and send reinforcements."

Jonqueen crossed the road as if nothing had happened, still holding Ronnie by the sleeve of his shirt, careful not to contact his skin. Ronnie was in shock; his face smudged with dirt, the whites of his eyes showing easily.

Helen was running from the house, panic in her eyes. "What in the hell just happened?"

"The Galv left behind an explosive device. I deactivated it."

Dust and debris drifted down, landing on their shoulders. "How much worse would it have been?"

Jonqueen stared at Helen without answering.

"That bad, huh?" Helen said as she brushed fine silt from her hair.

Jonqueen stared at her. He tilted his head slightly toward Emma. "We can expect a response from the local authorities. I am detecting heightened activity on the security communication bands. I will retrieve the Galv remains, then we must leave."

Emma brushed off the front of her jeans. "Agreed. Sam, it's time to go." She walked over to Helen, leaned forward, and gave Sam's mom a brief, awkward hug. She stepped back but held Helen by the wrists.

"We understand the concept of mother and father and family dynamics but have no experience in it. Thank you for sharing with me. What a marvelous gift your family has given me. I shall treasure it for the rest of my time." Emma said and bowed slightly toward Helen.

"Emma, I…" Helen tried to speak, but stopped. "At least let me give you an appropriate goodbye hug." She brushed away tears that clung to girls eyes and pulled Emma in tight. "Take care of Sam. Don't let him get in too much trouble."

Tears flowed freely down Emma's face. She smeared them clumsily. "I will, Helen Shepherd. I will protect the shepherd of the blue world with all I possess."

Helen let Emma go and cocked her head. "The shepherd of the what?"

Emma smiled and chuckled. "Just a phrase I grew up with." She brushed a loose hair out of her eye. "Be well, Helen." With that, she turned and walked to Sam's Camaro.

Sam opened the door, allowing Ronnie, still looking dazed, and Jonqueen to climb into the back seat. Sam jogged over to his mom. "Well, guess this is it. Text me Mr. Dellion's phone and address. I'll call him when we get to Florida."

"Be careful, Sam. Don't take any chances."

"Mom, really? I'm the King of 'take no chances'."

"Well, see that you don't." Helen grabbed her son and hugged him fiercely, then let go. "And don't let anything happen to that young lady."

"Mom, you know I won't. Besides, I think she's much tougher than we give her credit for."

Helen nodded. 'Okay, scoot. Y'all have a long way to go." She pulled a small wad of folded-up bills from her pocket. "This should be enough for gas, food, and a motel room or two if needed."

Sam took the money, thumbed through the small stack of twenties, then let out a low whistle. "Are you sure you want to give me all this? I have enough in my account."

"You don't know how long this will take, and I don't want you to worry about money."

"Thanks, mom." Sam hugged his mother again. "I'll call you tonight and tell you where we are." Letting go of his mother, he hugged his sister, then vaulted over the fender and climbed into the Camaro. The engine surged to life the moment he turned the key. Sam twisted around to look out the back window and fought to avoid laughing. To his left was an honest-to-goodness space alien. To his right was his ex-best friend, slash ex-best enemy. He backed into the road, dropped the car into gear, and punched the gas. The tires barked against the asphalt before gripping and thrusting the car forward.

"Y'know," Sam said to Emma. "If you guys can't go home, Jonqueen could make a fortune on the stock car racing circuit." He grinned at Emma's confused expression and pressed the pedal down harder. The car surged to sixty without so much as straining. As he rounded a long bend that led to the main East-West highway, he let off the gas as a trio of sheriff deputies flashed past, lights on and strobing.

"Dude, we got out of there in the nick of time." Ronnie said, twisting around to follow the blue lights.

"I guess I'll call mom later to see how she explained the explosion in the woods." Sam turned left onto Highway 31. "Before we get too far out of town, I need to top off the tank. I want to get as far down the road as possible before we have to stop again."

"You will not need any additional fuel." Jonqueen said evenly.

"Not now I won't," Sam replied, looking up in the rearview mirror. "But I don't plan on getting good mileage. I'm more interested in getting to Florida."

Jonqueen leaned forward, his expression mirroring humans more and more. "As I have stated, fuel will not be an issue. I have supplied a small amount of nanites to the fuel cell in this machine. They will continue to replicate the hydrocarbon-based fuel this machine needs to function."

Sam stared up into the rearview mirror. "Seriously?" Jonqueen leaned back but didn't reply. "Oh, yeah. You're always serious." He turned his attention back to the road. "How long will they last?"

"This machine can run at your current power rate for apoximately four thousand seven hundred and eight hours."

Sam looked back up in the rearview mirror. "That could be for years!"

"Correct. I calculate the fuel supply will last eleven point two years."

"What other things have your nanites improved?" Sam asked, grinning widely.

"The combustion chambers were extremely inefficient. My nanites have polished the chambers, filling microscopic cracks and pitting. They have also enhanced the fossil-based fluid used to lubricate the engine. You should not have to change this fluid ever. It has also reduced internal friction by forty-seven percent. You should experience an increase in power and efficiency of approximately twenty-two percent. I cannot give you an exact number of the improvement factor due to the primitive manufacturing of your machine. It will be substantial."

"That's crazy!" Sam brought his eyes back to the road and drove around a string of slower traffic. "But why did you do it? You have a limited supply of nanites available. Why waste them on something so— primitive?"

"Two reasons. One, the other vehicle, is inoperable. Returning the *Emissary de'tantel* to our time and place is far more valuable than my nanites." Jonqueen sat with his hands folded in his lap, eyes focused straight ahead.

Sam glanced up in the mirror, waiting for Jonqueen to continue. "You said there were two reasons. What is the second?"

For the first time, Jonqueen appeared uncomfortable, not his stoic, composed posture. He was quiet for several moments. "I find most of this planet lacking, primitive, having little of interest. But," he reached down and picked up the Pyrex bowl containing the Galv remains, "there are a few exceptions. One being this container. I have not encountered this material in my travels."

"Glass?" Sam laughed. "You've never seen a glass bowl?"

Jonqueen held the bowl against his lap but stared out the window shield.

Sam glanced at Emma. "Is he pouting?"

Emma focused on Sam, brushed her hair from her face, and laughed lightly. "Sam, you must understand, Jonqueen has traveled more than anyone I know, and has seen wonders too incredible to describe. And to find a material he's not familiar with on a planet that is, shall we say, not technologically advanced, is shocking to him." She smiled at Jonqueen, then turned back to Sam. "And yes, he is pouting… a little. Another side of him I have not seen." She stretched her arms forward, then leaned back in the seat. "Your planet it," she stared through the windshield as if looking for guidance in the clouds. "It changes you."

"And you've only been here a few days. Spend a week here and I'll have you eating hotdogs and going to a baseball game."

Emma turned slightly toward Sam, her eyes taking on a mischievous slant. "I know not of your canine food or games but think I would enjoy it." She reached over, took his worn ball cap off his head, and put it on. "How do I look?"

"Good enough that I want to turn this car around and say, 'to hell with the universe'."

"That is not an acceptable course of action." Jonqueen snapped from the back seat. "We must return the Emissary, otherwise billions will die."

"Quite the buzz kill." Sam groused.

Emma and Ronnie laughed hard. "I'm not sure what a 'buzz kill' is, but your sentiment comes through quite clear." Emma said, still laughing.

"But he is correct." Emma said, turning serious. "It's for the best I return home. But until then, let's enjoy our time together." She slipped a hand around Sam's right arm, leaned forward, and turned up the radio. "This music, it's unlike any of I've heard. What do you call it?"

Sam turned her way, a grin spreading across his face. "We call it 'rock and roll'."

"It's very rhythmic and powerful. I must take samples of it back with me." She turned up the volume.

"Just a warning before you do. It'll corrupt your youth, at least that what my mom says."

"Maybe we need a bit of corrupting to get us out of the rut we are in." She let go of Sam's arm and settled back into the seat. She rocked back and forth slightly. "It also has a strange persuasion over me. It makes me want to move to the music."

Sam nodded enthusiastically. "That's why we call it 'rock and roll', baby! Makes your body want to *move.*"

Turning up the volume, Sam matched Emma's body language as the Camaro sped down the highway and toward the coast.

Chapter Fourteen

They had been on the road for four hours when Sam exited I-95 north of the Georgia border and pulled into a rest stop.

"Why are we stopping?" Jonqueen asked. "You have sufficient fuel to travel for another eleven years."

Sam put the car in park, then shut down the engine. "Uh, maybe your nanites take care of this for you, but we humans have to stop every few hours to go to the bathroom—relieve ourselves."

"Quite an inefficient use of time."

"Well, it's that or pee our pants."

Jonqueen tilted his head slightly, a motion Sam understood as acquiescence. "My apologies. I forget you do not possess nanites to eliminate waste."

Emma sat up and ran her fingers through her hair. "I, for one, am pleased he stopped. My body is not accustomed to this diet, and I need to relieve myself as well." She unbuckled her seat belt. "Sam, if you will, please direct me to the appropriate building. I know your society has some taboos concerning the mixing of your genders, and I do not wish to offend anyone."

Ronnie yawned and leaned forward. "What did she ask?"

"She needs the lady's room." Sam whispered.

"Ah, gotcha." Ronnie said, blushing.

"C'mon, I'll show you," Sam unbuckled his belt. "It's the same as home. You just have to share the room with strangers." Sam sat on the edge of the hood of the

159

Camaro and waited for Emma. He couldn't take his eyes off her. She wore a pair of faded jeans and a tee shirt his sister had provided. Her hair was now in a ponytail and looped through the gap in the back of his hat. On her feet, she wore the same tan sandals she had worn since they first met, shoes that never seemed to get dirty.

"What, Sam Shepherd?" She asked, noticing his smile. "Why are you looking at me like that?"

"I am just amazed at how, well, *human* you look. You could pass for any of the girls in my school."

Emma stopped with her hands on her hips. "And you, Sam Shepard, could pass for any male on Shovain. Except they would consider you rather short and hairy." Emma winked.

"Are you calling me an ape again?" Sam laughed.

"No, I would never impugn the primates on this planet in such a fashion." She bumped hips with him, stepped forward quickly, and took him by the wrist. "Now, my hairy friend, show me the so-called lady's room before I burst."

Sam led the way, visited the men's room, and waited outside for her return. When she exited, her eyes were wide, her speech fast.

"Emma, is everything okay?"

She nodded quickly, then shook her head. "I am sorry, Sam. There are so many things about this world that are so *alien* to me." She stared at the sky as she held a hand to her face.

"Emma, what happened?"

"Oh, nothing really. I've just never been around offspring's before. Do they not possess a volume control?"

"No, ma'am, they don't." Said an elderly woman walking past, shaking her head. "You'd think they were all raised in a sawmill." The lady laughed at her own joke as she shuffled toward an elderly man waiting for her.

Sam watches the woman link arms with her husband and drift away. He turned to his friend. "Emma, she understood you. How is that possible? I thought you had to touch them or infect them or something,"

"Normally, that is the case. But the longer I am exposed to another culture or language, my speech patterns adapt, allowing me to converse. Usually I must spend many, many months in a new location. This is quite out of the norm."

"Is this because of Jonqueen's nanites?"

"Yes, and no. We all have a certain level of similar nanites in our blood stream from general contact. This has helped us communicate. But I also benefit from selective breeding over thousands of years. Over the ages, we have altered our brains to better understand and comprehend other beings. Some languages are still beyond Shovain physiology. Then we need artificial aids to communicate."

"So, you are human, more or less?" Sam asks, leaning against a split-rail fence near the bathrooms.

"Sam, I have never said I wasn't human. Or, more to the point, you are not Shovain." Emma took his hand, spread his fingers, and then placed her hand against his. "We each have two hands, ten fingers, two lungs, and our heart beats on the left side of our chest, pumping iron-rich blood through our bodies." She took his hand and placed it over her heart while placing her thin fingers on his wrist. "My heart beats as does yours. And I can feel your pulse as surely as you can feel mine."

"There are subtleties to our species as there are to the various races on this planet. But to the point of me being human or you being Shovain, we may never know."

Sam pulled his hand from Emma's chest, then held her hand with both of his. Her palm was warm, slightly electric. He could feel the same pulse of energy he experienced previously. But his time, it was more of a gentle vibration. "What happened the other day when you grabbed Ronnie and I stopped you?"

Emma turned away, took his hat off, and let the wind blow her dark black hair across her pale, soft face. "I'm not sure. It has never happened before. I was… overwhelmed with emotion. I thought the boy was there to hurt you and I felt—anger." She glanced down.

Sam gently touched her cheek, turning her to face him. "Is that bad where you come from? Are emotions forbidden?"

She smiled. "No, Sam Shepherd, emotions aren't forbidden." She interlaced her fingers in his and held them to her cheek. "But I am the *Emissary de'tantel.* In our ancient language, it means two things; one without emotions, and peace bringer." Emma dropped her hands and pulled him away from the fence. "Walk with me, Sam Shepherd." They crossed the wide green lawn, past picnic tables occupied by weary travelers. She raised her gaze toward the tree, her eyes almost closed. She inhaled deeply, then opened her eyes. "Your home, it's most beautiful." Emma pointed to a bird circling over the pines. "That animal, it's a bird, correct?"

Sam nodded.

"It's most majestic. We have nothing like it left on our world."

Sam laughed, noticed Emma's staring at him, then stopped. "I'm sorry." He wiped his eyes. "That bird is what we call a pigeon. Essentially a winged rat." Sam stifled a chuckle. "We have them by the millions. I'd be more than happy to send a few with you."

"And I'd gladly take it." She replied softly. They walked again. "But back to emotions and my title. On Shovain, most of the populace is quiet, outbursts of anger, or laughter are rare. We are all tested at birth for a genetic marker most possess. As you have seen, I'm able to touch individuals and share my feelings, fears and travels. It helps tremendously with negotiations."

"Are you one of the most powerful on your planet?"

Emma laughed harder than Sam had heard her laugh. "No, far from it!" She laughed again. "My ability is one of the lowest ever recorded. That's why I am an emissary. When I meet with other world leaders, they want to make sure we do not coerce the agreements, that their decisions are their own."

Emma steered them to an unoccupied shelter, sat on the concrete bench, and patted the seat beside her. Sam put an arm around her waist, and Emma leaned against him, resting her head on his shoulder. They watched the traffic enter and exit the rest area.

Sam broke the silence. "So that's why your planet is quiet. Everyone knows what everyone is thinking. There's no need to talk."

"That's a close analogy. On a normal day, I might say a hundred words out loud, usually to get someone's attention. Most of the ambient sound is transports carrying the citizens."

"Emma, I've got to ask you something, and I know you probably can't give me a straight answer, but how old are you?"

She smiled and shook her head. "Sam Shepard, somehow I feel that is an inappropriate question in your society."

"Well, sort of. But I'm curious. You look my age, but you talk like you're…."

"Old? Is that what you're going to ask?" She nudged him with her shoulder. "I'm not from your world, but I'm fairly certain that is not a compliment!"

"No, Emma, I mean," Sam turned red, flustered. "What I mean is…" He never finished his sentence. Ronnie came running toward them.

Emma sat bolt upright. "Sam, we need to leave. Jonqueen is quite agitated." She grabbed Sam by the hand, pulled him off the bench, and started running.

Ronnie was waving his arms. "Guys, the old dude says we have got to go… *now!*"

Emma and Sam race past Ronnie, who spun and chased them down the sidewalk. "I don't know if it's the gray guys or not, but tall, rough and scary is not a happy camper!"

The Camaro was running, with Jonqueen sitting in the rear, as stoic as ever. Sam opened the driver's door, pulled the seat forward, and Ronnie scrambled into the back. Sam jumped behind the wheel and buckled his belt as Emma fastened hers. Glancing into the rearview mirror, Same watched Jonqueen as he backed out. "What's going on?"

The soldier lifted the Pyrex bowl above the seat. "See for yourself."

The Galv remains were extremely active, bouncing and tumbling. They vibrated, turned into blocks, broke apart, and formed a mercury-like substance before separating again. "I do not believe the Galv have located our position. But these remains are trying to communicate. They might be picking up the Galv scanning array. If that is the case, we need to leave immediately."

"No argument from me." Sam dropped the transmission into drive and sped out of the rest stop and onto the interstate. He pushed the car to eighty miles per hour to keep up with traffic, then glanced into the rearview mirror. "Are the Galv parts still dancing around?"

"More than ever, man." Ronnie replied, licking his lips and grimacing.

"Jonqueen, are the Galv following us?"

The soldier stared at the bowl; the Galv parts jumped around like water droplets on a hot stove. "I do not believe they are tracking us. But they are in the vicinity. We need to increase our speed to put further distance between us and their ship."

Sam pressed harder on the pedal. The needle climbed to eighty-five. "I'm running fifteen over the posted limit, and don't want to push it too much and catch the attention of a patrol car."

"Sam Shepherd, you will need to drive faster. I believe they are using an intermittent transference beam. They are, to use a local colloquialism, 'hop-scotching' across this area, trying to get a fix on our location. I might have underestimated the ability of the remnants to communicate with the Galv transport."

"If the cops pick us up on radar, it is over for us. I can explain me and Ronnie, but you and Emma are going to be another story."

Jonqueen assembled a small black box he had been holding near his feet. "Artificial means will not detect us. If you pass a security vehicle, I cannot prevent them from visually seeing us. But their detection devices will not lock on us, nor will they function in close proximity."

"If you say so," Sam said, pushing the accelerator to the floor. The Camaro shot forward again, the needle on the speedometer resting between the one hundred zeros, the dotted lines becoming a solid white blur. Cars flash by before he was aware he was closing on them. He held his breath as a Georgia State Patrol passed in the Northbound lanes. The cop's lights remained dark as he vanished from view. Another five patrol officers ignored them over the next hour as they blasted down I-95 toward the Florida line.

"Sam, you can slow this vehicle. The Galv remains are no longer active."

"Are they dead?"

"No. They are simply no longer in contact with their vessel, not even peripherally."

Glancing up in the mirror, Sam could see that the shards of broken glass-like remains were docile. He let up on the accelerator and relaxed his grip on the steering wheel. "Whew, that was seriously nerve-wracking." Allowing the Camaro to settle down to a sedate seventy-five, he held the wheel with his knees as he flexed his fingers.

Emma took his right hand in both of her hands and gently massaged it. "Your hand is very tense."

"My entire body is tense. I've never driven that fast in my life." A dribble of sweat ran down his temple

"Well, you did excellent." She released his hand, then ran her fingers through his hair. "I could feel your anxiety, fear and adrenaline pouring off you in waves. It was…" Emma took a deep breath, her eyes growing wide. "… exhilarating." She patted her chest. "I didn't know how much more I could take."

"Seriously?"

"Seriously." She leaned forward, stretched, and then glanced at Sam from the corner of her eyes. "Can we do it again?"

Sam turned to Emma, his eyebrows raised, mouth open but not forming words. "Not anytime soon! My insides are still twisted up in knots."

"Maybe later?"

"You're an alien speed freak." Sam said with a grin.

She smiled and turned the radio volume up.

Chapter Fifteen

Sam drove another eight hours, keeping the needle on the speedometer hovering near eighty. The Galv shards hadn't so much as twitched since their earlier activity. They made a couple more stops for food and bathroom breaks. The sun had fully set, and the moon had risen over the ocean when they coasted into Cocoa Beach. Thomas Dellion's office was a few blocks away but closed. His mom had been in touch, updating Sam every few hours. Thomas still thought Helen was a crackpot but agreed to meet because of his feelings for Sam's father. He had even arranged for Sam and friends to stay at the beachfront condo he kept for honored guests.

Steering the Camaro into the condo's garage, Sam parked near the elevators and turned the ignition off. "Well, we're here. Now it's going to be up to you guys. Mr. Dellion is humoring mom. We need seriously concrete proof. And I mean almost Godly proof."

Ronnie leaned forward between the seats. "Emma won't work, but this dude beside me is positively mind blowing. That should be enough."

"I would think so but getting Mr. Dellion to release a billion dollars' worth of research to us is another thing. If we had Jonqueen's shuttle, it wouldn't be an argument. But we don't." Sam unbuckled and opened his door. Emma followed and pulled her seat forward for Jonqueen.

"Mr. Dellion texted me the access code to the elevator and condo." Sam waited for Emma to make her way around the car.

"After spending half an Earth day in your vehicle, I'm not so sure I want one right away." Emma smiled, twisting her body from side to side. "I have kinks in my body I never knew could kink." Sam and Ronnie laughed. Jonqueen said nothing as he retrieved the Pyrex bowl and equipment.

"You're getting more human by the hour." Ronnie said.

"I find no reason to speak to the Emissary in such a derogatory nature." Jonqueen added in a low, gravelly voice.

Sam and Ronnie stared speechlessly at the tall alien. Emma grinned, then clapped her hands and laughed. "Why, Jonqueen, I believe you just exhibited a bit of a sense of humor." She winked at the boys.

Jonqueen stared over the top of their heads with his black, flat, almond-shaped eyes. "It is an undesirable side effect of spending extended time near human adolescents." This time, they all laughed.

"C'mon, let's go find our rooms." Sam opened the trunk and removed their bags. He carried Emma's luggage along with his own. With Emma walking close by, almost leaning against him, Sam led the way through the garage and to the lift. When he tapped in the security code, the elevator doors shut and they ascended to the twentieth floor. When the doors opened, no one moved. A marble foyer gave way to plush carpeting and exquisite furniture. The far wall was all glass, providing a panoramic view of the Atlantic Ocean and stary night sky.

"Whoa, I think I have died and gone to heaven," Ronnie whispered.

"Sam Shepard, this is most unexpected." Emma walked slowly out of the elevator to the vast expanse of glass. She opened the door, then stepped out onto the balcony. She closed her eyes and took in a deep breath. "In all my travels, I've never experienced air this stimulating."

Sam walked up beside her, paused, and tentatively put a hand on the small of her back. "It's the ocean breezes. They always smell so clean."

Emma leaned against him, nearly nose to nose. Her voice was soft, peaceful, back to resembling snow falling through a forest of mountain fir trees. "If I can find a way to return to you, I will, Sam Shepherd." She put her hands on his chest and stared directly into his eyes. Sam could now see that they weren't just dark blue but dotted with specks of silver that seem to burst like micro fireworks. "But I first must return home."

"Emma," Sam breathed. "I know you do. And If I could, I'd return with you."

Emma stepped back, slowly shaking her head. "Sam, as the Shepherd of the blue world, you must remain here on earth."

Sam stared at her in amazement. "Why, because of some dimensional paradox where I can't exist in both timelines?"

Emma smiled, "No, my friend, who never ceases to bring joy to me. The vessel we are attempting to borrow can only accommodate two."

Sam stood momentarily speechless, then burst out laughing. "Y'know it's a bad sign when you've hung around with us long enough to develop a mean sense of humor." He winked at her. "C'mon, let's check out the rest of the condo while we wait for Mr. Dellion to call." Emma looped an arm through his as they walked through the many rooms of the penthouse residence. They caught up with Ronnie standing on the top floor patio, peering into the evening skies with a telescope he found in the condo.

"Sam, what's the chance you can talk Mr. Dellion into postponing his launch for a few weeks so we can hang out here?"

"Uh, probably not very good," Sam said, joining him.

"We need no further delays." A hard voice rasped behind them.

All three turned around to find Jonqueen joining them on the patio. "There is no telling how much time has elapsed on Shovain. If we have gone missing for an extended period, then it is possible that incalculable damage has occurred. I fear that further delays will doom any chance of peace."

Ronnie turned his back to the railing. "But you can't even be sure that you can return."

Jonqueen tilted his head slightly toward Ronnie. "That is true, but not attempting to return home is out of the question."

"Even if you can get those gray dude's ship, how are you going to get back to your time? Sam said you guys have traveled back something like five thousand—"

Jonqueen cut him off. "I have determined within a plus/minus factor of point zero eight percent that we have traveled four thousand eight hundred and nine solar years into the past.”

“Solar years?” Sam asked.

“Essentially, one-point-zero-zero-two of your years. A time frame you can conceptualize.” Jonqueen answered, staring at Sam as if he’d asked a stupid question.

“How can you tell?” Sam asked, now mirroring Ronnie’s position against the rails.

Jonqueen’s eyes narrowed on the boys. He then released a small huff, his equivalence to a sigh. “I’ve used the comboard retrieved from my shuttle and modified it to study astral charts. Even though this section of the galaxy has been rarely studied, there is very little of interest here. There are other charts programmed into it I have utilized to map the stars and their movement.”

“Which brings us back to the ‘when’. How are you going to return to your time?”

Jonqueen was silent for a few moments, his brow pinched. “It is my hope that the vessel we are to use will have enough explosive potential to force a compression wave similar to the one that brought us here.”

“Sounds like a lot of assumptions to me,” Ronnie said, still leaning against the railing.

The soldier turned his way, his posture minutely resigned. “It is. But I believe my nanites can reconfigure the engine’s detonation to provide enough energy to warp the spacial strings enough to return us to our time.”

Sam’s phone lit up. He walked to the corner of the deck and stood overlooking the pool, twenty floors below. His shoulders slumped, and he stared at the ground. He turned around, then dropped the phone in his pocket.

"Sam, what is it?" Emma asked.

"Mom said she had a long talk with Mr. Dellion. He's agreed to meet with us in the morning. But only to humor her. Mom said there is less than a zero chance we can even get near the launch site, much less get access to the ship."

"That is—unfortunate." Emma said as she sat heavily in a wicker chair facing the railing. She folded her hands under her chin and leaned against them. Jonqueen, showing rare emotion, walked to the patio's edge and stared at the moon, now fully risen over the Atlantic. The soldier gripped the metal rail hard enough to bend it.

"Mom says he's going to let us stay here until the launch, but then we need to head home."

Ronnie was looking at the beach-side condos with the telescope. He set it to the side and leaned their way. "This might sound crazy, but since we are in your past, which is our current, is there anything you know of that hasn't happened yet? Y'know, a star exploding, undiscovered comet? Anything?"

"Ronnie, just when I think of you as nothing but a slacker redneck, you come up with something smart!" Sam gave his friend two thumbs up.

"I have my moments." Ronnie responded, looking satisfied with himself.

"Jonqueen," Emma said, getting to her feet. "Your people have traveled and studied this quadrant of the galaxy far more that we ever have. Do you know of anything?"

Jonqueen's eyes narrowed as he tilted his head. "There has been a little exploration of this quadrant, as there are no resources, and no planets of interest. If we had full access to the databanks on my shuttle, we might find something. The comboard I have only has star charts."

"What about the Galv vessel?" Sam asked as he turned the telescope toward the moon. "That would be pretty good proof."

"It would. Unfortunately, exposing the Galv vessel would alert them they have been detected. They might move to a higher orbit or increase their security measures. That would make detecting them far more difficult."

The four gathered at the railing. Emma was leaning against Sam, no one speaking. The ocean rustled the palms, many floors below them. Splashing in the pool, a dozen young couples were having chicken fights, the girls on the boy's shoulders.

"Jonqueen," Sam drawled. "If the Galv remains are detecting some type of signal and communicating with it, is there a way to, say, 'piggyback' on the signal?"

Jonqueen turned slowly to Sam, his black eyes closing to slits. "Explain this 'piggyback'."

"It's two signals traveling together. One undetected. A very small signal buried inside a large one."

The soldier held his eyes on Sam. "A parasitic broadcast. It might be possible." Jonqueen turned from the wall and walked toward the row of sliding glass doors.

"Jonqueen, what are you thinking?" Emma called after him, now walking fast to match his pace. She caught up with him in the middle of the lavishly furnished living room. He was holding the comboard from his shuttle in one hand and the Pyrex dish in the other. Taking long strides, he hurried to the breakfast table and stripped off his outer armored shell. A wave of nanites burst from it, settling over the device like a hazy black mist. The electronic device mutated, changed. Jonqueen glanced up as Sam entered the room.

"Your communication device, I have need of it." Jonqueen reached for it as Sam pulled it from his pocket.

"Uh, okay. What do you plan on using it for?"

"As primitive as it is, I will need it to facilitate the communication with the satellite network orbiting this planet."

"But how will Mr. Dellion be able to reach us?"

Jonqueen releases another small snort. "Your device will remain undamaged. My nanites will clone the technology that allows it to interact with the satellites in orbit around this world."

"How will it work?"

Jonqueen glared at him again, his eyes returning to slits. He stepped back and crossed his arms over his chest with. "When I finish constructing this communications array, I will select the most viable Galv remains. I will then place the remains in the comboard along with your communication device. It will immediately start broadcasting a location sequence. I will then power up your communication device and have it map all the satellites in this sector. The Galv will reply to the remains with a reciprocating encrypted signal. At that point, your device will try to get a fixed location—"

"GPS. You're using the GPS function?" Ronnie said quickly, having entered the room quietly.

Jonqueen stared through Ronnie and continued. "The device will attempt to ascertain its global position. This will provide access to the computers aboard the Galv vessel. We will then be able to plot their course without alerting them."

"Jonqueen, can the scanning equipment on this planet detect the Galv landing craft? Maybe Thomas Dellion can as well."

The soldier slowly nodded while staring across the room. "That is my assumption. I hope we can provide him the crafts coordinates and scanning algorithms to help locate the ship."

Sam walked up to the heavy granite table, pulled a chair, and sat. "I think you'll have to give him more than that." He leaned back and rubbed his eyes. "His company, reputation… his life's work is at stake."

"Sam, what else can we do?" Emma asked, pulling out a chair beside him.

"Jonqueen is going to have to explain the faults of his ship and give him proof that will be overwhelming to anything else on the planet."

"Sam Shepherd, what is it you are asking me?" Jonqueen said, his eyes narrowed to almost entirely flat.

"Your nanite technology. That would revolutionize this world."

"Unacceptable."

"Why, Jonqueen? Why is it unacceptable?" Sam stood, facing the soldier with his hands on his hips.

"The technology is too advanced for your culture. Without the correct controls in place, you could very well destroy all life on this planet."

"You seem to have a way of controlling the nanites. Couldn't you provide a sample, a frame-work, if you will, on how to control the nanites?"

"Maybe dumb them down to a child's level of ability." Ronnie added, joining them at the table. "Don't give us the good stuff, just something that we could play with and learn from."

"That is not possible!" Jonqueen barked, his voice echoing off the walls. "I may not share this technology with any race."

"Helluva an ally you guys would be," Ronnie said as he pulled out a chair and dropped into it. "Would love to be in a foxhole with you."

"We are not allies." Jonqueen growled. "We are technically at war with the Shovain. My only duty here is to honor my father's order to protect the Emissary de'tantel and return her to the Shovain Star Empire. I will not see my father's death at the hands of the Galv be in vain."

"Well Sparky," Ronnie said with a heavy drawl, "looks like you're about to fail on all your plans."

"NO!" Jonqueen roared, slamming his fists down on the center of the granite table. The tabletop shattered and collapsed, leaving the others stunned. A cloud of black nanites exploded from his arms, hovered around his fist, then faded inside his skin. He rounded the remains of the table and closed quickly on Ronnie, his eyes drawn to slits as he drew the black cylinder from his coat and pointed it at the boy's chest.

Ronnie spilled from the chair, scrambling over the broken table as he backed away from Jonqueen.

Sam grabbed a chuck of the tabletop and leaped between them. "Settle down, man!" He screamed, drawing the chunk of granite back. "I'm sure those nanites can rebuild you, but I'm also certain I can crush your skull before you can draw your weapon." Sam's knuckles whited as he gripped the shard of stone.

Jonqueen's eyes flashed wide as streaks of silver raced across his flat pupils. His breathing quickened as his weapon raised.

"I'm warning you, man!" Sam snapped, taking a step forward, the jagged table fragment clenched in his hand.

Another cloud of nanites exploded from Jonqueen's coat, then settled on Sam, sinking into his skin. Sam recoiled and dropped the table shard as he tried to brush the vanishing specks off his skin.

"What in the hell did you do?" Ronnie shouted.

Jonqueen snorted, lowered the cylinder, then stepped over the table remains. "I gave him what he asked for."

"Jonqueen, what did you do?" Emma asked, her voice trembling. She joined Ronnie by Sam's side.

"The other boy is correct. If we cannot leave this planet, then all will be for naught—my father's death, the war, our civilizations. I have provided Sam Shepherd with enough nanites for Thomas Dellion to integrate the technology into his own."

Emma let go of Sam's arm and walked up to Jonqueen. "But why? What changed your mind?"

Jonqueen took in a long breath, the tension waning as he did. "I am still firmly against it, but the nanite collective mind decided on their own. When Sam stepped between me and the other human youth—"

"Hey, I have a name." Ronnie snapped.

Jonqueen ignored him. "The nanites decided that if he will defend his associate against overwhelming odds of destruction, then they felt the risk to be worth it."

Sam stared at his arm; the nanites now completely vanished. "The nanites are alive?"

"Not in the way you would describe life. But they are aware of their survival and function almost as a hive mind. They can, on rare occasions, act independently. The ones you now carry are infants. Their abilities are extremely limited. I will help you learn to interact with them."

"Will I be able to build things like you?"

"No. They will only be allow to assist Mr. Dellion with his next launch vessel research."

"So, how will this work? Will I just 'think' a question and the nanites will answer?"

Jonqueen retrieved his console off the ground where it had fallen when he shattered the table. He brought it over to Sam and held it before him. A slot formed and glowed softly. "Place your left hand in the opening."

Hesitantly, Sam complied. The front of the console molded around his hand. "What's going on?"

"I am creating a composite rendering of your hand."

"It tickles." Sam said, grimacing.

"That would be the nanites imbedding themselves into your skin, then returning to the console. Your hand will be a key. You will use the adapter I am creating to interface with the nanites and computer consoles.”

"And they will help create future launch vessels?”

"Yes.”

The console face opened, and Sam pulled his hand back, his palm rosy. He flexed his fingers, then squeezed them into a fist. "It doesn't feel any different.”

"It shouldn't. The nanites were creating a framework to communicate with the console.” Jonqueen carried the interface across the room, placing it on a table near the sliding glass doors. "Tomorrow, when Thomas Dellion arrives, I will demonstrate the possibilities of the nanites. I am sure that when I am finished, he will surrender his ship.”

Chapter Sixteen

Early morning sunshine was pushing through the curtains of Sam's room when his phone began ringing, waking him from a dreamless sleep. He rolled over and stared at the clock. It was nearly seven. He grabbed the phone off the table beside the bed. "Hello?"

"Sam? It's Thomas. How are you?"

Sam sat up quickly. "Mr. Dellion…"

"Son, when have you ever called me Mr. Dellion? Call me Thomas, or 'Uncle Thomas' like you did when you were a kid." Thomas cordially corrected.

"I called you Uncle Thomas?"

"Only every time we saw each other. You just started up one day and never called me anything else."

"Wow, I don't remember that. I remember going to the airport with dad and watching you fly gliders."

"That was a while back! I haven't flown gliders in many years. The last person I took up in a glider, if I'm correct, was your mom."

"Could have been. Mom said you took her once, said it was very peaceful."

"It definitely can be. And speaking of your mom, I'm glad she called. I miss spending time with your parents."

The phone went momentarily quiet. Sam thought Mr. Dellion was trying to figure out what to say next.

"Sam, the call I received from your mom…"

"Mr. Dell… Thomas," Sam said, correcting himself. "She's not on drugs or crazy or anything like that."

"I didn't say that she was." Thomas responded quickly. *"It's just that, what's she saying, asking is just too… crazy. You've got to admit, if I came to you and said I had aliens stored in my freezer, you'd think I was nuts."*

"Uncle Thomas, I know how it sounds. It's really, really weird. But trust me, if I can't convince you in five minutes, I'll give you the title to my car."

"You driving your dad's old Camaro?"

"Yes, sir, wouldn't give it up for anything… except this."

"I know how much that car meant to your dad. Okay, it's a deal! I'll see you in about an hour."

"Uncle Thomas, you won't be disappointed."

"Well, we'll see. And just to let you know I'm holding to your word, I'll be bringing a tow truck."

Sam laughed, then noticed that Thomas Dellion wasn't. "Uh, that's fine. I'm pretty certain that in a just over an hour, I will rock your world."

"We'll see, Sam. I'll see you in an hour."

The phone clicked off, leaving Sam sitting on the edge of his bed, tapping his foot on the carpet and staring at the ceiling. *Well, he'll either believe me, or I'll be taking the bus home.* He stretched, pulled on his shorts and tee shirt from the day before, and headed for the balcony. The condo was dim and quiet. He walked past the destroyed table and through the living room. As he approached the wall of glass doors, he could hear Emma's snowfall-like voice murmuring to Ronnie, her voice carrying easily on the breeze.

"Morning," Sam said, walking onto the balcony.

Emma glided over to Sam and wrapped her arms around him. "Good morning to you, Sam Shepherd."

She let go, slipped an arm through his, and dragged him to the railing. "The sunrise over the ocean was stunning. Never have I seen such an enormous expanse of blue water with such diversity of life. On my planet, blue waters are extremely toxic."

"That's hard to believe," Sam said after breaking eye contact with Emma's sapphire eyes. "Blue is a calming, peaceful color to me."

"Good morning, sunshine." Ronnie replied with a wide grin as he joined the pair. "Any word on Mr. Dellion?"

"He called me first thing this morning, going to drop by in an hour."

"How'd he sound?"

"Like he thought we were all lunatics. I think he's just going through the motions." Sam put his hands on the railing, held it hard enough to turn his knuckles white, and stared at the sky. "I really don't know what it's going to take to convince him."

"But you said the nanites would be all the evidence he needs." Emma's voice broke. "What more does he require?" She sagged against Sam, who put his arm around her waist, holding her close.

"He's just so… disbelieving. Without the nanites, we would have no chance. It's just, what we are asking of him is huge. We are asking him to risk being ruined with a slight chance of surviving financially." Sam stared over Emma's shoulder and down both lengths of the patio. "And speaking of the nanites, where is Jonqueen?"

Emma gently pulled Sam's arms away and stared at the roof. "He's using the building's height to scan for the Galv. He wants to make sure they haven't tracked us here. When he opens the dish holding their remains, they will know where we are. He just doesn't want them showing up too quickly."

"I take it he hasn't located the gray dudes?" Ronnie said, cupping his eyes to stare at the roof peak, thirty feet over their head.

"No, he has not detected them."

"Well, that's good news." Sam said. "Mr. Dellion will be here soon, so let's keep our fingers crossed the Galv don't crash our party." He turned to Emma. "Tell Jonqueen that whatever he has planned, he needs to be ready."

"I will, Sam Shepherd. And I'll tell Jonqueen to be convincing."

"Do you think he can?"

Emma's eyes darkened, and her mouth closed into a tight smile. "When Jonqueen wants to be convincing, he can do so very well."

"Cool, 'cause he will have to be very good." Sam took Emma by the hand and pulled her close enough that their chins almost met. "I'm going to get you home, Emma. One way or another, I'll get you there."

"I know you will, Sam Shepherd." She leaned forward, putting her forehead against his. "It's what shepherds do. They protect their flock, get them home safe and sound."

"That's a touch weird." Ronnie laughed, breaking up the silence that followed Emma's statement. "Now, where can I get a towel? I smell like the inside of an old Camaro."

Sam flipped him off, then pointed at a closet down the hall. "My guess would be there. Now don't leave a ring around the tub." Turning to Emma. "Have you eaten?"

"No, I haven't, and I am quite hungry. But I wasn't sure what I can or should eat."

"Let's see what's in the pantry. I'm sure we can find something." Leading Emma by the hand, Sam guided her through the kitchen to a small breakfast nook with a panoramic ocean view. She sat while Sam perused the food stores.

"Well, we have dry cereal and some fruits. Anything you want to try?"

"I trust you, Sam. Choose for me." Emma said with her back to him. She stared out over the ocean as gulls soared and floated on the air currents.

"I hope you like apples and dry cornflakes. That's pretty much all I see."

"That will be fine," Emma sighed, her eyes still on the blue horizon.

Sam opened the windows, and they ate silently as salty breezes flowed through the open glass. Ronnie startled them when he dropped his damp towel on the table.

"You two are awful quiet." Ronnie said as he pulled out a chair.

"Just thinking," Sam said quietly, his chin resting on his clenched hands..

"Well, you might want to finish your thinking 'cause your Mr. Dellion is going to be here in about thirty minutes."

"I know… just wish we had more time."

Emma placed a hand on his. "As do I." She let go and stood up from the table. "I'll find Jonqueen and make sure he is prepared." Emma pushed from the table and glided toward the patio, her bare feet hardly making a whisper on the tile floor.

"Man, she moves so quietly." Ronnie said as he watched her disappear out the patio door.

Sam nodded but didn't respond.

"What's weird is, I've only been around her a day and a half, but I'll be darned if she doesn't have some crazy effect on me. It feels like I've known her since forever and I'm watching her slowly fade from view."

"I know exactly what you mean," Sam said as he pushed the chair out and climbed to his feet. "I don't think I'll ever meet another person as fascinating as she is." His eyes watered.

"For sure, man." Ronnie patted Sam on the shoulder. "C'mon, time to get your head in the game. We need to make sure we get that girl and her scary friend off this rock and heading home."

Sam sighed, took a deep breath, and clapped his hands once. "Keep an eye out for Mr. Dellion. I'm going to take a shower and straighten up a bit. If he arrives early, tell Emma and Jonqueen to stay out of view, then let me know."

"Will do, brother. Will do."

Sam let the piping hot water seer his back and neck, the steam rising in thick clouds. The heat helped relax the knots kinking his muscles. If he were successful, he'd never, ever see Emma again. If he failed, he might doom billions of beings. "This is adult-level crap," he muttered and turned to face the water. He was shampooing his hair for the second time when there was a knock on his door.

"Hey, man. It's show time," Ronnie yelled through the door. "Your friend is apparently eager to prove you wrong."

"Tell him to hang on. I'll be with him in a minute. Where's Emma and Jonqueen?" Sam shouted back.

"They are out of view like you asked."

"Good." Sam turned off the water, grabbed his towel, and wrapped it around his waist. He cracked the door. "Tell Mr. Dellion I'll be within him in just a few minutes."

"I'll tell him."

Sam shut the door, brushed his hair, and then quickly retreated to his room to change. After he dressed, he found Ronnie and Thomas standing amid the ruins of the formal dining room table.

"Uncle Thomas, thanks so much for meeting with me."

Thomas turned, a big smile on his face. "Sam, it's great to see you again! My God, you look just like your dad at that age." We walked over to Sam and gave him a quick hug. He let go, then cast his thumb toward the destroyed table. "Your buddy says one of your guests did this?"

Sam closed his eyes and nodded. "I am very sorry. I'll take care of it for you. Might take a decade of cutting grass, but I'll replace it."

"Absolutely not. My wife bought that godawful table years ago, and I hated it. It was too big and bulky to wrestle through the house, and you can almost forget the elevator. It was nearly an impossible job getting it up here." He walked over and picked up the largest chunk of the tabletop. "Now it's much easier to move," Thomas said, laughing.

"So…" Thomas glanced around the room. "Where are these aliens of yours?"

"They'll be here in a minute. Ronnie, can you ask Emma to join us?"

"Your little green man is named 'Emma'? Kinda girly for an extraterrestrial."

Sam grinned. "He's a 'she' and her real name— actually, I don't know her real name. But here title is Emissary de'tantel of the Shovain Star Empire. We shortened it to 'Emma'." Sam heard approaching footsteps and glanced toward the patio doors. "She's a diplomat, was trying to stop a war. Hopefully, we can return her back to her people." Sam turned back, noticing Thomas' gaze turning toward the patio.

"Your mom didn't tell me you brought your girlfriend with you. She's… stunning." Thomas finished in almost a whisper.

"Uncle Thomas, I'd like to introduce you to the Emissary de'tantel of the Shovain Star Empire."

Emma stepped short of the destroyed table, hands folded before her, Ronnie at her side.

"Sam," Thomas said slowly, eyes on Emma, but words directed at him. "I sure hope this isn't a joke. Your mom and dad meant the world to me, but if this is a prank, I'm going to be very upset." He turned his back to Sam, his eyes narrowing.

"Emma, please say 'hello' to Thomas Dellion, the man who's going to help you get home."

Emma did as Sam requested. Thomas stared at her, not understanding.

"Sam, what's going on? Is she speaking an obscure French dialect?"

"Uncle Thomas, all will make sense in just a minute. But first, what did you hear when she spoke?"

Thomas glanced at Emma, then back to Sam, watching him from the corner of his eye. "What do you mean? I heard what sounded like gibberish."

"Not the words, the sound, the feeling."

"Sam, I really don't know what game you are playing, but—"

"Uncle Thomas, what did her voice *sound like?*"

Thomas shrugged. "What did it sound like? Do you mean the tone, the feeling?

Sam and Ronnie nodded vigorously. "Exactly." they said at the same time.

"Okay, I'll humor you. It sounded like…." He paused, searching for the correct words. "Wings. To me, it sounded like the wind over a bird's wing. The rustle of feathers."

"Wow, that's really good," Ronnie said, chuckling. "I heard gentle breathing. Sam said he heard snowfall."

"What in the hell are you getting at?" Thomas crossed his arms as his brow pinched.

"Uncle Thomas. None of us could understand her when we first met. Now, hold your arm out, and let her take your hand."

"What?"

"Please, it will all make sense. And to confirm we're not pulling a prank or drugging you…."

"Drugging me?"

"Ronnie's going to film every moment with his phone."

Thomas put his hands on his hips, his fingers flexing. "Last time, Sam. What in the hell are you talking about?"

"Trust me, please. Time is getting short."

Reluctantly, Thomas held out his right hand. Instantly, Emma was before him, faster than Sam thought possible. "Emma, are you ready?

She nodded, took a deep breath and held Thomas' hand in both of hers.

"So, what happens…" Thomas' eyes went wide; he cried out weakly as his knees buckled. Sam caught him before he hit the floor and gently laid him on his back.

"Guess we should have done this on the couch, huh? Ronnie asked as he continued to record.

Chapter Seventeen

Thomas gasped and sat up quickly. His vision swam as disorientation threatened to make him vomit. He collapsed back against the couch. "What… what's going on?" The room was dim, as if the day was pushing toward twilight. Taking a deep breath, he closed his eyes, then felt a cool cloth pressed to his forehead.

"I am sorry, Thomas Dellion," Emma said. "Your reaction was stronger than I had intended. Are you feeling better?"

Thomas felt the cloth removed from his face, then glanced around. The drapes were pulled, blocking the light from the patio. Sam sat a few feet away, hands knotted in his lap. The girl was kneeling before him, her eyes wide and skin pale as alabaster. "What did you do to me?"

Emma lowered her head, then met his gaze. "On my home world, we have mostly replaced speech with a direct neural connection. We can transfer a day's worth of knowledge with the touch of our hand. I have discovered that on your planet this can be overwhelming for some. I meant no harm or discomfort."

"The disorientation will pass in a few minutes, Uncle Thomas." Sam said.

"You've been through this?" Thomas asked, clumsily climbing onto the couch.

"Yep. Me, mom, Sharon, and Ronnie. It knocks some folks out, it did mom."

Thomas pushed up straighter, ran a finger through his hair, then wiped his face with his palms. "How long was I out?"

"About twenty minutes."

"Did I dream, or did the girl put these visions in my head?"

"You did not dream, Thomas Dellion. What I shared with you is the universe, the time I am from."

"What did you see?" Sam leaned forward, his palms on his knees. "We all see different visions."

"I saw… planets burning, ships exploding in space. Creatures that can be described as nightmares." He collected his thoughts. "I saw the earth from beyond the moon. How is that possible?"

"It is what we experienced as we approached your world."

"There was another… man, I guess that is what it was, with you. Is he here?"

"Yes."

"He's not human, is he?"

"No. His specie is called Kznas'ik. They are inhabitants of the Firestar Confederacy."

"But you," Thomas leaned forward, "are human?"

Emma sighed and shrugged. "I am a citizen of the Shovain Expanse. Our history goes back over five-thousand of your years. Where we originated from, no one knows."

"You look human."

Emma smiled her soft smile. "I would like to think so."

Thomas stretched, his eyes getting brighter. "Your companion, I'd be interested in meeting him."

Emma nodded, stared at the balcony, and then met his gaze. "He will be here momentarily."

"Is he psychic? How do you know he will be here soon?"

"Uncle Thomas, neither of them has physic ability. They just seem to communicate without speaking."

"We think it's Jonqueen's nanites." Ronnie added, ending the video recording. He put his phone in his pocket. "They do some crazy things."

"Nanites? You're talking nanotechnology?"

"Yes, sir. Apparently, this other dude is full of them. They are part of him." Ronnie said.

"A part of him, how?" Thomas asked, now fully recovered.

"They make up is armor and are integrated into his body." Sam replied, taking over the Q&A. "I've seen him create objects out of thin air *and* dissolve things by waving his hands over them."

"Yeah, and he put them in Sam, too." Ronnie added.

Thomas turned to Sam. "He put the nanites in you? How?"

Sam shrugged. "Not exactly sure. He just kind of balled up his fist and—they exploded, for lack of a better word—out of his wrist and landed on me and sank into my skin. It was weird."

"You could see them?"

"Sort of, they looked like a fine mist of pepper."

"Do you feel any different?" Thomas was now standing.

"Nope. He said he is going to create a bridge or console so I can interact with them."

Thomas ran a hand through his thinning blond and gray hair. He temples his hands before his face, then took a deep breath. "I'm sorry, Sam, but this is bordering on ludicrous! Nanites, aliens…"

"But Uncle Thomas, the visions you saw… you can't discount those." Sam argued as he paced.

"Sam, I don't know what I saw. Hell, I could have had a stroke." He laughed quickly, walked around the room, then stopped. "Son, I know *you* believe what you are saying, but nanites and trans-universe travel…" He stared at the teens. "I'm sorry, I just don't buy it."

"But Emma, what about her?" Sam pleaded.

Thomas shook his head. "Parlor trick?" He waved Sam's objection down. "Does this other person even exist?"

"Yes." Came a graveling, vibrating response from the patio.

Thomas spun around to find Jonqueen striding through the room, blocking out the light. His color was grayer, and his eyes narrowed. Thomas Dellion backpedaled and stopped at the edge of the couch. "Who in the hell are you?"

"His name is Jonqueen P'tonich, pilot and navigator of the Firestar Confederacy vessel Star Crucible. He is also my assigned protector." Emma announced, standing to join Jonqueen.

Jonqueen towered over Thomas Dellion and stared down at him. He turned to Sam. "Time is short." He held the Pyrex bowl out. The Galv remnants were dancing.

"Have they found us?" Sam asked, casting his gaze quickly between Ronnie and Emma.

"No, but it will not be long. I cannot completely block their transmissions. Enough of a signal is penetrating my dampening field to activate the remains. It will not be long before the Galv remains have enough of a signal-lock to broadcast our location."

"You are the other alien?" Thomas asked hesitantly.

Jonqueen glared at him, the muscles in his neck tightening, his nostrils now slits. "Sam Shepherd, it would be best if we moved into a subterranean location, if this structure has one. It would make it more difficult for their Galv signals to penetrate my shielding."

"These Galv," Thomas said, interrupting. "What is this, another governmental branch?"

"Parasitic beings that only conquer, kill and destroy." Jonqueen growled, his voice causing the windows to shake.

"These are the beings you showed me?" Thomas said, turning to Emma.

"Yes. They have destroyed many worlds and are growing stronger. We hoped having a common enemy could unite the Firestar Confederacy and Shovain Star Empire and end our own war. Our two civilizations might be strong enough to blunt, if not reverse, the Galv march through our galaxy."

"Sam, do you know of these Galv?"

Sam's jaw dropped as he stared at Thomas. "Are you kidding? They blew up my freaking house and almost destroyed the Camaro! Call mom, call the sheriff's department back home. They will tell you of two mysterious explosions—one being my house—and one being a Galv soldier mom killed."

Thomas glanced between Sam and the Pyrex bowl. "What does he have there?" Thomas said, pointing at Jonqueen. "Are those the Galv… beings?"

Sam shook his head quickly. "No, pieces of a Galv. They can teleport, sorta like Star Trek. Mom killed one as it tried to teleport, and this is what's left. But these parts continuously broadcast a signal, trying to be transported back and reassembled."

Sam turned to Jonqueen. "As for a basement, I don't know if there is one or not. We're at the beach, just above the waterline."

"There is a bunker below the parking deck, but that's it." Thomas said quickly. "We'll need my access code to enter." He avoided Jonqueen and hurried toward the door.

Sam ran after him. "Do you believe me now?"

Using a remote on his keys, Thomas summoned the elevator and held his hand against the panel listing the floors. "Sam, I will admit I have no explanations for your friends. This *being*, Jonqueen, is definitely not from around here." He paused and raised a hand to silence Sam. "And I'm inclined to believe they are not from this planet, and or even this solar system."

Thomas stayed the elevator until everyone was inside, then let the doors closed. "But I'm not convinced enough to abandon my launch and turn the ship over to you. If this launch doesn't go off as planned, me, my company, along with many others, will be ruined. We've invested everything into this launch. It is imperative that we succeed."

"Uncle Thomas, this is their *only* chance to get home. You're condemning billions to die!" Sam pleaded.

Thomas opened the control board and engaged an additional keypad that accessed the levels below the condo. The elevator descended. "Sam, my ship can only get to the moon and back. How in the world is it going to get them across the universe?"

"I plan to commandeer the Galv vessel and then detonate the engine core of your craft the moment we have a slipstream lock on the Shovain homeworld. If I can overload the engine, the subsequent blast should be enough to tear the spacial strings and deliver us back to our own universe and time."

"How do you know if this will even work?" Thomas asked as the elevator descended.

"I do not know for certain. I calculate our chance of success to be less than eleven percent. I am certain I can navigate back to our home system. As for reaching the correct *time*, I will not know if we have been successful until we arrive."

The elevator reached the bottom floor, and the door opened to a long, tiled corridor that slowed further down. Florescent lights flickered to life as they exited the elevator car.

Sam whistled lightly. "Wow, how far does this corridor run?" Sam asked.

Thomas led the way at a fast clip, his hard soled shoes echoing off the polished floor. "About two hundred feet. At the end we will be nineteen feet underground." The corridor led to massive steel door. Thomas typed commands into a wall-mounted keypad. The sound of electric motors could be heard before the door opened with a slight hiss. Thomas flipped on a bank of switches, and a series of recessed lights bloomed to life. The room was small and ornate, but not as luxurious as the penthouse apartment.

"What is this place?" Sam asked.

"It's my hurricane room-slash-operations center for the hotel. It's completely sealed from all weather and even flooding. We could stay here for several weeks and not run out of food or water."

"But why is it here?" Sam said as he took in the tech-laden bunker.

Thomas grabbed a remote control off a granite countertop and tapped several buttons. Six monitors came to life, three on top of three. Four showed the corners of the building; one provided birds-eye view from the top of the building, and one from the bottom floor of the parking garage.

"You've probably never heard of Alvin Petersmith. He was big-tech before big-tech ever existed. Man was a visionary, incredibly intelligent. Alvin was on the periphery of the Apollo missions. Just a junior engineer but his concepts, ideas…" Thomas shook his head, "were so far advanced, folks considered him a kook. Solar Xploration actually based a lot of our research on his early work.

"Anyway, it was his desire to build a smaller version of Kennedy Space Center right here," Thomas pointed at the ground. "This site is built on a bit of knoll, a rare high-spot in Florida. He built this underground bunker to safely watch his rockets launch. I have, obviously, updated what he started here."

"What happened to him?" Ronnie asked as he studied pictures of the first Apollo crew.

Thomas shook his head and stared at blankly across the room. "He had a heart attack, literally worked himself to death. He had a great mind, was working on a new project, was very excited about it, said it was going to 'revolutionize space travel'."

"Any idea what it was?" Sam asked.

Thomas shrugged. "No clue. Whatever it was, it died with him." Thomas took a deep breath. "Anyway, welcome to my command center. I have dozens of cameras spaced around the hotel, showing every angle. And from here I can cut power to the elevators, any floor or the entire building. My team and I can also access everything at Solar Xploration." Thomas typed codes into the remote, and the top monitors faded, then returned to show images of the spaceport.

"But why such an advanced room below your parking garage?" Sam asked.

"Because you never know when your security is at risk." Thomas worked the remote again, and all the monitors returned to displaying random images from around the hotel. "When you have a billion-dollar project on the launch pad, you can't be too careful."

"Your launch will not be successful," Jonqueen said as he prowled around the room, the Galv remnants inactive.

Thomas watched him circle. "I assure you, we will be successful. We've tested the engines, the craft countless times. Only thing that can prevent a successful launch is the weather."

Jonqueen stopped beside a monitor showing the spaceport. "I did not say your launch would not succeed. In fact, the approach to your moon will be a success. When you exit the moon's orbit and begin your approach vector, the stresses on the outer hull will cause it to fracture and delaminate. It will never survive contact with your planet's gravitational fields."

Thomas shook his head vigorously. "There you are wrong. The engineering team designed the outer skin to withstand gravitational forces and the heat of reentry."

"Once again, in that respect, you are correct. If your craft were to fall unpowered into the planet's upper atmosphere, it would survive mostly intact. It is the engine's harmonics, combined with the skin composition, that is the problem. The vibrations from the powering of the engines will breakdown the molecular bond of the skin causing it to dissipate. It would not be possible for your engineers to be aware of this issue, since your engineers have never built an engine of this type." Jonqueen turned to Thomas, his voice softening with respect. "I am, though, impressed with what you have accomplished with the limited amount of technology available to you on this planet."

"There is no way you can know that!"

"As we approached your planet, we recorded every transmission we received. When my ship's AI detected this construct, it intrigued me. We accessed your systems and examined your design. It will, as I propose, disintegrate upon approach."

"Not possible…" Thomas argued.

Jonqueen pulled a hand-sized data pad from inside his coat. "I am currently transmitting my findings to your lead engineer. Have him run these simulations. I am sure he will concur."

Thomas stormed to the corner of the room and
called his engineer. He glanced at Jonqeen several times
before closing his phone. "I do not know how you
accessed our systems, but my engineering team has
acknowledged the receipt of your data and is running
scenarios."

Thomas nervously fidgeting with his phone. After
fifteen minutes, the device chirped. Thomas answered it
instantly. "You're absolutely certain?" He said after
listening silently. "Thanks, Hanson, I'll call you back."
He disconnected the call but remained standing before
the wall of monitors. "This is unbelievable."

"Did you engineering team confirm my findings?"
Jonqueen asked, his hands still at his side.

"Initially, yes. He's running more tests, but there is
some accuracy in your assessment."

Jonqueen's eyes narrowed as his nostrils flared.
"Some accuracy?" A cloud of nanites burst from his
hands before settling back into his skin. "The accuracy
of my 'assessment' is not in question. What is in
question is your scientists ability to understand the
truth."

"Listen here!" Thomas shouted. "I would trust my
life…."

"Jonqueen!" Sam grabbed the Pyrex bowl and held it
up. The Galv remains were dancing and jumping.

Chapter Eighteen

Jonqueen hissed. He grabbed the bowl, waved his arm over it, and growled deeply. "We need to evacuate this facility—now!"

"What's going on?" Thomas asked.

"The Galv have detected us." He slipped the data pad from his coat and reconfigured it as he stared at the monitors. The device changed from a flat tablet-style computer to one with a parabolic antenna. Jonqueen walked to the back of the room and pulled the power cable from the monitor showing the front of the hotel. The monitor died as the cable erupted in a shower of sparks. He stripped the wires, then inserted the leads into the data pad. He coiled the rest of the wire and held it in his hand.

"Jonqueen," Sam said, backing away. "The last you tried this, you blew my house apart."

Without acknowledging Sam, Jonqueen turned to Thomas. "Is there another exit from this location?"

"There is an emergency exit," Thomas said, pointing to a flush-mounted door at the rear of the bunker. "Another corridor runs about a hundred yards to the West and leads toward the highway. But these 'Galv' you talked about, how strong are they? We're locked behind a six inches of hardened steel and concrete. This room is practically nuclear bomb proof."

The elevator light dinged to life, and the numbers started falling.

Thomas opened a keyboard mounted on a counter and rapidly typed commands. "This will bring them to a halt." He finished typing and stared at the elevator display. The numbers continued to drop. "What in the hell? I cut power to the elevator shaft!" Thomas typed again his fingers pounding the keyboard, his jaw set hard. He glanced up and pushed the keyboard across the counter. "I have no idea how they bypassed the shut-down code, but they won't get far."

"Your steel door will be no match for them. It will hold momentarily before they burn through it."

The indicator above the door showed the lift sitting at the basement level of the condo building.

"Sam, you, the Emissary de'tantel and the other youth must leave."

"I'm telling you, this place is a fortress." Thomas pointed at the door. "We're safe here." Thomas stepped up to Jonqueen. "No one is coming through that door."

Ronnie pried the faux wood covering off the far wall, struggling with the heavy escape access. Jonqueen rushed over and jerked the door open as if it was weightless. The long corridor behind brightened as emergency lights glowed to life. Ronnie held the door open as Emma; then Sam bolted through.

"Leave, now!" Jonqueen ordered.

"I'm telling you, nothing on Earth is coming through that door!"

"The Galv are not from Earth." Jonqueen snapped and backed away from the hardened door, dragging Thomas by the sleeve with him. As they retreated toward the escape tunnel, the room vibrated, slowly at first, then with the heavy staccato rasp of cutting. Dust fell from the ceiling as the monitors broke loose from their moorings. The soldier drew his black tube from his coat and screwed it into the data pad. He pushed Thomas toward the tunnel.

The elevator door appeared to slough off its metal jacket, then crumble like sand. Inside the doorframe stood two Galv soldiers. They turned in unison, bringing their weapons up as they moved. Jonqueen fired first, catching the Galv on the left in the chest, and driving him against the other soldier, knocking them both into the corridor. Smoke poured from their armor as the transmission field faded, then strengthened.

Grabbing Thomas by the neck, Jonqueen threw him across the room and into the escape tunnel. He then turned, training his weapons on the ceiling, and blasted the walls around the elevator entrance. Concrete exploded, leaving steel girders and wiring exposed. He fired again, slagging the metal supports and bringing the ceiling down in front of the doorway. The room collapsed as the walls buckled and hardened steel braces crashed to the floor.

"Go!" Jonqueen roared, pushing Thomas back as he continued to fire. Additional concrete fell from the ceiling. The heavy vibrations returned as the fallen concrete cracked and disintegrated. Jonqueen pulled the barrel off the pad, wrapped the electrical cord around it, and pressed the firing stud. The cylinder twisted and warped as it gave off an ear-splitting howl. The soldier tossed it into the room, slammed the outer door shut, then ran up the corridor, pushing Thomas ahead of him. Halfway down its hundred-yard length, the walls and floor shook as the cylinder exploded. The concussion blew the exit door open, the shockwave knocking them off their feet. Fire surged after the men as the sudden influx of oxygen fueled the inferno. Jonqueen staggered, grabbed the stunned Thomas as if the man were weightless, and stumbled out of the tunnel, exiting on the far side of the condo's property. He carried Thomas clear of the exit, slammed the door shut, and engaged the locks. He dropped to his knees, his palms smoldering from the contact with Thomas.

Emma raced forward and dropped to her knees, careful not to touch him. "Jonqueen, are you okay?"

He glanced up slowly, his face grayer than ever. "I am fine," he managed after a moment. "Though my nanites are severely depleted. It will take some time for them to replicate in sufficient numbers."

Thomas staggered to his feet, brushed the dirt off his hands and shirt, and then turned toward the parking garage. The tan, concrete structured towered several stories over the surrounding trees and palmettos. Smoke rose around it, briefly obscuring the building before the center began to collapse and fall inward. The outer walls followed as a large plume of black smoke rose skyward.

"What just happened?" Thomas cupped his eyes to block the glare of the Florida sun.

"I believe Jonqueen saved all our lives," Ronnie said, joining the founder of Solar Xploration. "Those Galv are some seriously bad dudes. They chased me and Sam for almost a mile through the woods." A muffled 'whump' shook the ground, and the sinkhole deepened, taking with it the shattered garage. Birds took flight as more steam and smoke billowed out of the crater. "I think one of the Galv just detonated."

"It must have been trapped, and unable to transfer back," Jonqueen said as he climb to his feet. "We need to keep moving. There should be at least three more soldiers, not including the pilot. We can expect them to materialize in this vicinity."

"And go where?" Thomas asked, still focused on the smoking depression. "If those—things—can get through that hardened door as easily as they did, there is no safe place."

"I don't know, Uncle Thomas. But we need to get them home." Sam said. "The longer we stay here, the more danger we are all in."

Thomas pulled his shades from his pocket and carefully placed them on his face. "You don't understand, you can't, you're too young." Thomas said with a clenched jaw. "But my life, every damn thing I've worked for, my entire existence is tied up in that launch. If it doesn't go as planned, I'm ruined." He stared blankly across the expanse of palmettos and saw grass. For several minutes, no one spoke. "Now look." he pointed to the smoking pit, not talking. "The authorities will be here any moment. What in the hell will I tell them?"

"I'm truly sorry, Uncle Thomas." Sam said quietly.

"And if my launch has a 'malfunction' on top of this? You can forget about Solar Xporation surviving. No one will lend me a dime to rebuild."

"If this 'dime' you speak of is currency, you will not be destitute long. I have transmitted everything I have on this solar system—mineral compositions, comets and asteroid trajectories, planets and moons you haven't discovered yet—to the scientist in your compound. The program I have installed will release the information in timed intervals, creating the illusion that these are 'new' discoveries. They will hail you as a visionary." Jonqueen offered in a soft voice.

Thomas was about to address Jonqueen's point when his phone rang. "This is Thomas," he said and walked a dozen feet away, standing with his back to everyone. His eyes flicked to Jonqueen. "Are you serious?" More conversation from the caller. "Okay, I'll get back to you ASAP. And yes, tie in every data server we have. Erase them if you have to."

Thomas dropped his phone into his pocket, walked slowly to Jonqueen, and stood with his arms folded over his chest, glasses pressed firmly on his face. "I don't know how you hacked through all the security we have in place, nor how you reconfigured our data storage networks to increase the capacity by thousands of gigabytes," Thomas said evenly. "But the engineer in charge of my IT department says our servers are overloading, that our storage networks are maxed to capacity, Yet the storage subroutines continue to rewrite themselves, adding more compression than we've ever theorized."

"You will need more available storage; the computers you have are inadequate to the task. When capacity is reached, the data flow will stop. It will resume when additional storage is available."

"What about after you leave?"

"It will continue. When we approached your planet, I accessed every data network on this world, both civilian and military. I have downloaded all the data we captured into the satellites in orbit and every academic computer on your planet. They will continue to transmit the data until everything has been transferred."

"Won't all this data and information be noticed?"

Jonqueen tilted his head slightly. His lips parted to a tight slit. Emma would have recognized this for what it was: a smile. "No more than you would recognize one more grain of sand on your beach."

Sam stepped around Ronnie and Emma, his eyes wide. "So, you're going to help?"

Thomas shrugged. "What do I have to lose?" He said with a weak laugh. "My engineers have already confirmed that the data stream is unbelievable, that the information provided is decades—at minimum—ahead of anything we have." He cocked his head toward Jonqueen. "Plus, I'm sure there is a catch to all this data."

"A catch? I am not sure I understand." Jonqueen said evenly.

"Come now, you're smarter than that. You wouldn't just *give* this treasure trove of data to us without a backup plan. What if I were to say, 'no dice' on the launch? You wouldn't give us access to all the data in the solar system without having a way to control it. Control us."

"Uncle Thomas, what are you talking about?"

Thomas gazed over Sam's head. "He is leveraging this information against my launch. I only get access to the data if he gets access to the launch vehicle." Thomas nodded at the soldier, than softly laughed. "We have at least one thing in common. I would do the same."

Jonqueen spoke evenly. "I encrypted the data to Sam's DNA sequence. The nanites in him will only be able to interact with your computers through my console. Not all the information will be released at once. The program will parcel it out as needed. The data is a blueprint. Successfully create section one, section two will then integrate into your systems. Do not circumvent or deactivate the encryption. If an attempt is made, my nanites will instruct your data centers to erase all traces of the information. Lastly, should any harm come to Sam's life, the nanites will expire at the same time."

"In other words, someone can't cut his hand off and use it to access the data."

"Precisely."

Thomas smiled at Sam. "Well, son, looks like you are a ward of my company. It's in my best interest to keep you healthy."

Ronnie carried the bowl containing Galv's remnants to Jonqueen. "Uh guys, these things are stirring again. I think we need to get a move on it."

Jonqueen hissed. "I do not have enough nanites to add an additional layer of shielding. We are too exposed here."

"My car's not far," Thomas said. "Thankfully, I didn't park in the garage."

Chapter Nineteen

The Galv remains quieted during the drive to Solar Xploration. When Thomas presented his ID, the security official waved Thomas's Chevrolet Tahoe through the gate. They drove across the sprawling launch site until they reached an eight-story building of gleaming white marble and gold reflective windows. A man exited the front door, holding it open for them.

Thomas spoke quickly over his shoulder. "Do not say anything, touch anything, or move without my approval. We are now three days within the launch window and my staff is very much on edge."

"What have you told them of us?" Emma asked in her soft voice. "They will not understand me and will take notice of Jonqueen immediately."

"Jonqueen will remain in the car until I come for him. I have told my staff that I'm giving you three a VIP tour of the facility, and that I will allow you to remain on site during the launch. They know of Sam through my relationship with his father. You and Ronnie are his cousins, but you almost never speak because of an auto accident."

Sam stared at Thomas, his mouth open in surprise. "You told them she has a head injury?" He and Ronnie laughed. Emma continued to sit with her hands folded in her lap.

"It's the best I could come up with in a hurry!" He snapped. Thomas turned to stare out the window, then gripped the wheel tightly, flexing his fingers. "I'm sorry.

I didn't mean that like it sounded." He turned the motor off and unbuckled his belt. "Just…pretend you're quiet church-mice tourist, smile and follow me."

All four opened their doors simultaneously, and the passengers exited. Thomas walked quickly around the hood, motioning subtly with his hand for them to line up behind him. He walked briskly toward the front door. "Horace, good morning!"

Horace Wainwright, tall, fit with touches of salt and pepper in his brown hair, smiled. Despite the muggy, sub-tropical Florida air, he waited outside for them wearing dark slacks, a perfectly pressed shirt, a tie, and tailored jacket, unbuttoned. He turned toward Thomas; the sun glinting off his dark aviator glasses. "I take it these are our guests?"

"You are correct." He pulled Sam around. "Do you remember little Sammie?"

Horace lifted his glasses off his face. "Crawdaddy's little boy?"

Thomas nodded.

"Well, I'll be," he says, smiling. "Sam, it's been a long time." he shook Sam's hand warmly. "You look just like your father did in high school. Are you into aviation as well?"

"Yes, sir. Wanted to follow him into the service, but my hearts got some issues, no way to pass the physicals. But, yeah, I love to fly RC planes."

Horace motioned toward the beach and the distant launch pad. "Out there was your daddy's dream. If it could get off the ground, ol' Crawdaddy wanted to be on it."

"You called my dad 'Crawdaddy'?"

Horace and Thomas laughed. Horace wiped his eyes, then put his glasses back on. "Oh yeah, all the time! When your name is 'Crawford', and you grow up near a southern swamp, someone's gonna make fun of you. So, we tagged him 'Crawdaddy' many years ago. He hated it at first, eventually realized we would always call him 'Crawdaddy', and finally came around to embrace it."

"I never knew that." Sam said, shaking his head.

"I'm not surprised. You were little when we worked together. When he joined up with the air rescue guys, the job got a bit more serious. They called him by his last name. But we had some good times." Horace pulled the front door open. "Well, gather up your friends and we'll get this show on the road. First stop is the lounge and quasi-museum. We have a suite to watch the launch from. We might have a few more guests before it's all said and done. So, you guys go ahead and claim dibs— do y'all still say that? —on the best seats."

"Only about ten times a day." Sam confirmed, nodding.

"Well good, then. You guys claim the good seats, and we'll let the exes fight over the rest."

Sam motioned for Emma and Ronnie to follow. Horace led them through the ornate lobby; plaques and memorabilia lined the richly paneled walls. A showcase was filled with acknowledgments of Solar Xploration's successes over the past twelve years. Leather chairs and couches were arranged around a glass table, providing a cozy environment for guests to sit and talk. And on the far wall was a reception desk with a woman deftly cycling through phone calls. Her hair was pulled back in a loose ponytail; she wore a tailored dark blue dress sporting a Solar Xploration name tag.

"Catherine," Horace called across the room, his voice echoing off the stone floor and glass windows, "These are our honored guests. Can you please provide them with their VIP badges?"

The woman stood and walked around the desk, her polished heels clicking on the tile floor. She had three badges in her hand, each with a lanyard containing a name. "Welcome to Solar Xploration, lady and gentlemen! Sam, this one is yours." She said cheerfully. "You must be Ronnie," she continued, handing out badges. "And this must be for you, sweetheart." Catherine handed Emma her badge. When Emma reached for it, their fingertips touched. Catherine's eyes flew wide, and she stumbled. Ronnie grabbed her by the elbow to keep her from falling.

"Are you okay?" He asked when the receptionist regained her balance.

She blinked several times, ran a hand over her hair to smooth it, then smiled sheepishly. "I must have stood up too fast." Ronnie helped her around the desk, where she gingerly retreated to her chair. "I think I almost fainted." Catherine pulled her chair closer to the desk, stretched her arms out, and then clasped her hands together. She took several deep breaths.

Thomas glanced from Emma to Sam, then turned to Catherine. "Why don't you take the rest of the day off? You look a bit pale."

Catherine managed a wan smile. "Thank you, Thomas." She grabbed her purse and climbed to her feet. "I suddenly don't feel too well."

"Call me later and let me know you made it home."

"Yes, sir." She pulled a pair of sunglasses from her purse, and held them with a shaking hand. "I think I'm going to take a nap the moment I get home." She waved goodbye, slipped on her sunglasses, and left the building.

When the door had closed behind Catherine, Emma met Thomas's gaze. "I am so sorry. Our hands barely touched. Incidental contact should not have influenced her so," she said, almost in a whisper.

"It's fine. Don't worry about it. But let's move on. I need to get you guys settled in before our other guest arrive."

A middle-aged black security guard waited in an open elevator, holding it for them. "Good Afternoon, Mr. Dellion, I take it these are the first of our dignitaries?"

"Yes, they are, George. Please make them feel welcome."

"Absolutely." George tipped his hat slightly. "If you have questions my number in on the back of your VIP tag. You can call me from any phone." He turned back to Thomas. "Mr. Dellion. Will you be heading to the operations room?"

"Yes, George, eventually."

"Very well, sir." George reached into the elevator, inserted a long metal key into the panel, turned it several times, then withdrew it. "You guys enjoy your stay," He finished with an open smile.

The teenagers entered the lift first, followed by Horace, then Thomas. When the doors shut, Horace said, "That incident with Catherine, was that…."

Thomas held a finger to his lips, then pointed up. The elevator rose quickly before stopping smoothly on the eighteenth floor. The doors opened to a horizon-wide view of the Florida Atlantic coast. Several miles to the North-East, the launch facility's bright concrete gleamed in the sun.

"Well, what do you guys think?" Thomas said, breaking the silence.

"Wow…I mean, WOW!" Sam blurted out.

"What he said," Ronnie echoed. "I thought your penthouse apartment was sweet. But this… this is incredible!"

Emma walked to the windows and faced northeast toward the launch pad. "Your ship, is it over there?"

Thomas nodded.

"Thomas, you can understand her? I am fluent in French, German and Spanish, but her words, they are…" Horace shrugged.

"Alien?"

"Might as well be. She's the girl you told me about? Where's the other?"

"He'll be here soon," Thomas said, joining the teens by the windows. "You've talked with Nichols in R&D, seen the data?"

"I have. I thought he was out of his mind." Horace joined Thomas by the wall of glass.

"And now?"

"I think you two have drank the same Kool-Aid."

Thomas laughed and slapped his friend on the back. He walked across the room and past a row of recliners facing the launch pad. Beyond the chairs was a bank of monitors and data terminals. He powered each one. The video screens warmed to show various angles of the launch pad. One zoomed in on the launch vehicle, an army of yellow-shirted technicians swarming around it. Grabbing a remote control off the wall, he retreated to the wall of recliners, sat, propped his feet up, then kicked his shoes off.

"I thought that Sam's mom had been drinking and was drunk when she called. I only humored her for Crawford's sake, thought that maybe she just needed a break. And when Sam showed up in his dad's old Camaro with a couple of teenagers and some strange looking old guy, I was *sure* I was being played." Thomas pushed back in the recliner, extended the footstool, and stretched out.

"You don't think so now?" Horace asked, his eyes discounting the words of his business partner.

Thomas laughed again. "What do I think? Personally, I think this has turned everything I have ever known inside out, just mangled it." He pointed to Emma. "Sit down and shake her hand, then you tell me."

"That's it, huh? Just shake her hand and she will reveal all?" Horace replied with a smirk.

"It's up to Emma. If she's willing."

Both men turned to the Emissary. Emma took a deep breath before nodding. "I will do as you ask."

"Did she agree?" Horace asked.

"She did. Now have a seat and hold on to your ass."

Horace glanced warily between Thomas and Emma but did as requested. He sat in the recliner next to Thomas. "Okay, what next?"

"Hold your hand out."

Horace held his hand out in a half-hearted attempt, an unconvinced smile on his face. Emma glided across the floor and took his hand in hers. Horace rolled his eyes at first, then sat upright in his chair.

"Sam, quickly!" Thomas shouted as he jumped from his chair. Sam ran over and put a steadying hand on Horace's shoulder.

Horace's jaw clenched, and his eyes rolled back in his head. He groaned, flailed feebly, and went limp. Emma let go and slumped to her knees, her head buried against her chest.

Sam let Horace sink into the recliner, then dropped quickly beside Emma. "Hey, are you okay?"

Emma put a hand on her forehead, then nodded that she was.

"Are you sure?"

Emma pushed a lock of hair out of her face, then turned his way. Her lips parted in a weak smile. "I am fine Sam Shepherd. The connection took a lot out of me." Using his shoulder for support, Emma climbed to her feet. She walked over to the windows and resumed staring at the spaceport.

"Emma, what are you not telling me?" Sam asked, joining her by the glass wall.

"Sam, you know that if it were within my power, I would stay here with you on Earth."

"Emma," Sam said sharply, then winced, not meaning to be so rough, "I know that. We have talked about it. Every fiber in my being wants you to stay here, but I understand your need to return home. And I'm okay with it. I won't lie to you. It's going to hurt knowing that I'll never see you again." Tears fell from the corner of his eyes.

Emma gently wiped away each tear with the tip of her finger, smiling the sweet smile that could induce a cold star to flame again. "My Sam Shepherd, one thing I will miss the most about your home is the openness of your people to share their emotions. In all my years of travel and all the worlds I have visited, only the people of Earth share this ability. It makes you a very rare being." She leaned in close enough for Sam to smell the slight hint of cinnamon on her breath. "Sam, there is another reason I can't stay." Emma glanced down, biting her bottom lip. "I think I am dying."

Sam recoiled against the windows, his hands on his face. "What? No…you can't be!" He lowered his hands and stared at her over his fingertips. "Why do you think so?"

Emma reached out and gently took his hands in hers. "My Sam, you can't hide behind your hands. I can still see you!" She raised the back of his hands to her lips and kissed them. "I wasn't sure, but Jonqueen had his nanites scan me. He confirmed that something in the air or water is causing my cells to degrade."

"How long do you have?"

"Weeks…maybe a month or two. We don't know."

"Can your people heal you?"

"Yes, our physicians are very skilled. Once home, I will be fine." Emma pulled him close and wrapped Sam in a fierce hug. "If our healers could learn the power of this embrace, I think they could cure anything." She whispered in his ear. "Maybe the stories of the blue world aren't entirely false."

Sam sagged against her, put his head on her shoulder, and breathed in her skin's soft, clean scent. He reluctantly looked up when a shadow fell on the windows.

Ronnie nodded toward the recliners. "Hey lovebirds, our doubting Horace is waking up, and he looks seriously freaked out."

Chapter Twenty

"Okay, thanks." Sam said, releasing Emma. He wiped his eyes clear with the back of his hand, then turned to see Horace leaning forward, his hands on his knees. "Mr. Wainwright, are you okay?"

Horace slowly shook his head and looked up. His pupils were dilated, eyes red-streaked. "What in the hell did you guys do to me? Did you drug me?"

"Quite a rush, isn't it? I was just like you, wanting to know what they drugged me with. But give it a few minutes. Your head will clear and then all the images will settle down."

Emma approached, but Horace held a hand up, keeping her at bay. "Hang on, sweetie. Let my head clear before I throw up all over Mr. Dellion's expensive leather chair."

Emma stopped several feet away from the men and waited. "I am sorry, Mr. Wainright. It wasn't my intention to make you ill, but to share with you the universe I come from. Sometimes it is very intense."

"Yeah, it knocked me for a loop," Ronnie added, filling the silence in the room.

Horace sat up straighter. "So, all of you have experienced this? Seen these…creatures, for lack of a better word?"

"And the world's burning, ships exploding, and seas boiling," Thomas said. "Horace, she and her friend are what we have been holding out for, searching for all our lives. Now it…they…are here. And they need our help."

"In what capacity, Thomas? I'm rather short on intergalactic space craft at the moment."

"Jonqueen, you haven't met him yet, has offered us technology the world has never seen before, and might never. Including a detailed map of every planet, moon and asteroid in our solar systems. This includes an analysis of core materials. There is enough raw material within our grasp to revolutionize this planet."

"And you trust it?" Horace said, finally regaining color in his cheeks and sitting back in the leather recliner.

"I do, without a doubt. I've seen the data, had R&D go over it and they say it's like nothing they've ever seen. And I've experienced what these other aliens, these Galv can do." Thomas turned to stare straight at Horace. "These…aliens destroyed the bunker as if it was balsa wood. That room could practically survive a nuclear strike, and they entered as if there was no door."

Horace leaned back against the recliner, gripping the sides hard enough to make the furniture creak. "We will be ruined. Never get this chance again."

Thomas stood, then paced along the wall of windows. "I agree. It will be a setback. Will take years to get the financial backing to launch another vehicle. But I disagree on this being a fatal setback. More of a lateral setback. We'll regroup, reform into something better."

"And what of the staff? We'll lose our brain-trust. They'll jump to Space-X, or NASA. Without financial backing, we'll never get this level of talent again."

Thomas shook his head vigorously. "There you are wrong. Check with Philco. Robert called me a couple of hours ago, said 'someone' is downloading petabytes of data, maybe as much as exabytes into our servers. Everything is overloading, data storage is at max. We can't even stop the downloads. And the amazing thing is, it keeps compressing at rates I've never even heard anyone hypothesize."

Taking a deep breath, Thomas relaxed and continued. "The data is encrypted, allows only snapshots before the data vanishes. But Robert said the information is beyond brilliant. We have complete scans of every planet, moon, rock—you name it—in our solar system. This includes practically every microbe, spore, mineral, and molecule. It's incredible on a level I can't comprehend yet."

Horace climbed to his feet and walked to the windows. He stared toward the launch pad. "But what good will it do us, Thomas? All the knowledge in the world is useless without a way to access it. If we give up our one chance to test the launch vehicle, we will not get another. I'm sorry, I just can't go along with you on this."

"Then you have condemned billions to death." Jonqueen said in a low, gravelly voice. He stood just inside the door, filling the frame.

Horace spun around, his eyes wide, mouth open. "You…are the other alien?"

Jonqueen ignored him as he turned to Thomas. "I have reviewed your security, and it is inadequate. The Galv will penetrate it easily and eliminate everyone in their path."

launch vehicle, we will not be able to build up a pressure wave to distort time."

"Where would you put your odds of achieving this with our ship?"

Jonqueen took a breath and focused fully on Horace. "There are many variables involved, but I would approximate that there is an eleven percent chance of success in reaching the correct time stream."

"So, what you are saying is, you want to destroy our launch vehicle knowing it won't be successful? That will leave us with the stigma of failure." Horace stood with his hands on his hips. "Thomas, I'm having a hard time believing you'll risk everything we've worked for on a fool's errand. I think we need to look out for number one, and that's Solar X."

Thomas glared at Horace. "I believe in these beings, Horace. I have seen what the Galv can do. If the Galv can contact their home world in our timeline and bring ships back, I doubt we will put up much of a defense. So, this *is* for Solar X and for every man, woman and child living on the planet." Thomas pulled a small computer tablet clipped to his belt and began typing. "I feared this would be your reaction. I am terminating your access to all Solar Xploration files, buildings, and equipment. Security has been notified to remove you on sight."

"You can't do this!" Horace shouted. "We are equal partners in Solar Xploration! The board is the only one who can take this action." He snarled.

Thomas held his ground against the younger man. "You are correct. We are forty-nine percent to forty-nine percent, with the final two percent being held privately by CD, Inc, as you well know. I've already spoken with Marshall Cox in our legal department. He advised me that CD, Inc's chairman can vote with whatever partner they wish. CD, Inc notified the board an hour ago that they are putting their vote in the hands of a proxy. I feel certain the proxy will vote with me."

Horace's face reddened; his lips trembled with anger. "You know this wasn't the plan! You can't do this, Thomas. I'll have my attorney file an injunction before the day's over." Horace's eyes narrowed as he stood in Thomas's shadow.

"Well, I just did. And by the time you get this in front of a judge, the launch will be over." Thomas walked past Horace and to the back of the room. He opened a refrigerator mounted flush with the wall, pulled out a beer, and popped the top. He took a long pull. "Oh Horace, don't bother the board. They've already been informed that CD, Inc. will side with me and have accepted the decision of the proxy."

"But the proxy hasn't voted. We're still at even percentage." Horace growled.

"Well, let's ask him." Thomas used his near-empty beer to point at Sam. "So, Sam, as the proxy for CD, Inc., do you throw your percentage in with me? That will give me, us, controlling interest in Solar Xploration."

"What in the world are you talking about?" Sam asked, arms out, palms up. Glancing between Thomas and Horace.

"What they're saying, buddy," Ronnie chimed in, "Is that some company called CD, Inc owns a tiny percentage of Solar Xploration. They have said you can vote for them. If you vote with your uncle, he will have a majority ownership, and can do as he pleases."

Sam gawked at his friend. "How do you know this?"

"I'm not a complete moron." Ronnie said, laughing. "Last semester, one of my elective classes was an AP business class. We studied corporation structures. They actually learned me something."

"I'll be darned." Sam shook his head. "Okay, I don't know who CD, Inc is, but if they'll help get Emma home, I vote with Uncle Thomas."

"You know this won't stand up in court!" Horace snapped. "I'll have you kicked off the board, Thomas, and all your interests dissolved." He stormed out the door, slamming it shut behind him hard enough to knock pictures off the wall.

The room was quiet, everyone facing the closed door.

"Well, that went better than I expected," Thomas said dryly.

"Uncle Thomas, what is CD, Inc?" Sam asked, still staring at the door.

"Ironically enough, it was Horace's idea to create CD, Inc. We both took forty-nine percent, leaving two percent to a third, uninterested party. That way, neither of us would have a controlling interest."

"So, who owns CD, Inc?"

Thomas smiled. "You do, son."

"Me?"

"Well, not completely. It is owned by your mom and sister as well."

"Does mom know this?" Sam asked, walking to stand by Emma.

"She didn't until today. We created CD, Inc. without her knowledge to honor your dad, and hopefully a future windfall for you guys. I called her today, explained the situation."

"My dad was CD, Inc.?" Sam asked

"Yeah, your old man," Thomas confirmed. "It actually cracked us up when we came up with it." Thomas regained his composure and smiled at Sam. "CD, Inc is short for 'Crawdaddy, Inc'."

"So, what do we do now?" Sam asked.

Thomas joined Sam and Emma by the bank of windows. He pointed to a location in the far corner of the facility. "Jonqueen thinks we should lure the Galv to that power station. My guess is that the frequency of the current will affect the soldiers. "

"That is correct," Jonqueen said evenly. "The power station will have an adverse effect on their transference beam. There is an enormous amount of energy leaking from the transmission coils. I should be able to reconfigure my weapon to use the electrical charge surrounding the area to destroy the Galv."

"How long will it take before you are ready?" Thomas asked.

"I am practically ready now. Once we reach the power station, I can configure my weapon depending on the amount of ambient power leaking from the location. Once I am in position, I will release the dampening field on the Galv remains. The Galv should respond almost instantly."

"Then let's do it now, before Horace can stop us," Sam said.

Emma walked over to him, held his arm, and rested her head on his shoulder. "Our time is almost over," she coughed, then stared up at him. "I'm getting weaker, Sam Shepherd."

"If it's the last thing I do, I'm getting you home, Emma." He ran his fingers through her silky, jet-black hair.

Emma smiled up at him, her dark crystal eyes heavy with emotion. "Well, let's hope it's not the last thing you do, my Sam. I want you to do so much more."

Sam nodded. "Just a saying, Emma," he sighed as he leaned his head against her. "Just a silly Earth saying."

"Do we need anything else?" Thomas asked as walked to the door, followed by Jonqueen.

Jonqueen held the matte black tube he always carried and a small tablet console his nanites had just completed, and slowly shook his head. "If young Ronnie will carry the Galv remains, it is all I require."

Thomas held the door for everyone, Emma and Sam, the last to exit. As they did, he squeezed Sam's shoulder with his free hand. He then locked the door and joined everyone at the elevator.

The ride down was uneventful, the lobby dark when they stepped out. "Horace must have sent everyone home," Thomas commented as he locked the elevator. "This way, guys." He nodded in the direction he wanted Sam and his friends to go. "We can exit the building about a hundred yards from the power relay station."

They walked through a maze of corridors and offices before pushing through a nondescript door into the intense Florida sunshine. Emma leaned against Sam, taking him by the arm once more. She squinted and used her free hand to shield her eyes.

"Are you okay?" Sam asked, moving strands of hair from her face.

"Yes, Sam, just tired. Your sun, it is very intense, much brighter than home." She smiled at him. "But the heat feels good on my skin." Emma took him by the hand, leading him forward. "Come, let's catch up with Jonqueen."

The soldier reached the power substation and assembled his weapon as a haze of nanites swarmed the comboard. Every few moments, he would stand and wave the tablet toward the horizon, then move a few feet forward and repeat the action. Ronnie stood close by, then motioned for Sam and Emma not to approach any closer.

"He's a bit testy right now. I wouldn't get in his light or ask him questions." Ronnie cautioned. "I asked him where he wanted me to put the Galv remains, and by his expression, I feel fairly certain it was a place I wouldn't like."

"Please understand that he means well," Emma said. "When he prepares for battle, it completely consumes him with the task. When he's ready, he will let you know."

"I didn't take any offence." Ronnie said, smiling. "I get his attitude. My dad was like that when I was a kid." His eyes dimmed, and his good-natured attitude waned.

Emma walked over to him and brushed the base of his neck with the back of her hand. "You are still young, Ronnie. You will have many years with your father yet."

Ronnie nodded, put on his best smile, then turned away.

"We are ready," Jonqueen announced without preamble. He clamped the tablet-console board to the edge of the fencing surrounding the relay station. Jonqueen then mounted a small directional antenna to a signpost several feet away and pointed it toward the eastern horizon at a forty-degree angle. A slight hum emanated from the antenna. Jonqueen turned and faced Thomas and the teenagers. "I highly recommend that you retreat to a safe distance and take shelter."

Thomas backed up, sweeping the kids behind him. "Jonqueen, what would you consider a safe distance?"

Jonqueen cocked his head to one side as he stared at Thomas. "I am unsure. There could be an electrical discharge in a radius of 20 yards. It might also result in an explosion that could level the power station, though that is unlikely."

"How unlikely?" Sam and Ronnie asked at the same time.

"No more than twenty-seven percent."

"C'mon guys, let's retreat to the corner of the building," Thomas advised.

"One more thing," Jonqueen advised, strolling forward. "Young Ronnie, I need you to smash the container with the Galv remains."

Ronnie blinked. "Smash it? Why?"

Jonqueen stopped walking and glared down at him. His lips peeled back, showing rows of sharp, small teeth. "Why your species must ask a question with every command is beyond me. I would execute you on the spot if you were my prisoner."

Ronnie froze, afraid to move.

Jonqueen tilted his head a few degrees, and Emma laughed. "Jonqueen, now is not the time for humor!"

Ronnie turned slowly to look at Emma. "That was a joke?"

"Admittedly not a good one, but for his species, it is quite funny." Emma said, her face brightening. She rejoined by Sam and Thomas as they backed away. "Now, Ronnie, do as Jonqueen has instructed and smash the dish."

"Alrighty, if that's what tall, dark and scary wants, that's what he gets." Ronnie raised the glass container far over his head and threw it to the ground. The Pyrex dish shattered.

Chapter Twenty-One

Jonqueen walked over to the broken container, the glass crunching beneath his boots. He waved his hand over the remains. A black swarm of nanites descended to the ground then returned. "You did well." He said to Ronnie. "The Galv remnants are properly agitated. My nanites have detected a transference beam signal. It is too weak for the Galv to receive at the moment but is growing in strength. I suggest you retreat while I amplify the transmission."

"Okay, but a couple of quick questions, and please don't execute me," Ronnie said, backing away.

Jonqueen inclined his head again. "You were in no danger of execution. Ask your questions."

"First, were you laughing at me again?"

Jonqueen stooped and leaned forward until he was almost nose-to-nose with Ronnie. "Yes," he hissed. "Of the humans I have met, you amuse me the most."

"Uh, okay." The teen said, taking a big step back. "But I'm curious. Why did you have me shatter the dish? Couldn't you have done so?"

The soldier stared at him, thin gray lips twitching, then he softened a bit. "I could have easily smashed the container. But the Galv remains might have detected my nanites. I did not know how they might react. Even though they are just shards of a Galv soldier, each piece contains sensors and basic command functions. The remains might have decided I was trying to trap the rest

of the creature and remained dormant." Jonqueen
walked away from Ronnie, toward the power station.

"You would have been of no consequence to the
Galv. They would not have perceived you as a threat."
he pointed his black tube at the console mounted to the
fence. The board began to flash and change colors.

"But why did you have me smash the glass instead of
simply removing your protective force field or whatever
you put on it?"

"No real purpose in smashing the container except I
thought you might enjoy it." Jonqueen stepped back and
aimed his tube at the small dish antenna. The dish
transformed slightly, then hummed. "You need to take
shelter. The Galv are retrieving their remains and will
send soldiers to investigate."

Ronnie jogged back to where Sam, Emma, and
Thomas were taking shelter behind the building, each
leaning out as far as they dared. The Galv remains
vibrated and expanded. When they reached the size of a
deck of cards, streamers of gray smoke glittered
skyward. With a final crackling sound, the remains
vanished, and the hum diminished. Jonqueen unclipped
the comboard from the fence and studied it.

"I am detecting Galv Transference beams. They are
locking onto this location." Jonqueen snarled as he
backed away from the relay station. Instantly a pair of
soldiers materialized, their forms wavering, sputtering.
He raised his cylinder and pointed it at the first soldier.
Copper light flashed from the tube in a high-pitch howl.
The beam caught the soldier mid-chest. The Galv
oscillated; its form swelled and darkened.

The Alien's color changed to grayish-black ash, then exploded. The blast hurled Jonqueen across the road. Sparks jumped from the relay station as the transformers burst into flames. Electricity arced into the sky, sizzling and crackling. Black smoke poured from the burning wiring. The second soldier vanished in a staccato flicker of light.

Jonqueen climbed to his feet, then turned his attention to his tablet. "I have eliminated one soldier, the other was retrieved by its ship." He continued to walk away from the burning relay junction. "The explosion and disruption of power to the electrical grid is setting off alarms. I am now detecting local security forces in route. It would be prudent to leave."

"Agreed," Thomas said. "With the power out, we won't be able to access the building from here. We will need to walk around the complex."

"Security personnel are approaching from the South-West corner of the facility. We will need to hurry."

Thomas began to run but stopped when a black Chevrolet Tahoe came speeding up the gravel drive between the building and the power station, dust flying behind it. "Oh crap, not now."

Sam moved to stand beside his uncle. "Who is it?"

Thomas held his hand up, motioning for them to hold still. "Horace, I think. I should have figured he wouldn't have left."

Jonqueen stepped onto the road, raising his tube. "This delay cannot be permitted." The cylinder whined, the pitch increasing.

"No, don't do that. He's not the enemy."

"If he is preventing us from returning home, then he is the enemy." The soldier growled in his, rusted metal voice.

"Get the kids out of here, then contact me when you do. I'll handle this."

Jonqueen rumbled deep in his throat. "I will acquiesce to your decision, though I think it is a poor one." He packed his weapon into his coat, spun in the road, and raced to the corner of the building where the teens were waiting. "This way," he said as they ran along the building, staying close to the shadows.

Thomas stood in the middle of the road as the SUV slid to a stop in front of him. He walked over to the driver's side. The tinted glass was halfway down. As he expected, Horace was behind the wheel.

"Get in," his partner snapped.

Thomas shook his head. "We've been over this. I'm turning the launch vehicle over to Emma and Jonqueen."

"I know that," Horace said and slammed a fist on the wheel. "Just get in before the cops get here."

Thomas ran around the front of the Chevrolet, opened the passenger door, and climbed in. The truck was in motion before he shut the door. "Horace, did you finally see reason?"

"Let's just say I'm not in the least bit happy—and that's putting it mildly—with your decision. But I checked with Philco. He confirmed what you said, that the information being downloading into our servers is revolutionary, unlike anything he's ever seen before."

Thomas held on to the strap above the door as Horace made a sharp turn down a seldom-used dirt road. "And he convinced you just like that?" He snapped his fingers for emphasis.

"That and watching one of those—Galv, is it?—soldiers materialize, then explode. I've seen nothing like it in my life."

"So, you believe me now?" The truck took another hard turn, the rear-end fishtailing.

"I believe that what we have here is not from Earth. I believe that the technology is absolutely extraterrestrial. What I don't completely swallow is the need to destroy the vessel we've spent our lives designing."

"We've been over that. The only chance these people have of getting home is the detonation of the launch vehicle engine core."

Horace gunned the truck as they sped down the narrow road. His hands gripped the wheel hard, his knuckles turning white. "That's why I'm showing you this." The road ended at a series of abandoned metal warehouses. All were rusted, and some near collapse. "If he can commandeer the other spacecraft, he can land it here. The woods and buildings will prevent anyone from getting a close-up view of it."

Thomas stared out the passenger-side window as Horace drove around the empty lot. Decaying buildings and machinery littered the hardscrabble terrain. A two-story warehouse loomed on the ocean side of the property. The metal sheeting was gray and pockmarked with rust. "I've never been over here. What is this place?"

"Originally a fish packing plant. Boats would dock at the pier, long gone now, unload their catch and take back to sea. The reason I know of it is because my grandfather used to supervise the unloading of boats. And the only entrance in is the road we came in on. The trees near the water and around the perimeter will provide cover."

Horace parked the Tahoe facing the remains of the pier, the ocean a mile out through a network of jetties and canals. He switched the engine off. "What do you think?"

Thomas stared out his window, surveying the tall, broad water oaks and old buildings. "Looks good to me. If Jonqueen brings the craft down quickly at night, they should be able to board and get off the planet before anyone notices."

Horace agreed, nodding.

Thomas pivoted slightly to face his partner. "Just so that we are clear, you know what we're going to get out this, don't you? Within forty-eight hours, the country is going to see our launch vehicle explode on its maiden voyage. The government is going to be all over it. The scientific community will deem us failures, our funding will dry up, and Space Xploration might fold. Are you sure you can handle this?"

Horace tightened his hands on the wheel, the leather wrap crinkling under his grip. His jaw locked hard as he stared out the windshield. "Of course, I know all that!" His hands flexed. "I also get the opportunity to see all my future standing in the aerospace community collapse and my career crumble. I will get ulcers and sleeping problems from not being able to respond to a question with a straight answer," Thomas tried to interrupt, but Horace waved him off. "I also get the consolation prize which is the chance to save billions, and possibly, humanity." His voice was tense, raw. Horace let go of the wheel and fell back against the seat. His hands dropped into his lap. "But I've seen what those aliens can do. If sending your friends back will keep us safe, then I'd be a fool to try to stop them."

"I know that when you woke up this morning, this was the last thing you could imagine. Trust me, a couple of days ago, I was in your same shoes." Thomas said as he watched seagulls dive into the water, then relaunch themselves skyward. He reached over and put a hand on his friend's shoulder. "It'll be alright. Trust me on this."

Horace sighed and stared out the windshield. "It will be, what it will be. Let's get it over with." He started the engine, backed the Tahoe away from the building, and aimed toward the gap between the trees lining the entrance. He was pulling out when a vintage Camaro rolled through the gates at the far end of the field. "Who is that?"

"Relax," Thomas said, laughing. "Our friends are here."

"How'd they find us?"

"Not sure, but I think when the girl touches you, it leaves a marker they can follow. Turn the truck off. We need to plan our next move."

The Camaro idled across the hard ground, slowly angling toward them. Thomas opened his door, stepped out, and waved them over.

Sam parked beside the Tahoe. "Man, oh man, is this place crawling with cops," he said in a rush. "The power company is also out here. They are inspecting the relay station. They have no clue what knocked it offline."

"How did you know where to find us?" Horace asked.

Sam motioned toward Emma. "I'm not sure how she does it, but she seemed to know y'all would be back here." Sam stepped away from the vehicles and studied the buildings. "Is this where you think Jonqueen should bring the Galv vessel down?"

Thomas pointed toward the open space fronting the buildings. "Horace came up with this place. I didn't even know it was back here. He thinks there's enough room here to accommodate the Galv craft. If Jonqueen brings it in at night, the trees and buildings will hide it."

"I concur," Jonqueen said, his voice deep and, grave. "I can bring it down over the ocean. Your scanning installations will not detect it. Once I land the vessel, I will breach it and destroy the last of the Galv. It will then take a few of your hours to retrofit the controls and environmental systems to support us. I will then launch and take a stationary orbit over your launch facility."

"You're sure you can do this?" Horace asked, finally exiting the truck.

His armor creaking, Jonqueen turned slowly to stare at the smaller man,. "Yes." He pulled the tablet console from his jacket, the device now transformed back to its basic flat display. "The Galv took the bait and transferred the phone's operating system and global positioning programming into their computers. My nanites are currently deactivating all security protocols."

"How to you plan on commandeering our launch vehicle?" Horace asked with more than a trace of bitterness in his voice.

"I have analyzed your flight plan. Your craft will break free of your planet's gravitational field in approximately forty-nine seconds. When the main engines shut down and your prototype drive engage, I will override your programming from the Galv craft and change the trajectory of your launch. It will appear as a minor course correction. Once clear of your satellites and on its approach to your moon, I will use the grappling beams aboard the Galv craft to snare it. With the engines of the launch vehicle at full burn, the Galv vessel will not show up on your scanners. I will then open a slipstream point. When the wormhole has fully materialized, I will push the engines of your craft to maximum, then explode them eighteen seconds later."

"And this will send you home?" Horace asked as he kicked at the hard ground with the toe of his shoe.

"It will, hopefully." Jonqueen replied.

Chapter Twenty-Two

The following afternoon, a box truck was parked under the swaying branches of a massive water oak, the wooden arms draped over the top, leaves scrubbing against it. Drifting over the ocean, a dozen gulls followed a small commercial fishing boat as it returned to port. The seabirds flocked around it squawking loudly as the fishermen tossed scraps of bait into the air. Sam leaned against the hood of his car, the sea breeze ruffling his hair. Emma relaxed in his arms, eyes closed. She coughed suddenly, the sound wet and raspy.

"Sam, take me for a ride in your vehicle," Emma said.

"Okay, sure. Where?" Sam said, digging the keys out of his pocket.

"It does not matter. Jonqueen says the components Thomas Dellion delivered are crude, but he can create an interface between the launch vessel and the Galv ship. But it will take many hours." She turned and smiled at him. Her eyes were not as bright as the day they met. "I would like to see the sun set on your world once more before we leave, someplace over your marvelous blue water. Is there a place we could be alone to watch it?"

Sam nodded. "We'll have to drive about two hours, but yeah, we can go watch the sun set over the gulf."

"I would like that, my Sam." She leaned into him again. "Please take me there."

Sam put an arm around the Saint's waist, and half carried her to his car. He helped her in, then jogged around the front. Ronnie stepped from the back of the box truck.

"Yo, man, where are the two of you slinking off too?" Ronnie asked with a grin.

"Gonna, drive over to the gulf to watch the sunset. Should be back in a four to five hours."

Ronnie made his way over to the car, glanced in, then at Sam. "She doesn't look good."

"I know. But she wanted to see one more sunset before they leave." Sam started the Camaro.

"Well, according to tall, gray, and scary, he won't be ready until this evening. Wants to bring the Galv ship down around midnight when the skies are quiet. So, you've got time."

"Good," Sam said, nodding. "See ya' in a few." He dropped the car in gear, and drove across the abandoned factory site, out the gate, and toward the highway. Twenty minutes later, Sam pulled onto the interstate heading west.

Emma lay her head back on the seat, letting the wind stir her hair. "Play music for me, Sam. Music you would play for a girlfriend."

"Uh, okay. I've never had a girl in my car except my sister and mother, so… let's see." Sam leafed through his CD case, thumbing past selection after selection. He finally settled on a one. "This is a compilation disc, a bunch of various artists. I hope you like it." Sam slid the disc into the player, put an arm on the back of her seat, and drove toward the retreating sun.

They reached the west coast of Florida two hours later. Sam pulled up to a beachfront pavilion and parked facing the water. He shut the motor off. Emma turned his way slowly, her hair falling in tangled strings across her face and shoulders. The color was fading from her face; her eyes were now pale blue. She managed a weak smile. "Your music, it is…interesting." Emma brushed her hair from her face. Sam was relieved to see some of her color return.

"You didn't like it?"

"On the contrary. I liked it very much. It was, as is much of your world, discordant, unpredictable, chaotic." She laughed softly. "Compared to my world, it is soothing in its randomness." Emma unbuckled her belt, then struggled to push the car door open. "Walk me down your beach, Sam. I want to feel the last of your sun on my face and this gulf water on my feet."

Sam met Emma at the front of his car, where she leaned against the warm hood. She held her hand out, Sam took it and led her down the earthen walk to the quietly shushing waves.

They splashed casually through the surf, Emma reaching down, cupping the salty water in her hands, and tasting it. She inhaled deeply, then coughed and staggered against him.

"Are you okay?" Sam asked, stepping in front of her, putting his hands on her waist, and steadying her.

Emma nodded.

"Are you sure? I'll take you to a hospital if you need me to." Sam stroked the back of her hand nervously.

"I am perfect, my Sam." She squeezed his hand and laced her fingers in his. "Let's find a place to watch your wonderful sunset."

They walked without talking, Emma leaning slightly on his shoulder, their hands clasped tight. As the sun's fiery edge hovered over the Gulf of Mexico, they came to a small dune between towering palm trees fronting a resort. "Up here," Sam said as he pulled her up the dune. They sat on the small hill, Emma sitting between his knees, leaning against his chest. The sun turned the wispy high clouds violet and orange, the nearly flat gulf reflecting the colors across a watery horizon.

The sun melted into the glassy Gulf of Mexico, the calm water absorbing the fiery colors and diffusing them as far as the eye could see.

A photographer walked by, noticed the pair framed by the palms, and took their picture. "You guys look really content," the man said, handing Sam his card. "I'm sorry, I should have asked your permission, but was afraid you would change position. I work for the Tradewinds Resort, and I've been searching for the right shot for our next brochure. You guys are perfect."

"You're fine. Any chance you could email me a copy of the pic?" Sam asked.

"I can do better than that. Give me fifteen minutes and I can give you guys a framed copy."

"That would be great," Sam replied, then watched the man jog toward the resort, his flip-flops kicking up sand as his camera bounced on his back.

"That man, what was he inquiring about?" Emma asked, her face showing puzzlement.

Sam laughed. "Apparently, you guys don't have tourists on your planet. He's trying to find a good-looking couple to put on their advertising, and apparently we fit the bill."

Emma rolled her eyes. "There are many things about this planet I don't think I'll ever understand."

"Trust me, I've lived here all my life and there are lots of things I still don't understand." Sam leaned down and kissed the top of Emma's head.

Emma sighed and snuggled against Sam. He slipped an arm around her shoulders and pulled her in tight. "Your sun's setting. It is quite beautiful. I've never seen a sunset over a blue body of water before. It is quite unique." She yawned and drifted heavily against him.

The last rays of the sun were disappearing below the far horizon when the photographer returned. "Here you go…" he said and paused. "Is she all right?"

Sam glanced up quickly, not having heard the man approach. He could see the concern in the photographer's eyes. "Emma," Sam cried, sitting up fast and turning to face her. Emma's eyes were half-lidded, and a trickle of blood ran from her nose. Sam dropped in front of her, wiped away the blood, then shook her gently. "Emma, please, talk to me!"

Emma's eyes closed, then slowly opened. "Sam…" she said thickly.

"Hold on Emma, I'm taking you to the hospital." Sam jumped up and moved in front of her.

She reached out and took him by the wrist, her hands incredibly strong. "No, Sam. They won't be able to help me. You must take me back. Jonqueen can put me in stasis." She managed a slight smile. "I'll be fine."

"Hey man, I think she needs to go to the hospital," the photographer said as he pulled out his phone. "I'll call 911."

"No!" Sam snapped a little too quickly. "She missed her medication today. She's, uh, diabetic. I just need to get her home where she can take her insulin." Sam carefully pulled Emma to her feet. "Please, help me get her to my car."

The photographer nodded, took Emma's other arm, and helped Sam walk her to the Camaro. Once they belted her in, he handed Sam the picture. "If she's feeling better in the future, I'd like to take more pics of you guys. She's so…striking. You're a lucky young man." He grinned and patted Sam on the shoulder.

"Thanks, I think so too." Sam started the Camaro, dropped the car in reverse, and backed out fast, the rear tires spitting sand and gravel. He pulled out onto the highway and pressed the accelerator hard. The Camaro's speedometer topped eighty when Sam felt a hand on his elbow.

"Sam, it will be okay," Emma breathed. "Please do not get in trouble with your authorities." She coughed into her hands. Sam winced when he saw dark red speckles in the palm of her hand. "Jonqueen has already commandeered the Galv craft. He will land it about the time we arrive." She coughed again, the rattle coming from deep in her chest.

"You're getting worse, Emma!" Sam cried, then handed her several napkins that he kept beside the console. Emma wiped her hands and nodded.

"That is true, I am. But we have plenty of time." She turned to face him. "And I don't want my last memories of your face being lined with worry." Emma slid her hand gently up his arm. "Relax, my Sam, and please turn your music back on. I find it soothing, even in my condition." She smiled at him.

Sam slowed the Camaro under eighty miles per hour, then turned the compact disc player back on. He looked over at Emma. She sat with her head back on the seat, eyes closed, breathing shallow. *You better be right, Emma. You better be goddamn right.*

The Galv ship was on the ground when Sam pulled the Camaro across the hard-packed gravel lot. It was smaller than he imagined, only about one hundred feet long and half as wide. The ship was matte gray, all light sinking into its oval shape which resembled a stone you could skip on a river. A pale blue light glowed from beneath it.

Jonqueen ran to greet the Camaro. "You should not have taken the Emissary!"

Sam opened the door for Emma and she struggled to her feet. "Do not blame Sam, my friend," she said to Jonqueen. "There was plenty of time for Sam to bring me back." She smiled, then collapsed.

Jonqueen wrapped her in metallic foil, only exposing her face. He waved his hands over Emma and a wave of nanites descended, forming a clear shield just above her skin. "This will slow the progression of her condition. I need to put her in the Galv ship immediately."

The foil shifted, and Emma's hand reached through it, not tearing the foil but piercing it like water. "Sam, may I have the picture?" Her voice was weak, muffled.

"Yeah, sure." Sam said and hurried to his car. He returned with the framed photograph. Her arm was now back inside the metal wrap.

"Place the image on top of the shroud. It will pass through undamaged," Jonqueen said softly, the gravel in his voice fading.

Sam did as requested. The small wooden frame sank through the sheeting and vanished. "Emma, can you hear me?" A tear trickled down his face as his throat tightened. The Saint's eyes were closed, her face ashen.

"Sam Shepherd, she is now in stasis. She can no longer hear you. My nanites will keep her safe until we return." Jonqueen kneeled and slipped his hands under the woman. He lifted her as if she was weightless. Sam followed the soldier to the Galv vessel, where Jonqueen stopped and faced him. "You cannot enter. The atmosphere is now toxic; you would not survive." The hatch opened, and Jonqueen stepped inside. The door closed instantly behind him.

"How is she?" Thomas asked, now standing beside the Camaro.

"I...I don't know. She started coughing up blood. Then she got real weak." Sam wiped his eyes with the back of his hand.

Thomas put an arm around the boy's shoulder. "I'm sure she'll be fine. C'mon over to the van. We need to get you prepared."

The box truck's roll-up door was open. Inside, banks of computer screens and consoles lined the walls. Horace feverishly worked at one, his hands a blur, his eyes flying from the keyboard to a bank of monitors. Several technicians bounced from station to station, keying in commands and watching the results scroll across a second bank of monitors.

"What's going on?" Sam asked.

"Jonqueen's nanites are busy linking our launch controls with those in this truck. In a few hours, you get to take the center terminal. According to Jonqueen, the nanites inside you will 'meld', for a lack of a better word, with the ones here. Soon after we launch our vessel, you will take control and navigate from the pre-planned flight path. Jonqueen will intercept when it reaches orbit and take command."

"Why me?"

"Because your nanites will have to communicate with Jonqueen's. Plus, no one can know what's going on. Flight control will assume the vessel is having navigation issues." He patted Sam on the back. "Don't worry. We will be feeding you the coordinates to input. All you have to do is enter them into the interface. That way I can be on site the entire time looking upset," Thomas laughed. "And with Mr. Happy over there grousing around the control room, everyone will buy it."

"I thought you canceled all his clearances," Sam said, nodding toward Horace.

"No, only made him think I did. I knew—hoped— he'd come around."

Sam sat on the truck's bumper and pointed toward the Galv craft. "Jonqueen was early with the ship. You don't think anyone noticed it landing?"

Thomas shook his head. "Absolutely not. It was almost invisible coming in, just a heavy vibration, felt like a train running close by. I had our launch team scanning the airspace around here. They didn't detect a thing." Thomas joined Sam on the bumper. "Now, military radar is better than our own, but we don't think they even picked up an echo or shadow. Maybe some calls from people who thought they felt an earthquake, but nothing else."

"Have you seen inside the ship?"

"Me? No. But guess who has." Thomas cast a thumb behind him.

"Your partner?" Sam asked with a laugh.

"Yeah, I couldn't believe it. Jonqueen brought the ship in—which was deserted. We don't know what happened to the remaining Galv soldier or pilot. Jonqueen confirmed it was safe, vacated the atmosphere, and took Horace in. Whatever Horace saw in there calmed him down. I still had some concerns with him."

"And you weren't allowed in?"

"Not even for a peek." Thomas laughed, stretched, then checked his watch. "All right, Sam, it's time we get ready. Our launch window is in sixteen hours. Horace and I need to head to the flight center. I'll secure the truck here."

A slight hum from the Galv ship caused them to turn. A door that wasn't there moments earlier slid open. "Sam Shepherd," Jonqueen said in his rusty voice. "Has Thomas Dellion apprised you of your duties?"

"Yeah, for the most part. I'm not one hundred percent sure of what I am to do but have a decent grasp of it."

"Good. Any questions you have, the nanites will answer for you."

"Seriously? How?" Sam and Thomas blurted at the same time.

"When you interface with them, they will relay the mission parameters directly to you. It will be the sensation of a whisper. It will initially be uncomfortable, but you will eventually learn to tolerate it."

"Wow, sounds fun," Sam said flatly.

Jonqueen tilted his head; his lips parted slightly. "Humor. I think I might just miss you after all." He walked over to Sam, held his hand just above the boy's shoulder, and then seized it. A cloud of nanites billowed out, followed by wisps of smoke. When he pulled his hand back, his gloves were smoking.

"Jonqueen, why did you do that? That had to hurt like hell!"

The soldier tilted his head down and stared into Sam's eyes. "Your pain. The Emissary's pain. Now my pain. I had to share. My father held my shoulder when I left on this mission. It was his pain as well." Jonqueen managed a weak, human smile. "Farewell, Sam Shepherd."

The side of the craft closed the second Jonqueen entered. A heavy vibration stirred the dust and sand. Thomas and Sam retreated to the tree line as the Galv vessel rose; the compression of the atmosphere by the engine's power made the air visibly pulse. The craft lifted vertically, slow at first, then with increasing speed until it was a pale blue dot against the dark Florida sky. The blue glow flashed once and vanished.

Sam swallowed hard. "She's gone," he said in a whisper.

Thomas put a hand on his back, patted him, and then gave his shoulder a firm, fatherly squeeze. "Sam, it was time. They had to go."

Sam nodded and this time let the tears flow.

"C'mon, I'll drop you back at Solar X. Your pal Ronnie is already there. I'm having food delivered, and I'll have a driver bring you back in the morning." He steered the teen toward a black Tahoe.

Sam shook his head. "I'll drive my car, if it's okay with you. I'd kinda like to be alone."

"I understand." Thomas pulled out his phone. "I'm going to text you the security code for the gate. It's only going to work once, so when you pull in, don't leave again." He rubbed Sam's shoulder. "It'll be okay. Maybe not tomorrow, or next week, or…"

"Never," Sam said, interrupting.

Thomas smiled. "Never is a long time, son. But in time, it will."

Sam sighed, then gave Thomas an awkward hug. He released his uncle and shuffled to his car with his head down. He slid in, fired the motor, spun the Camaro around, and sped out of the gate, trailing a cloud of dust.

Chapter Twenty-Three

The moon was swinging past midnight when Sam pulled the Camaro into the parking lot of Space Xploration. He parked in the 'presidents' reserved spot, figuring if he was the deciding vote on CD, Inc, he deserved a better parking spot than one marked 'visitor.' The door to the lobby opened as Sam stepped from the car.

"Good Evening, Mr. Shepherd." George Conway, the captain of Solar Xploration's security team, said to Sam. "I've heard it's been a long, emotional night."

Taking the captain's outstretched arm, Sam shook his hand warmly. "Yes, sir, it's definitely been that. Is Ronnie here?"

"Yes, sir. He's been waiting for you for some time. I notified him of your arrival when I saw your headlights. He's been holding onto a pizza and a beer for each of you." George winked at Sam. "I told him I wouldn't tell on you guys."

"Thanks, I've only had a sip with my mom and dad, and that was a long time ago. Probably not the best thing for a high school senior, but what senior launches his alien girlfriend across space and time?"

George shook his head, then clapped Sam on the back. "No one I know of, Mr. Shepherd."

"Okay, you gotta stop with the 'sirs' and 'Mr. Shepherd,'" Sam said, managing a tired grin. "Just call me 'Sam'. I've still got a few years of just being 'Sam' left in me."

"Understood, Mr. Sam," George said, smiling, then motioned toward the open lobby door. "Elevator's standing by. When you step in, the doors will close automatically. Enjoy your stay."

"I will. Thanks for all you've done for us."

"Think nothing of it," the dark-skinned man replied. "Safe travels, Sam." He shook Sam's hand again before stepping away and letting the boy pass.

The elevator doors closed upon his entering, the lift rising fast enough to make him sag. He reached the penthouse without stopping. Ronnie was waiting in a recliner, the pizza on a warming stone, and two cold beers floated in an ice bucket.

"Hey, there he is!" Ronnie boomed across the room. "Man, I've been waiting for you for what seems like forever! Hurry man, I *really* want to open this beer, eat pizza, and chill. In honor of your friends, I figured we'd watch Star Wars: Return of the Jedi on your uncle's eighty-inch screen. Tried to get a six-pack, but your uncle said 'no', that 'your mom would skin him alive'. He tried to buy me off with some sparkling cider. I whined and pouted until he broke down and slipped us a couple of Buds."

Sam nodded and worked up a wry grin. "It's things like this that get you in trouble."

"So, you want to trade the Buds for Cokes?"

"Gods no, let's eat! I'm tired, my head and heart hurt, and I'm freakin' hungry as all get out."

Ronnie plucked the beers from the ice bucket, tossed one to Sam, then waited for his friend to collapse into the matching recliner. When Sam was settled, they popped the tops simultaneously, the beers hissing and foaming. He tipped his beer toward Sam. "Here's to good friends, close by and soon to be very far away." They tapped the beers together.

"Amen, brother, amen."

"So, what's the plan for tomorrow?" Ronnie asked between bites of pizza. He swallowed, then wiped his mouth with the back of his hand.

Sam shook his head, wondering how slightly over three days ago they were bitter enemies. And now they are having a beer in a million-dollar apartment while eating pizza and watching Star Wars on a gigantic screen. He leaned back, wiped his mouth with a napkin, and sighed. "Dude, could you have not waited just a bit more on that question?"

"Sorry man, this is hard, isn't it?"

Sam nodded, his throat tightening. "Yeah, it's like losing a sibling or something. I only met them this week, but it feels like a lifetime. And tomorrow afternoon, if Jonqueen is correct, she'll be blasting across the universe and hopefully back to her own time." Sam bit his lip, his emotions threatening to overwhelm him.

Ronnie reached over and punched Sam lightly on the shoulder. "It's all right, dude. Go ahead, let it out." He stared down at his friend; his eyebrows raised in concern. "And if you're not going to finish that beer, can I have it?"

Sam laughed hard enough to spit bites of pizza across the room. "You know where you can shove your concern, don't you?" He laughed again, this time completely losing control and gasping for breath.

"Oh, man, I think I needed that!" Sam rasped when he could regain control of his breathing.

"Yeah, you were getting kind of girly back there, if you know what I mean."

"Yeah, right," Sam said, drawing out his words. "Now turn the television up. I don't know about you, but I always thought Princes Leia looked hot in her slave girl outfit." Sam turned to Ronnie, and they high-fived each other.

"Definitely a hot slave. So, what time do you need to be down at the van?"

"Uncle Thomas said I should be plugged in and ready to go by nine in the morning. They said it will take a while to synchronize the computers in the truck with C&C. Launch will be twelve-ten if the weather cooperates. By one-ish I'll be flying the launch vehicle by remote control. We figure Jonqueen will intercept approximately three hours later. Then my work is done."

"What happens after that?"

Sam shook his head and shrugged. "I don't know. I guess we come back here, clean up, pack, and go home."

"Just like that?"

Sam nodded. "Yep, just like that."

"Wow, kinda anti-climactic, if you ask me."

"For sure." Sam shifted in his chair and extended the footrest. "Then the real fun begins for Uncle Thomas. He will have to explain what happened to his ship, how his bunker blew up, cops being called here…."

"You plan on hanging around to help?" Ronnie asked, now pulling up his footrest.

Shaking his head, Sam said, "No, sir. We're going to hit the road first chance we get. When the crapola hits the fan, I want to be miles and miles from here." He grabbed the remote off the table between the recliners. "To be honest, I'm about ready for all this to be over with and go back to being just another loner kid in high school."

"You realize that your loner life in school is over?" Ronnie picked up his beer and drained the last. "After this week, son, you're going to be a major curiosity."

Sam waved away the comment. "Dude, when I get home—wherever that might be with my house blown up—I just want to curl up in front of a TV and veg out for a few days."

"Oh, yeah, your house kinda blew its top. I had completely forgotten about that." Ronnie laughed. "The lengths you will go to avoid cleaning your room."

Flipping Ronnie the bird, Sam pushed back in his chair, reclining almost all the way. He then increased the volume on the viewscreen and folded his hands behind his head. Sam's eyes closed before the first lightsaber battle took place.

Sam sat bolt upright in his chair. The TV was off, leftover pizza was on a table nearby, and the bright Florida sun was barely edging over the Atlantic. His head was buzzing, and it wasn't from the beer. Ronnie slowly sat up, peering at him with half-lidded eyes.

"What's up?"

"I think the nanites are communicating." Sam climbed stiffly from the chair and walked to the large plate-glass windows providing a panoramic view of the ocean and the beach. "This is a freakin' weird sensation."

Ronnie leaned forward, dropping his footrest. "What are you talking about?"

"The nanites, the ones in me and at launch control, seem to be—talking. It's like I have a low voltage wire vibrating my brain. I'm not a real fan of it." Sam rubbed his temples as he opened one of the glass doors. He stepped out onto the patio and turned mechanically toward the spaceport.

"You're not gonna jump or anything, are you?"

Sam laughed. "No, I just have this feeling I need to be here and looking this way." A flash of light followed by a low sonic boom creased the air in the upper atmosphere. The buzzing in Sam's head ended abruptly.

"What in the hell was that?" Ronnie asked, meeting his friend on the patio.

"A flyby. I think the old soldier is getting soft from his time on Earth."

"Shouldn't he be heading to the moon or something?"

"I'm sure he is. Just wanted to say goodbye before he did," Sam broke into a wide grin. He slapped Ronnie on the back. "I'm going to take a shower. Do you want to ride down to the launch site or sit with me in the truck?"

"I figure the launch site's gonna be hectic. If it's okay with you, I'm gonna chill here. Not too often I can watch football on a screen that makes the players life-size."

"Probably a good idea. If you see the explosion in the sky, you'll know it's all over."

The morning air was cool and clear when Sam pulled into the abandoned fish processing plant. A small army of technicians swarmed over the box truck, running cables from it to the to the roof of the abandoned plat. They erected a satellite dish on the far end and pointed it toward the Northeastern sky. Sam sat in his car, checking his watch continuously, staying out of the way as best he could. At 7:45 am, a familiar black SUV pulled through the gate and parked beside him. The tinted driver's window rolled down. Horace glanced out, took a deep breath, and forced a shallow smile.

"You ready, son?"

"I guess so. Or about as ready as I can get."

"And that, son, is an understatement." Horace smiled briefly, then climbed from the truck. "C'mon, time to you get you prepped. Your soldier friend is anxious and not very patient."

"That sounds like Jonqueen," Sam replied, opening the car door and climbing out. "I take it he's in position?"

Mr. Wainwright nodded and pointed up. "Yes. Somewhere about sixty miles up, just waiting for us to launch."

Standing with his hands in his pockets, Sam nodded toward the truck. "Hey, I know you hate this, that the idea of blowing up your ship is killing you."

"Yes, it is." Horace shrugged a shoulder slightly. "The technology we've been given will be groundbreaking. But the short term will be disastrous." He took a deep breath and scuffed the dirt with the toe of a once-polished, now dusty shoe. He gritted his teeth and grimaced, then walked toward the box truck. "It's time to wire you into the system. Do you have any idea of what you're in for?"

"No sir, not really."

"Me neither." Horace confided, then released a long exhale. "We're all flying blind on this one. One way or the other, none of us are ever going to be the same after today."

Sam was surprised that the time to 'wire him up' was reasonably quick. Jonqueen had designed an interface console for him to place his hands in. Once inside, the console warmed and melted to encapsulate his palm and fingers. He had to keep from recoiling as the nanites connected his hands to the comboard. The sensation resembled dozens of granddaddy longlegs crawling up and down his hands before sinking into his skin. Then the feeling subsided as a dozen monitors hummed to life.

The techs left the van, closing the door behind them, leaving Sam and Horace alone in the truck.

"Jonqueen said you should hear or feel whispers in your head. That is the nanites synching with your cerebral cortex," Horace said as he watched the monitors warm and sparkle to life.

"I felt that this morning. Very weird sensation. Not sure I like it very much."

"Interesting. Jonqueen didn't think they could communicate from a distance. Apparently they can." Horace leaned back, rolled his neck on his shoulders, then started typing commands into his keyboard. "Okay, I need you to think about Jonqueen's position."

"Just think about it?" Sam asked, turning slightly.

"Yes, just think about it."

"All right, let's see what happens." Sam relaxed and thought about the Galv boarding craft, Jonqueen, and then Emma. A monitor above and to his right flickered, turned black, then resolved to show a distant speck silhouetted against the moon. The speck enlarged, focused, and expanded again to provide a clear image of the craft.

"Wow," Sam said after a moment. "That was really bizarre. It was as if I imagined with one part of my brain, then sharpened and zoomed with the other."

"Incredible," Horace whispered. He leaned forward. "Now, the launch vessel."

Sam could feel the connections being made as Horace spoke. A monitor in front of him glowed to life, showing the vessel on the pad and technicians crawling all over the ship.

"One last test. Bring up the control room."

"Yes, sir." Getting accustomed to the feelings of voyeurism, Sam took a deep breath. The monitor directly to his left brightened. The camera angle was from the rear of the room. Rows of operators sat behind monitors and keyboards, their hands in constant motion. Commands were being given that he could not hear. Sam saw Thomas walking across the floor, occasionally stopping to look over the shoulder of a system engineer. "I think I can access any of the displays you want me to. The nanites have control over all the video systems."

Horace leaned back, nodded, and ran a hand through his hair. "This is astonishing. With the nanite interface, you can control all these systems."

"Yes, sir. It's like they can almost read my thoughts and are already doing what I want them to do before I know I'm going to ask. It's rather freaky, if you ask me."

Using a standard keyboard and mouse, Horace moved to sit beside Sam and brought another bank of monitors to life. "We have a couple of hours until the launch. While you continue to get acclimated, I will work on our press releases and talking points. Today will be a nightmare when it's all over."

Sam nodded but said nothing. The nanites were a soft buzz in the back of his mind. He was absently aware of monitors flickering to life and launch control making final preparations for their only flight. Command and control was a hive of nervous human anxiety. The Galv ship rested quietly in orbit—a new monitor focused on Ronnie sitting with his feet up, a football game about to start. Then a hand on his shoulder made him jump.

"Sorry, didn't mean to startle you," Horace said with a smile that warmed his eyes. "You haven't moved in the past hour, but the monitors have been a blur of activity. And you apparently tapped into the security cams at Solar X. For a few minutes, all the monitors showed your friend watching TV."

"Really? It feels as if I've only been sitting her a few minutes."

"It's almost noon. I'm heading over to the control center now. I think it's important for the captains of a ship to be at the helm when she goes down."

The console loosened its grip on Sam's hand. He stood and held his arm out. "Thanks for all your help, sir. As I said earlier, I know this is the last thing you wanted to be doing, but I'm sure it will all work out."

Horace shook Sam's hand. "I hope so. What I've seen this morning gives me hope. But, you never know." He powered off the terminal he was using. "Take care, son." He palmed a switch on the wall, and the door rolled up. It closed moments after he stepped through.

Sam put his hand back in the console, felt it meld to his touch, and the spiders crawl into his skin. A countdown clock glowed with soft light. The red digits started with seventy-three minutes and began counting down.

The monitors stretching across the wall changed. One showed the Galv craft, the operation center, and the launch vehicle. All he had to do was think about them, and they appeared. Wondering how far he could push the technology, he brought a fifth monitor to life, showing his Facebook page. Grinning, he updated his status by mentally typing. Today, *I launched my alien girlfriend to space and her own reality.* He laughed as the words appeared, followed by the cursor backing over them, replacing the words with *today's going to be a great day!* and a smiling emoticon. He could sense the nanite's disapproval in the back of his mind.

"Okay, wondered how far you buggers would let me get."

Seconds later, the monitor dimmed, and the one showing the Galv craft moved front and center. The image zoomed in closer; the ship filling the screen. Then the image changed to the interior of the vessel. The cabin was barren. There was a central display panel and banks with digital feeds and readouts he couldn't comprehend: no chairs or other amenities. The walls shimmered as if electricity coursed through them. In the middle of the ship was a center dais with controls not designed for human hands. And standing at the dais was Jonqueen. The image swept around so that he was facing the camera. He nodded to Sam.

"Jonqueen," Sam said, unsure if the alien could hear him.

"Sam Shepherd, our time is short, but I felt compelled to inform you of a few items." Jonqueen crossed his arms over his chest as he leaned against the panel. "It has been my honor to serve with you these last few days. You have proven to be a worthy and courageous being. I have traveled between worlds and served with warriors both stronger and more-fierce than you, but none have the keen intellect and fearlessness you have shown. There is also an element of your world that cannot be duplicated."

"Really? I mean, are you sure?"

Jonqueen tilted his head subtly; his lips cracked just a hint. "And it is not this aggravating trait of your species to constantly question." He tilted his head again, the grin growing minutely. "It is your desire to put yourself in harm's way for another being, despite the risk to your own self. It is both remarkable and rare."

"Thanks, Jonqueen. I guess it's a human-thing."

"Indeed." Jonqueen turned toward a display Sam couldn't decipher. "Time is scarce, and there is one more item we must discuss. Emma," Jonqueen said, with some effort, "would not be happy with me for divulging this, but she knew of your desire to join your nation's astronautical fields."

"Can't, I have a heart defect that keeps me earth bound."

"No longer, Sam Shepherd."

"What do you mean?" Sam leaned back in his chair.

"The reason Emma is sick is that she transferred an enzyme to you that keeps her species safe on alien planets. Without it, she cannot survive."

"Why?"

"I was unsure at first. Apparently, it was your decision to risk your life for an enemy that triggered her desire," Jonqueen said as he leaned closer to the camera. "Sam Shepherd, the contact we had with you will change our galaxy for the best." The soldier's fingers squeezed into a fist and flexed, another human trait of nervousness. "If we survive, I feel certain you have given both our species what we need to prevail against the Galv. You and your world will never be forgotten."

"Obviously," Sam said, half laughing, half crying. "You have ancient texts talking about us."

Jonqueen lowered his head. When he glanced up again, his face was almost grinning. "That is true." He turned his back to Sam and tapped quickly on a display. The screens behind him changed to show a distant constellation of stars. "I, as Commander in the Firestar Confederacy, grant you Commander status in our fleet."

Sam watched in amazement as a section of his console opened and a flat, circular medallion appeared. It was embossed with a pair of lightning bolts piercing it. "Should you ever make it through time and space and find yourself in the Firestar Confederacy, this insignia will allow you free passage, and to commandeer any ship you see fit. Farewell, Commander Shepherd." Jonqueen stood, raised a fist to his chest, then slightly bowed. Sam followed suit.

The screen with Jonqueen's image changed to show the ship silhouetted against the darkness of space. The engines glowed bright blue as the ship moved away. A droning buzz filled his mind. He glanced up as the monitors now displayed the inside of the flight control building and the exterior of the launch vehicle. A subtle message echoed in his mind—*almost time.*

Sam felt his breathing quicken and the tingling in his hands increased. The clock was counting down, now showing three minutes to liftoff. He could sense launch vectors being verified, power couplings detaching from the craft, and the main engine priming. He thought about Ronnie, and a monitor to his far left flickered to life. A Security cam found him standing outside on the balcony, wind ruffling his collar-length hair and his hands on the railing as he faced the facility. The television was off, and their bags were packed and sitting next to the door. The monitor and all the others flashed once and became one continuous screen. He could see the Solar Xploration's ship and The Galv shuttle all at the same time.

The countdown dropped below fifteen seconds. Then ten. The engines of the craft fired. Sam had a nauseating sensation of vertigo and slumped in his chair.

All will be fine, the nanites assured him. The sickness passed. Sam felt contacts under his fingers. *Control will be surrendered in ninety seconds.* The Solar Xploration craft rocketed across the Florida East Coast, leaving a trail of smoke and orange flame in its wake. Sam sensed gravity falling off, the air thinning, the sky turning black. *It is your time.*

Sam thinly smiled as he programmed the vessel to deviate from its assigned path. He could feel the confusion, sense the panic in the control room. In one corner of his mind, Sam saw Horace shouting orders, sweat pouring off his brow as he requested the launch be aborted. *He is a fine actor,* the nanites whispered.

"Yes, he is," Sam replied quietly. He felt an overwhelming sadness for the controllers as they frantically tried to correct the flight. *All will be fine, my Sam.*

"Emma? Is that you?" Sam asked frantically, his attention broken. He stared wildly around the truck. His heart raced.

I will always be with you, my Sam. Always. As long as I remain in your heart.

Sam cried, then felt the ship abruptly change direction. The nanites released his hand. As the last of the tendrils pulled free, he heard a final whisper, *Thank you, Sam, for everything.*

It was irrational to think he felt it, but Sam swore he could sense the ship's engines pushing toward critical, the phase-couplings overloading and exploding. The center monitor showed the Solar Xploration ship's engine glowing incredibly bright, and then the vessel was gone. An explosion whited out the screens. When the glare cleared, there was nothing remaining of the craft. He sagged in the seat and closed his eyes.

Sam jerked upright when he felt a hand on his shoulder. He turned quickly to find Ronnie standing beside him.

"Sorry, man, didn't mean to startle you."

"What time is it?"

"It's almost three o'clock."

"How did you get here?" Sam asked as he pushed from the monitors.

"Your uncle sent a car for me. I think they sensed you would want to leave as soon as possible."

"I never want to repeat this day." Sam said dropping his head into his hands and crying.

"You did good, Sam, considering this was you first time piloting a rocket ship." He smiled and clapped Sam on the back. "The news crews are climbing all over each other, trying to find out what happened. It was actually kinda funny to watch."

"How's Uncle Thomas?"

"Seems to be holding up okay. He's using all the standard answers like 'not knowing what happened' 'vowing to get to the bottom of it', saying the ship experienced a 'rapid unplanned disassembly'". Ronnie leaned against the wall of the truck as the screens bounced between the launch pad, the control room, and the news feeds. "You about ready to cruise? I grabbed your things and put them in your car."

Sam nodded and stretched. "Yeah, I think it's time we headed home. Help me power everything down and we'll hit the road."

Ten minutes later, Ronnie palmed the switch for the door, and they jumped from the rear of the box truck. "So, do you think they made it?"

"I don't know." Sam shook his head. "I just don't know" he repeated. Sam pulled the car keys from his pocket and faced the coast. "The nanites were talking to me right 'till the end. I kind of thought they'd give me some kind of indication."

"What's your gut tell you?" Ronnie asked as he opened the passenger door.

Sam shrugged and sadly shook his head. His eyes were becoming wet again as a lump formed in his throat, making it hard for him to talk. He wiped away a tear that threatened to unleash a torrent more. "Don't know, guess we never will." He dropped into the driver's seat and fired the engine. They drove across the hard-packed lot, leaving a cloud of dust behind.

The sun was pushing toward late afternoon when Sam merged with traffic heading up I-95 North. He picked up the medallion Jonqueen's nanites had created for him and pinned it to his chest, just over his heart. The insignia seemed to melt into the shirt and warm his skin. For a moment, he felt the nanites enter his chest and withdraw, leaving his chest feeling clean and healthy. But before they did, a voice whispered, *home.*

"Did you say something?" Sam asked Ronnie.

"Me, no. Why?"

"Nothing, thought I heard you say something." Sam sighed quietly and relaxed in the seat. He pushed the accelerator down and let the needle sweep up to seventy-five miles per hour. Sea air filled the sports car's interior as palm trees flew past in a blur.